THE
BLUE STAR

R O B E R T
F E R R O

•

THE
BLUE STAR

E. P. DUTTON, INC.   NEW YORK

Published in the United States by E. P. Dutton, Inc.,
2 Park Avenue, New York, N.Y. 10016

Library of Congress Cataloging in Publication Data

Ferro, Robert.
The blue star.

I. Title.
PS3556.E76B58   1985   813'.54   84-25882

ISBN: 0-525-24321-6

Published simultaneously in Canada by Fitzhenry & Whiteside,
Ltd., Toronto

DESIGNED BY EARL TIDWELL

10 9 8 7 6 5 4 3 2 1

First Edition

FOR MICHAEL GRUMLEY

I am grateful to Laura Wood Roper for her estimable book, *F-L-O, A Biography of Frederick Law Olmsted,* Johns Hopkins University Press, 1973; and to Peter Partner for his sober history of the Knights Templar, *The Murdered Magicians, the Templars and Their Myth,* Oxford University Press, 1982.

R F

ONE

·

THE
BARDOLINI

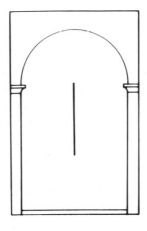

In June of 1963, when I arrived in Florence, the Pensione Bardolini was in its ninth decade. Seasoned boarders invariably made the claim that E. M. Forster had written there all or part of *A Room with a View,* calling it the Bertolini. I had heard the name on the train from Rome. Ease of travel in those days, before the tourist boom, coupled with the confidence of a twenty-one-year-old whom life had scarcely noticed, seemed to lead me to it naturally. At the tourist agency in the train station they spoke to the Signora by phone, and a very low price was quoted: 1900 lire a day, meals included, which then was just over three dollars. The taxi left me at the *portone* of a red palazzo on the river. The room I was given looked up and down the Arno, at the Ponte Vecchio in the morning mist, at pink, atrocious sunsets in the evening. For symmetry's sake within the frame of the window—and in an otherwise perfect situation—the Duomo might have been moved a foot or two to the left.

Signora Zá-zá was an attractive, childless widow inclined to show affection for those she liked. She always used the formal *Lei,* but with varying degrees of intimacy, from friendly to cold and abrupt. As a result I think she seemed slightly different to all her guests, like a team of sisters who greatly resemble each other. She was a small woman, probably only about forty-five at the time, who did nothing to glamorize herself. She wore housecoats and flats that slapped the bottoms of her feet down the long corridors; this sound of her arrival preceded her, giving us a moment to collect ourselves for the *padrona* and precluding surprise, which is anathema in a hotel.

It was not apparent at first but the clientele of the Bardolini was hardly orthodox sexually. I recall one or two elderly English couples, but everyone else was younger and single; not surprisingly, since Zá-zá did not bother with transients and preferred long-term boarders, and who else but young loners would be abroad for months at a time? When someone new rang the bell unannounced, which was common, Zá-zá would size him or her up according to some inner, hosteler's instinct that had nothing to do with the availability of rooms. In the year I was there a few troublemakers slipped through her net but these, when they declared themselves—a theft, rudeness, a pregnancy—were sent packing without a qualm. I wonder now if this instinct of hers wasn't basically sexual. I once asked how she had made up her mind about me, by telephone, and she said she had asked the agency at the station to describe my footwear. She said she always looked at the feet. But I think she looked into our eyes and judged us by the degree to which we knew what we longed for.

In the dining room she always seated a new arrival at a table alone, at least for the first few nights. Then a group table was selected according to her choice. This period of adjustment, as if the new people were divers coming to the surface in stages, might last days or weeks.

The June nights, like the days, were hot, even excruciating.

This and something else drew me into the streets around midnight. It seemed I was too excited for sleep, too warm, too young. After a few hours of writing in my room, I told myself a walk would calm me, and that Florence was beautiful at night. But the walking was like the writing. I didn't understand the purpose of either—only the mechanics. Putting the words down on paper was the same as putting one foot in front of the other in the empty streets.

These night walks were soon ritualized. After a few hours of work, on countless beginnings and fragments, I would go out. It wasn't clear to me that the writing was a preamble to the walks, an excuse, rather than the walks being a decompressing coda to the writing. Gradually the work interval was shortened. The moment of departure, like a decree, came earlier, and the walks lasted later into the night. By the beginning of July, I no longer wrote after dinner, and only prepared for the night.

The fifteen-foot portone downstairs, which lay open all day, was closed and locked at night. Beside it a stone lion face gradually smiled as the sun went down. The sound of the heavy door closing behind me, with its stony reverberations, meant freedom. Each time I felt I was turning suddenly to face a new life—all at once, a fresh, different existence in a new place nearly out of time.

At that hour you would have thought the years had flown away. Except for the streets along the river, or perhaps in Piazza Repubblica, no cars went by, and scarcely a carriage. In the narrow, cobbled streets of the perpetual past, in the shadows down a long, unlighted *vicolo,* it seemed whole centuries melted away in dark theatrical gloom. I was as if transported to a vague, operatic past, within elaborate tableaux—lifelike but unreal. And my impulse was to picture a role for myself within the spectacle in which these convincing street-sets and cleverly lit night skies might have some personal use. Florence and me. It seemed that at night the place was abandoned to sensation and a whole new set of inchoate longings I scarcely recognized. Nothing was clear; nor did I suspect any motive behind the walks other than appreciation for the city and the formation of a new, unorthodox but sophisticated pattern—so different from life at school—that now suddenly was open to me. I felt some compunction to be in bed by dawn—when anyway the magic stopped—or at least before breakfast was brought in; but sleep was a matter of indifference, while the exquisite disregard of all previous patterns and rules gave me for the first time the impression of an inner life; as if, each night, as I slipped silently down the darkened stairs and through the vaulted hall, counter to all of life's currents, I was hurrying to a meeting with a new self—someone like me, but different.

This naiveté as to what I was doing lasted about a week. I remember the exact moment when the balance was tipped. It came in my second week there, as a kind of retrospective revelation that swept everything away. I had been looking at the river from the Ponte Vecchio. It was very late. A man walked toward me across the length of the bridge. He approached and in Italian asked the hour. I wasn't wearing a watch, and realized, as I looked at him, that he was not interested in the time. He had stopped in the light, and I saw in his luminous eyes, or thought I did, the two of us embracing—two sets of figures so tiny that only he and I would have recognized them as ourselves. He smiled, with what I understand now was a smile of self-congratulation: his instinct, even at fifty feet and in the dark, had not failed him. He had seen at a distance what I had not yet perceived within myself.

He might as well have struck me. Instead he said, "Thank you just the same, and good night," and walked on down Por Santa Maria. I pretended to look again at the river, the while listening to the sound of his receding footsteps.

Wandering at random through the streets, one after another, I think I wanted to walk until something happened. I walked along the Arno and into the park. I approached the train station as if to leave the city, or as if meeting a lover's train. I took a bus to the outskirts up the valley and walked back. At other times on other nights, I set up a circuit of visits to cafés in order to see the faces of men well lighted and close at hand. In these places I would try to blend in, to speak minimally but convincingly as a Florentine. I bought other clothes and cut my hair, fitting myself out in the manner, perhaps, of a young Italian student. This meant looking less American, less middle-class, less white, less male, less of everything I was—and more of this other thing.

A few weeks after I arrived, a Moroccan homosexual checked into the Bardolini, exotic and effeminate, the first such person I had seen at close range. In the evenings Rashid appeared at dinner wearing kohl on his eyes, discreet but discernible, and belladonna in them, he subsequently explained, which gave them a bright, bluish, myopic, doll-like gleam that was quite unnatural and mystifying. He wore also scent, and the kind of fine silk tops one's mother would wear in the 1970s. Rashid too was seated at a table alone but came over to mine at the first opportunity, choosing me out of all the others naturally and automatically, as though attracted I feared by a spoor, a sign, a physical invitation. This was embarrassing. What had he seen, I wondered, to choose me? What did it mean to the other diners that we sat, nightclub fashion, as in the whirling vortex of scandal?

I knew I was not like Rashid, but I knew I was not completely unlike him. I knew I would never wear eye makeup, but I was already conscious of the fact that I had appealing eyes, meaning they were a sexual tool I might use, if not to the same exaggerated degree.

Rashid's faulty English provided a screen behind which I managed to hide. When he asked what one did of an evening in Florence, I suggested the opera. When he asked if there weren't *certi posti*—certain places—where one could find *da fare*—things to do—I gazed blankly into his crystalline eyes. But the next night we encountered each other in the street. Rashid looked at me strangely and said, "Are you drugged?"

"No," I said firmly.

Then what was it, Rashid wanted to know. "Are you in love? Are you with child? I can always tell."

"I'm free," I said rather simply.

"Well, you have the strangest look in your eyes," Rashid said. "I suppose it might be freeness."

"Freedom," I corrected.

"You mean, of course, freedom to chase men," he went on, with a great cheap wryness. He looked at me and raised his chin. Regarding me speculatively, he said, "In Morocco they would take you like a ripe melon. Wait . . . they will come to you."

As late as the nights were, I would rise when Zá-zá or her niece Rosa brought in the breakfast tray. One or the other of them would knock briefly and come in, setting the tray down on the desk. Zá-zá always said something when she opened the shutters —"*Che bella giornata!*" or, as the days wore on, "*Che bel caldo!*" She would take the desk chair by its back, set it beside the bed, seat first, and remove the tray from the desk to the chair. I lay back against the pillows and looked through the open window at the sky. You could hear the city outside, and the pensione through the door.

Zá-zá's niece Rosa was a big-breasted, short girl with a beautiful face obscured and distorted by thick glasses. It was impossible to tell if she was eighteen or twenty-eight. Occasionally she released the bun of dark hair behind her neck and removed the eyeglasses, and like a lovely blind girl at home, would deftly navigate the halls, avoiding the furniture by memory.

Alvaro, the houseboy, was someone's cousin. He was also short, but slight and birdlike. From his manner with everyone he seemed to maintain a strangely low opinion of himself and was given to little fits of subservience. He cocked his head to one side to make himself shorter, kept silent, did his work; and two nights a week drank himself to sleep, so that on the following mornings he looked green and ill and miserable.

Beside these three—Zá-zá, Rosa and Alvaro—four others made up the Bardolini household. Babbo, Zá-zá's father, was old, rheumy, obese, but still quick and humorous, and was cared for in the kitchen and treasured like a rare, dear pet. Rosa-mama, who was in fact Rosa's mother, was Zá-zá's sister-in-law. Orazio, Zá-zá's brother, was a laborer, a dark, thick man seldom seen, and then only in the kitchen like Babbo at mealtime, when you came in after lunch to say you would or would not be in for dinner. Their son Lorenzo was fifteen and had, through some trick of fate or ecstatic pact between Rosa-mama and her saints, been lifted from Caravaggio's erotic dreams and given to them all to worship. His beauty, of the heart-stopping variety, was something even the family could not get used to. Under its cover Lorenzo came and went unfathomed, unknown, but like visiting royalty indulged to the edge of belief.

Zá-zá's husband had been killed in the war. One afternoon as lunch was ending and a few of us sat at a table by the open window over the river, someone asked her what it had been like during the war, when the city was spared but many of the bridges were blown out of the water by the retreating Germans.

"Ah, *cari miei* . . ." she began, waving away the memories, the experience, the shattered windows and bullet-riddled walls. At the window she leaned pensively against the railing. "They fired from Fiesole," she said and pointed across the city to the hills beyond. "We were serving lunch. What did we know? These little popping sounds in the distance, and the window glass broke, the chandelier shattered and my poor husband fell, there . . ." She indicated a spot beside me on the floor. "After that we had terrible times, *tempi duri* . . ."

In the late morning, having carefully shaved and dressed, I rushed down the hundred steps to the street, carrying my note-

9

book of fragments. I had formally asked the owners of various cafés if I could sit at their tables by the hour, writing. Some refused, some thought me eccentric and possibly dangerous, some claimed to be honored. One owner near the pensione thought me an improvement over his regular trade, which included an unusual number of amputees from the war, cripples and deficients. There being no social programs for them, these types had chosen the bar as a place where, as a group, they would not be interfered with. I did not understand this until one morning, while at a table in the corner, I was seized by a feeling of anxiety and looked around to see a quartet of deaf-mutes engaged in a vicious but silent argument. Red-faced and gesticulating, they cursed each other with swooping hands and enraged looks. The bartender was required to calm them. It was then I noticed the man with no legs in the makeshift wheel-chair, the man with the bandage covering what had been his nose, the woman with two eyes on the one side of her face, the blind man with the tiny, white, vigilant dog, the little men shorter than the backs of chairs who held up their coffee cups for sugar from the bar.

In the afternoons I took naps, as did the rest of the population except the tourists, if for different reasons. Wandering all night, with only a few hours' sleep in the early morning, the day's felling heat gave me an excuse to sleep from after lunch until just before dinner at eight. I felt this new schedule qualified me for the life I knew must exist in Florence, as I imagined it existed in cities everywhere: an underworld, the back half, the obverse, the hidden part of life. My writing attempts during the day—intended as cover as much as an occupation or self-expression—were misera-ble little failures that went nowhere. You would have thought from these fragments that I was luxuriating in some nineteenth-century way in the glories of Florence and the freedom of youth unfettered, youth released. Perhaps I was, or was at times. But inside I was crazed by a dilemma I was at last allowing myself to face. At the same time, as I sat staring in the cafés, I realized how dull and uneventful, how banal life had been until then; or at least how usual and common. It seemed to me, suddenly, that the only aspect of my nature worth pursuing was this new, horrifying urge. Poverty of experience—so galling, so embarrassing to the young writer—caused me to change my mind, again in an instant, about all of it.

I was sitting on a marble bench in Piazza della Signoria. It was well after midnight. The little cars came along one edge of the piazza, outlining the square with bright red dashes of light. I felt certain—in the way you are sometimes certain of the inevitability of the next move, as if you had already taken it—that now was the moment, the end of avoiding the issue, and that the next man who presented himself would, within reason, as in a kind of lottery, be accepted.

I looked across the square and saw a figure leaning against the railing of the fountain of Tritone, which the Florentines call *Il Brutto*, for Neptune's ugly face. The body however is glorious and the face only streaked by weather. The man leaning against the railing with his arms crossed over his chest was watching me, as well he might, since for the moment we were the only two people in the piazza.

I stood up, with the same sudden deliberateness with which one leaps from a great height, and started toward him across the cobbles. It seemed, in this walk of perhaps fifty yards, that the whole piazza was tipped in his direction and that I fell toward him lightly, according to a natural gravity.

As I drew near him he smiled a little smile, without which, who knows, I might have faltered and changed directions, and on account of which I give him credit for the seduction, such as it was. I find it ironic to think I didn't recognize him, having searched for his eyes in each passing face for two weeks: the man from the Ponte Vecchio.

But he remembered me, and with a kindly, a sweet, indulgent smile, he said, *"Sa l'ora?"* Do you know the time? This in spite of the thirty-foot clock face just over our heads in the Arnati tower.

"It's you," I said, blushing and wondering at the coincidence.

"It's been me a few times," he replied. "It seemed to me you knew that, no?"

By which he meant, he later said, that several times he had been just across the street, or on the other side of the nave of a church, or passing the door of a café in which I sat gazing distractedly into the street.

I do not now remember his name. He was perhaps thirty-five, which then I considered middle-aged but which, now that I am myself past forty, seems simply mature. I was fortunate in choosing him, for he was gentle; he less so in accepting me, because I didn't know how to act. In the end, after two confusing weeks, we both gave up, as two people do who face each other over a torrent that would sweep them both away. He was an artist; all of this was beyond me. My Italian was rudimentary and dim; my expectations, as I followed him home that first night and the nights thereafter, were based on the tribal nonsense of high-school and college sweethearts, and on the marital confusions and humiliations of my parents. His antidote for this was minimal conversation, with nothing beyond pleasantries, and the simple directives and questions necessary for logistics. His eyes soon mocked me, or so I thought.

But all that came later. The first night was magical, a delicate, polite dance; he treating me like the alien species I was—young, wild and liable to bolt—and I regarding him with devotional awe, as teacher, expert and master of these new mysteries and sensations.

I see him differently now—now that I have become him, and have again become what I was. He is demystified. Even the fact that he lived nearby, in a street just behind the piazza, reduces him somewhat, to a kind of provincial boy-chaser preying on tourists just outside his door. This maybe was cheap and easy. The conflict that developed between us came out of my need for some real connection—which, from his point of view, would only have served to complicate the purpose of our meeting: sex. I see now how right he was. But I remember standing in the doorway of his bedroom saying loudly that I was not an animal, nor yet a piece of meat, but an artist too, like him.

The patience he showed in his lovemaking easily carried over to handle these outbursts; but it was in turn this stoicism that drove me away. I raged at the spongy depths of his dark, eloquent eyes. After several scenes, he made no effort to stop me from leaving, and I left.

But that first night he gently took me to bed and caressed and kissed me—not the approximation or imitation of lovemaking, but the real thing, ending in a physical connection that I had had no inkling was possible between men.

I left his bed with the palpable feeling of pride and discovery, and the next day could not wait to tell Rashid, who listened raptly, a knowing half-smile on his lips.

"*Che debutto!*" he kept saying. What a debut. And, "*Troppo puro*"—too pure, too pure. Rashid's doctored eyes glistened with envy, I saw, and quickly I was asked a succession of questions—How old? How tall? How big? Who was he? Did he have money? Did he have hair?—which made me realize that after a full night together I could not remember the man's face. It was gone.

"But Rashid," I said, whispering unnecessarily in the dining-room din, "I had no idea that . . . you could . . ."

"Could what?" Rashid asked, fascinated.

". . . that men could fuck each other," I whispered.

Rashid said nothing and only stared at me with something

like distrust, not believing me. Then looking again and deciding I meant it, he said, "Ah, this is excellent." He leaned closer, across the table, pausing for me to lean in as well. "It is the wonder of Europe," he said, "that American boys can all be so stupid, and so good with their mouths."

The night after the artist affair ended, like a jockey under different colors, I was out on the street looking for another mount. This new and powerful mode of expression—cruising with intent—which seems now to be nothing like it was, distracted me completely, like a rich, jaded gambler in the salle privée, so that my feelings for the artist—my indignation, confusion and frustration, all of which obscured the deeper, larger issue of coming out—were themselves replaced by a sense of excitement tinged with danger, glamour, romance, sexual longing. Before I knew it the artist had been replaced by a man who stopped his car by the river to ask directions with his fly open and his cock out. You did not resist such directness, for why then have put yourself in front of it in the first place? Why walk along the river at night unless you were a whore or wanting to act like one? Why say no to anything that was not plainly repulsive? By whose standards did it attract or repel?

I roamed the streets and parks, as far removed from the idea of art and pretense as I could take myself, discovering there the kind of truth I was supposed to be setting down on paper; and setting down on paper a rendition of life in Florence that might please professors and critics; and in the end not even that.

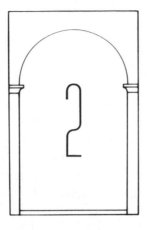

The Bardolini occupied the top floor of a palazzo on the river. The rest of the house below was a grand private residence. The top floor, divided into two irregular stories, was connected here and there by narrow staircases, and over the years parts of an additional story had been added on the tile roof, so that the impression was of a warren on many levels.

Signora Zá-zá had about twenty rooms for rent, perhaps twenty-five, although one day I counted forty-four. Six or eight of these were for family use, others for laundry and storage. Several were too large to heat in winter, too hot in summer, or too remote; some of them lugubrious and dark. Also, I think Zá-zá let only those rooms that she, Rosa and Alvaro could comfortably handle, twenty being the approximate limit. The Bardolini had two public rooms, the *ingresso* and the dining room, which were connected. The ingresso, about thirty feet across, had a refectory table in the middle and over it a skylight through which a net of sunlight fell upon a bowl of flowers. Our mail was arranged on this table each morning. The ochre plaster walls of the ingresso and the dining room, indeed the walls of the corridors as well as of all the rooms, were hung with bad paintings given in lieu of rent by a long line of artists who had stayed there over the years.

The dining room had a fireplace, or rather a mantle out of which a cast-iron potbelly stove took root. An enormous gilt mirror, too tall to go straight up the wall, leaned out over the stove and duplicated half the room at a slant. At one end two tall French windows were filled with views of the city, the sky and river, lending the room all the credentials of a great and gifted interior. More paintings—portraits and still lifes, in courses à la Palazzo Pitti—lined the walls. Twelve or fifteen tables of varying sizes had white cloths, and chairs that did not match. The chandelier, damaged the day Zá-zá's husband was shot through the window, was a blue Murano and something of a treasure.

Among the other guests I preferred vestigial anonymity and the automatic formality of Italian hotel life—which gives you a free hand between meals and at night—although Rashid was increasingly avid for details. And it was a relief to have someone in this part of my life who knew something of the other, growing, mysterious part.

"Puttana," Rashid said softly as we sat down to lunch.

Rashid claimed kinship to the nobility of Morocco, a country where, it seemed, you were either destitute or rich beyond measure. I took this to mean that his family no longer kept goats in the lounge, that they had reached a level of sophistication at which it embarrassed them to have spawned a hermaphrodite— at any rate a creature unable to ride a horse or bear a child—and whom they thought it to their social advantage to maintain in Europe. Rashid was not yet thirty, although he took these few years between us as a measure of difference that, when added to my inexperience, gave him the upper hand in all our conversations. Nothing could I say or claim I had done the night before that he had not already done or seen earlier. And for all the information I gave out, he gave little in return, or little that was believable. I doubted he spent all his evenings in the lap of a great Florentine lord, as he claimed, and imagined him instead, like St Genet, sitting backwards in a tall urinal doing piecework, to while away the time between penises. His favorite subject at meals was speculation on the possible tastes and habits of new arrivals. He would not discuss women "over food." The appearance of a new young man would send him into a loop of automatic mating responses—hand to hair, lips pursed—which, as I came to know him better, was drawn out or abbreviated depending on his opinion or state of heat. Or he could be disdainful of an old favorite, with cruel, cynical comments muttered under his breath.

"Puttana," he repeated in salutation as we settled into our chairs, and then looked past me in open-mouthed wonder at the person entering the room. It was the first either of us saw of Chase Walker.

In those days anyone as fine as Chase was automatically taken for a model, as in an earlier period he might have been thought a saint or later on a rock star. He smiled, at everyone and the room in general, and—looking out the window from the desirable table Zá-zá had automatically assigned him as his due—at the view in particular.

Rashid had colored. *"Mai visto,"* he said two or three times, trying to catch Chase's long-lashed bright blue eye.

The white tablecloth before him took light from the window and threw a soft glow up under Chase's chin. Direct sunlight lit his shining blond hair. He was twenty-one. He was perfect. Before I could stop Rashid, he half rose from his chair and asked in French if Chase would join us for lunch—an incredible impropriety, to which Chase responded with a graceful, priestlike gesture that described, using both hands, the entire circle of the world, saying, *"Mais c'est tellement beau ici, devant la fenêtre . . ."*

And after a moment's pause—a long moment to show that his heart was not in the invitation—Chase asked if, instead, we would join him there, *"pour ne dissiper pas la vue."*

He and Rashid spoke French, he and I English, the effect being that of a genteel, rather aimless conversation about arrivals and departures punctuated with flat footnotes in English. He was from New York and might stay the summer. How had he heard about the Bardolini? One knew about the Bardolini, he replied, from friends.

My reaction to Chase was unequivocal enough for me to dismiss him initially. His opening remark was the most affected I had ever heard, and in the ensuing conversation I detected such smugness and condescension as to put me off completely. After lunch we had coffee, minus Rashid, in the amputees' bar downstairs. This change of venue seemed to encourage an additional frankness between us—some remark was made about men—and he said he had thought at lunch that I was flirting with him with my eyes. "It's a trick," he said, "of looking at the forehead, which widens the eyes most becomingly."

Any reply would have been rude, or perhaps flattering, and I let it all go. I thought this façade of gentility, by which we were all meant to be charmed, must hide the wreckage of his real personality, whatever that was. I had never met anyone who had gone to the trouble of erecting a façade—in fact the idea of such a thing came new to me with Chase—and it took some time to discover I was wrong about him.

I suppose Rashid should thus be credited with the confluence in the dining room of its three principal sexual inverts. Subsequently a young and very pretty American girl named Margi was added to give the table balance—important in Zá-zá's view —and who acted as chaperone and frequently caused Rashid's eyes to roll. Between Chase and Margi the sexual line was blurred. All here was blondness, beauty and good manners, the brother-sister version of the same Wasp ideal, as similar as they were separate. It was Margi—for whom all of life's institutions and customs were invented, for whom life's wishes and hopes seemed translated into reality with such apparent ease—who happened one day to meet a young, dark Florentine of good family, who dated, delighted and married him, a kind of prince, and who moved into a kind of palace, just as Rashid or Chase or I thought we might like to do.

We came and went, each of us pursuing our new life in Florence like a game, meeting back at the pensione, usually for lunch and always for dinner. Chase spent the next few weeks in museums and churches, and I recognized in his brand of thorough, guidebook tourism—so different from my own system of untutored emotion-alism—the fact-finding scholarly approach of the "A" student, a large difference between us, and one that caused me to see him as other than a pretty fop. I was impressed too by many of the things that at first had put me off—the precise manners, the blue blazer, slacks and fat necktie, the crisp click of his heel on the tiles. His choices of costume, props and stage business for each of us new things of our own devising—seemed most apt for a situation and schedule that, at heart, were still essentially Edwardian. I had seen the Bardolini as merely Italian; Chase made me realize it had been invented for foreigners, specifically the English, and that hardly any of it had been altered in eighty years.

He collected stamps, he wore fat ties, he whistled the love aria from *Samson et Dalilah*. He lavished loving respect on the bindings of books and the collars of his shirts. I see him in the tradition of Sebastian Flyte, of whom I had not then heard; but less overbred, less outrageous and perhaps more handsome—the sort of boy a girl's mother might see at a country club or smart day-school dance and think of as It, and be as wrong and foolish in her choice as if she had selected for her delicate daughter a bum from the streets or a maniac out of Bedlam. For it was in this mold —of the perfect young man for the perfect young lady—that

Chase had been bred and raised, first by his parents and then, after the age of fifteen, by himself—as camouflage. This was the façade behind which there hid something, as Rashid would have said, *inattendu.*

I have before me a large portrait photograph of him as he was the year after Florence, when we had both returned to the United States, he to Harvard for his final year and I to a writer's workshop in the Midwest. In it he looks as he did the day I first saw him—just beyond being a boy, not quite a man, practically an angel. Though the picture is black and white, you can see that his eyes are blue, the left in shadow, the right iris catching a point of light at the edge of the pupil like the moon of a planet; and that his hair is a shiny light brown, tending to "summer blond," he said. It is a high square forehead; a short straight nose, fleshy bottom lip and the beginning of a cleft; a square jaw. The side of his face in shadow is a soft, dunelike line that rises past the cheekbone into the delicate gold confusion of a sideburn. The directness of his gaze, from the point of his eye, extends outward and inward along the perfect alignment of two mirrors set up to reflect infinity. This seems to mean he sees precisely into the center of the lens, the young animal attracted to a sound there that has just caught its attention.

In August the Bardolini emptied out. Rashid went to Switzerland, Margi to Greece, Chase to Rome, to see the churches, he said. The dining-room shutters stood closed to the stuporous heat and flannel wind.

"*Tutto solo,*" Zá-zá said compassionately, and set a plate of pasta before me.

At night the streets were empty. But always, one way or another, something happened, with men I had never seen before and never saw again, whose lives were merely interrupted, in the moments I knew them, by desire, but whose lives afterward returned to normal, as if for them nothing had happened.

In the mornings when she brought in the breakfast tray, Zá-zá would say, "Why don't you go somewhere, Piero? Get out of this heat."

"Where?" I asked, wishing now I had gone to Rome with Chase, not that he had invited me.

"Does it matter? Away from this!" She gestured toward the gorgeous view. "Go and *see* something," she said, in the way my mother had suggested I turn off the TV on a beautiful afternoon and find the others. But I stayed, held by the habit I was acquiring, this frantic preoccupation, and by the same heat that had driven everyone else off; by inertia; by the patterns I had devised for myself: the daily and nightly repetitions and rituals. I wondered if any of this would travel, or if it would be there when I returned.

Chase came back at the end of August. I was in the ingresso and he invited me into his room while he unpacked. He threw his dirty clothes into a corner for Zá-zá.

"Number five," he said to himself wearily.

"Number five?" I repeated.

"Number five means, 'Where will it all lead us?' These are statements one makes so often that numbers are easier."

"What's number one?"

"Number one is, 'If I don't have Chinese food in an hour I'll die.' Number two is, 'If I never see Chinese food again it will be too soon.' Number three," he said, carefully removing a new camel's-hair jacket from his suitcase and spreading it over the bed, "is, 'Do you love it?' Via Condotti, twenty-three thousand lire . . . Number four is, 'Which of us isn't/wouldn't/doesn't?' And the most profound and often asked, Number five—'Where will it all lead us?' "

I asked about Rome.

"Rome," he said, "is very adult, very grown-up. The Devil lives in Rome. He only spends weekends here."

"Then why don't you move to Rome?" I asked.

"Because I've already ordered stationery." He looked at his watch. "Come," he said. "It's supposed to be ready today."

Pineider was then right across the river. Chase's stationery was cream stock with light blue ink. He and the salesperson thought I must have some too and the three of us designed it like a small room. Afterward we went to the American Express to see about renegade mail; Chase was handed a letter from New York. Over coffee at Doney's he read parts of it aloud.

'I would say it's safe to come back,' the letter said. 'The manager understands you're not coming in temporarily but can't see why you should want to quit over something like that, and be upset enough to leave the country and all.' Chase put the letter down and looked sadly across Piazza Repubblica. "It all happened in the space of two days," he said. "I had a summer job at Brentano's. Someone from the *Times* came in about the Best Seller List. I said *Giovanni's Room* was doing very well. The next day in the paper it said, 'The pretty blond at Brentano's said it was our best mover.' In the *Times,* you understand . . . Meanwhile two truckers picked me up on an overnight haul to Montauk and back. The next day someone called and asked Mother if she knew her son was a faggot."

I said this was awful.

"Awful, yes."

"Did your mother know?"

"When I was a child she once asked why I didn't bounce like other little boys—but no, I don't think she did. . . . People don't, you know, unless you rub their faces in it. Anyway, I took her to lunch in the Park, at the zoo, and told her it was true. She said she was sorry because it would be a lonely life."

We walked back along the river; he asked if my parents knew about me, and I said that until my arrival in Florence there had been nothing to know. From this angle the river looped along the waist of the city through belt-buckle bridges.

"You came out *here?*" Chase said excitedly.

"More or less."

"I came out when I was fifteen," he said. "I was watching a parade on Fifth Avenue and a man winked at me. I still see him sometimes downtown, getting older and older. Paul was one of the original twelve homosexuals of New York."

We went back to the pensione, and in his room, killing time before dinner, Chase whisked the chenille spread from the bed and wrapped it around his waist. He flounced the ends of it into a bustle at the back and tied a black ribbon in the collar of his white shirt. He brushed up his hair and held it at the back of his neck with one hand, a cigarette in the other.

"Consuelo Vanderbilt, on the point of becoming the Duchess of Marlborough," he said; then added, "Outside I am a man, inside a woman. But inside her is another man, hard as nails. *That's* who I am, should anybody ask."

Abruptly the weather went from high summer one moment to fall the next, the switch coming simply as a change in the direction of the wind. The fresh air brought with it an escalation of Chase's Edwardian bent and of our friendship, these two things being linked in my mind. His stylishness attracted me, not sex. The engraved stationery, for instance, was a tool that formed only part of an extensive philosophy about letters and letter-writing—together with his beautiful handwriting, a bound Pineider notebook in which he copied all letters sent and received, special boxes with ribbons to store the letters in, and attractive modern stamps, themselves an adjunct of his own stamp collection, inherited from his grandfather and to which he constantly added; all this, plus of course the content of his letters, many of which he read to me, seemed powerfully sophisticated and smart, the letters just daring and brittle enough, and always wonderfully funny and fresh. His correspondents were his schoolmates at Harvard, now in the final year he was putting off. I think that what he was doing at the

Bardolini—which was what I so liked about it—was recreating the patterns of his life in Adams House. It was as if, in coming to Florence, he had returned to the anglophile dream of English-men abroad, which over the years has inspired and informed American Ivy League life. And I'm sure his letters struck the same chord in Cambridge that they did in me—a fine, high note of comic androgyny and disrespect, as if one's smart grandmother, who happened to know all about sex and everything else, had written them.

The woman whom Chase spoke of as being within him and who often emerged in the witty and genteel pronouncements he liked to make, was patterned on an actual person—his father's mother, Anne Starkweather Chase, for whose family he was named and from whom he had already inherited the first of two fifty-thousand dollar trusts. It had never occurred to him that she was not the perfect model to emulate, and though she had been dead for several years she was still the person he most admired. The irony was that had he been born female he might have developed into what his family had most naturally desired in a daughter of the house: a traditional, Jamesian young lady familiar with the rules of society, who is comfortable anywhere, who dresses beautifully, who collects and entertains and paints and writes charmingly, who then marries well and becomes the more-than-wished-for wife. Margi, in fact.

That Chase instead had been born male and homosexual, but still admired these things, seemed not to matter to anyone, really. The family had other sons, had in any case lost its money and scattered. But to Chase, who was the repository of a whole set of ideals and traditions that had skipped a generation, the irony of what he actually was, compared with what he might have been, was vivid. His grandmother Chase, whom they called Grandmère though nothing about her was French but some of her clothes, had honeymooned in China in 1908. Here you had it all, in this one image: a woman in white chenilles standing in the high stern of a Chinese junk, her skirts whipped about her legs, while around her stand little men in straw hats with their hands in their sleeves. This tableau an artist subsequently transposed into a design for her dinner plates. In the Crash they had lost control of one of the world's great copper mines—such an inconvenience. Only memory remained, and now only in Chase. From the number of times he mentioned her, I understood that she occurred to him constantly.

Margi returned from Greece, Rashid from Switzerland. A few new regulars arrived for the winter—a young man with a guitar whom we amused but who was as if anesthetized or distracted; an older American woman named Loretta with a pageboy and a past who lived off the landing between floors and often kept her door open; a younger English girl who took the room next to mine and apparently lived on nothing. She could not afford wood and occasionally would ask for a "stick" from my abundant pile, to take the chill off.

My room was directly over Chase's, up a narrow staircase just outside his door. His smoking caused him to cough once, nervously, every time he came in and out, like a territorial doorbell, or as if touching a mazuzeh, and I could always hear him arrive and leave. He spent mornings shopping for stamps or having clothes fitted, or drafting letters in cafés I had put him on to. He especially liked the amputees' bar, where his looks made him an object of wonder to the cripples. Or he went to his barber. Sometimes he sat on the bed talking while I shaved and dressed. Usually he would say, "Why don't you put on *this?*" It was Chase who taught me Coco Chanel's rule of always removing the last thing you put on before you go out the door. After lunch we would go somewhere for coffee, then spend an hour or two investigating a church, always with guidebook—or a room of the Bargello or the Pitti; never a museum, but one room of it; never the whole church, but one of its altars or paintings. I saw that I had been taking everything whole. Chase, dressed to witness, slowed it all down.

Margi had come back from Greece looking like a goddess, with very blond hair, a flawless tan, blue violet eyes, and a new white cotton wardrobe that she wore all at once in many layers. Thus enhanced, in the first week back she overwhelmed her Florentine boyfriend and got engaged. She was radiant and happy and overconfident and not very pleasant to be with. To anything she might not agree with, she would say, "Oh come on . . ." Rashid decided one evening, publicly, that he hated her.

"You will drive your boyfriend to subtraction," he said, flinging down his napkin, "just as you have all of us, you silly bitch."

Margi deftly reached across the table and slapped his face. In a moment Zá-zá was at the table demanding, *"Che succede?"*

"This . . . person, called me a bitch," Margi explained.

Zá-zá looked from Margi to Rashid. *"Via!"* she said immediately. *"Via, su!"* She pushed at Rashid's chair until he stood up, then pushed him through the dining room door into the ingresso. Contemptuously she used the *tu* form. *"Sei sempre stato un'annoia a tutti."* You've always been a bother to everyone. "Get out. Pack your bags and leave."

Margi was appalled—as were Chase and I—at her power. The slap had become something of an execution.

"Signora, no," Margi began. *"Non è necessario da . . ."*

"Sì, sì, lo so," Zá-zá said, *"ma basta con quella."*

Rashid left that afternoon and we never saw him again.

At night now I had company. After dinner Chase and I would
change into tight pants, a thin shirt and dark jacket—this is all
I remember of the original uniform. Definitive fashion statements
did not come until later. The point here however was the same;
that we were looking for sex, were in fact dressing for it. The hour
and the endeavor seemed to indicate one angle of the sartorial
spectrum: dark colors, against the chance of being seen in the
shadows; sturdy shoes or boots, as much to anchor oneself to the
ground in a masculine way as for all the trudging required; a short
jacket or sweater, to leave the crotch and buttocks unobscured.
On my own I would simply have changed into something comfortable. Chase initiated me into the arcana of an early dress code
—before such refinements as hanky color and the display of keys
—not a code but an idea. In our clothes, in our minds, we dressed
down—for the streets and parks, not cafés or nightclubs or discos,
which anyway didn't exist. I remember sneaking through the

darkened halls and ingresso and down the hundred steps as if in outrageous drag, when all we had put on was what you might wear to rake leaves or muck out a barn. But our clothes represented our intentions, so that all could see them and understand.

Proof of this came as a shock one afternoon much later, when spring was arriving again and we were about to leave Florence. Chase and I had both commissioned three-piece cream-colored gabardine suits; we had taken the tailor with us to a movie theatre to show him the cream suit Marcello Mastroianni wore in *Yesterday, Today and Tomorrow*. There followed fitting after fitting, with refinements that included ten working buttons at each cuff. Wearing the suits for the first time, we went for an afternoon walk; not a block from the Bardolini, two women passed us on the sidewalk, and one of them said conversationally to the other, *"Due omosessuali . . ."*

Chase and I looked at each other and blushed, then turned to watch as they walked off down the street, two middle-aged borghese women in hats warning each other to mind the shit. Chase said, "So much for three-piece cream-colored suits."

Slipping through the big portone into the street one night, Chase declared, "Isabella of Spain and a lady-in-waiting used to dress like whores, and the two of them would sneak out of the palace after midnight and turn tricks for money." He paused. "How else would a lowly sailor ever get near the Queen of Spain? How else would Isabella ever imagine the world was not fucking flat?"

We spurned the amputees' bar as low, heading across the Trinità bridge and up Via Tornabuoni, along an ellipsis that held the Bardolini on one side and the Duomo on the other. Alternative directions we might have taken ran each way along the Arno: between the Ponte Vecchio to the east and the Cascine, a public park at the western end of the city. In addition, we sometimes went for coffee at the train station, always considered a special occasion. Also, but less important, on the ultr'Arno behind the

Bardolini, a street called Borgo San Frediano ran parallel to the river like a back hall. This way was used only when we wished to be incognito. To take Via Tornabuoni or Borgo San Frediano was to choose, as Proust pointed out, one evening over another. Up Tornabuoni we would turn at the Palazzo Strozzi into Piazza Repubblica, linger there, or go through it to Piazza del Duomo, by which time one of us was certain to have peeled off, like a Thunderbird dipping out of formation, wing over wing.

Chase took the glance from a passing stranger not as an invitation or even a vague sign of interest, but as an insistent command, rather like a ringing telephone. It took precedence and must be answered. I would rather have walked on with him, or have sat together at a table in one of the squares. But for Chase the spontaneity of a sudden encounter was the first ingredient of sex. It caught him up immediately, like a mail bag snatched by a speeding train. In a moment, with a smile at once pleased and regretful, he would be gone.

On a night I remember in particular we were walking under the arcade in Piazza Repubblica, the little bars and shop windows like ambulatory chapels in an immense church of sophistication dedicated to the soigné. In a situation like this we were severely underdressed. Because of Chase I had given up my campaign of cryptic coloration; and as obvious foreigners we were entitled to wear what we chose, being strange, and who knew *what* colors we painted our bodies in the barbaric fastness of our own forests? Chase interpreted the attention we attracted as benign interest rather than implied criticism, and took focus gladly. Lacking his confidence I was less oblivious, and turned to notice a few derisive smiles among the passersby. A situation like this might be all wrong, until presently someone would appear, would declare himself; would, in a way, as with a flipped switch, glow red in the dark or sprout flags and pinwheels from his head and shoulders, if only for us to see. Queer. It was as if we were insects inspecting a flower, perceiving marks and tracks and brightnesses invisible to everyone else. It took only the extra moment of a held glance—a quick stare, mind to mind—to make contact. Chase said, "We are the first men in history to stare at each other without meaning harm . . . If you do that to a gorilla it will begin to seethe."

They are gone now, but at that time, at one end of the arcade, around a blind corner but redolent, was a *pissoir,* the first stop—*vaut le detour*—on this end of the circuit. Rashid had shown it to me. Now, as a gift, I presented it to Chase, who immediately became serious. Turning to me with pleasure expressed in a slight widening of the eyes, he went in and I followed him.

Through the open doorway was a sharp turn into a short, arched tunnel about ten feet long. Our footsteps resonated in the vault so that those inside could immediately hear us coming and have three and a half seconds to become fully dressed statues of men about to piss. It was the sort of pissoir you find in European train stations: a tiled room with urinals along one wall, closed cubicles—with holes between pairs of raised cement footprints—along the other. It was momentarily empty. Chase's seriousness fell away and he turned a full circle, as if viewing a new apartment.

Footsteps in the entrance sent us reflexively to the urinals, four or five apart. A middle-aged man entered and went to the one next to Chase. Discreetly, as part of the whole presentation, I slipped away and waited in the arcade. A minute or two later Chase came out and we resumed walking under the arcade, now nearly empty. When we got back to the pissoir, he went back in alone.

The next morning I asked Zá-zá if Chase was in or out and she said he didn't feel well and was still in bed. I went to his room, knocked and went in. The shutters were closed, his breakfast tray untouched.

"Chase," I said. "What's the matter?"

"Oh, Christ, Peter," he muttered in his pillow. "What a mess. . . ."

I opened the shutters as he slowly sat up in bed. His left cheek was discolored, his nostrils caked with dried blood.

"What *happened* to you?"

"Some guy beat me up," he said simply.

"Who?"

"*Who!* I don't know. . . . Some guy." He groaned and lay back again.

"Where?" I asked, amazed. I saw blood on the pillow, and on the washstand his bowl was filled with cloudy, rust-colored water.

"He tore my clothes," Chase said sadly, indicating a messy pile on the floor. "He also raped me, not that that in *any* way excuses his rudeness."

"Raped you! Not really . . ."

"Really. He theoretically strangled me, and my nose may be broken." He sat up again. "Oh God, I ache all over. . . . Bring me that coffee. Maybe it's still hot."

I said, "Tell me what happened. Was it that guy in the pissoir?"

"Who? Oh no, no . . . After that." He drank the coffee and closed his eyes. "I was walking back along the river and this man stops his car and asks if I wanted a *piccola passeggiata.*"

I suggested he was going to have two black eyes. He slumped back against the pillows.

"Shouldn't you tell the police?"

"Oh, yes, of course, the police. . . . Wouldn't they love it. Three in the morning strolling along the river."

"What happened?"

". . . I got in the car and we drove into the park somewhere." Chase shifted and groaned in pain. "He was rude to my ribs," he said.

"What did he look like?"

"Big, dirty and mean—just the way I like them. He never said a word."

"Chase, you've been beaten and raped. This was not a romantic interlude."

He smiled wanly. "It does sound divine . . . Tell Zá-zá I won't be down for lunch. When I wake up this will all be over and my beauty will be restored. Now go away and let me sleep."

Later, in the afternoon, I saw him in the street, in sunglasses and rather overdressed.

"Why the suit?" I asked. "You look like a lesbian."

He raised the sunglasses momentarily to reveal a dark half-moon under each eye. "The costume is to divert attention." He was on his way to Doney's for tea, since apparently life went on.

"Tell me," I said when we had settled in, "what was it really like?"

"Peter, both heaven and hell. Terribly exciting and frightening. It hurt and it felt good. I think what made him so mad was my enthusiasm for it all as an idea." He sighed.

"He could have killed you," I said.

"True. But he didn't. And all my life I will have this delicious memory. In the end, you know, we have only our memories. This will be among my most treasured."

He continued to make light of it, referring to the incident in funny ironic ways long after the bruises had faded and the half-moons disappeared. But now I can only think that this rape affected him as nothing ever had. I believe it changed the way he thought of himself. It seemed afterward that he began to complain about the inadequacies of sex, its inevitable disappointment. He no longer rhapsodized over it, except in a way one would call tangential: the specifics of what attracted him were narrowed to the externals—the rituals and theatrics of sex, rather than its physical actualities. He was as apt to respond to someone's muddy boots or idiosyncratic clothes as to his eyes, finding in an accoutrement the intense point of sexual interest usually assigned to all or part of the person: in short, fetishism.

"Look at that man's overalls," he said to me one day in the arcade.

"What about them?"

"Well, aren't they exquisite? Such a color, such softness—like a mouse's underbelly."

"Chase," I said, "they're overalls, not slipcovers."

"But wouldn't you love to crawl all over him and smell him?" he said dreamily.

This kind of talk embarrassed me, though clearly it should not have. It showed Chase's sexual nature in what seemed a peculiar, unfamiliar, unflattering light.

One evening he received a phone call during dinner inviting him to tea the next afternoon. When he returned to the table—Rashid had been thrown out and Margi was dining with her fiancé—he dabbed his lips with his napkin and said, "Count Niccolo Virgiliano has invited me to view his Caravaggio. I said you were visiting and he invited you to come too. He lives in Palazzo Virgiliano in Via Virgiliano and has an arrangement with the Questura to keep him informed of all new gay arrivals."

"How do you know him?" I asked.

"Grandmère knew the family. Their Caravaggio has never been photographed."

The next afternoon, after an extensive toilette, we presented ourselves at Palazzo Virgiliano, which abutted the Pitti and was favored with a private entrance to the Boboli Gardens. A butler in a striped coat took us up in a small mahogany elevator, delivering us into a three-storyed paneled library in which the floor, tables and all the chairs were covered in bright green baize cloth.

"Numbers three and five," Chase muttered. A door opened and the count came in.

Virgiliano was over sixty, very tall, thin and gray, and had crossed over that line between the truly aristocratic and the truly effeminate. In the fifteenth century his family had enjoyed its great historical moment with the Humanists and had lived in the reflected glory of this connection ever since. Grandmère Chase and Count Niccolo's mother were contemporaries and had met in the forties. Chase said Niccolo had known every gay tourist to visit Florence since the Brownings. English translations were his hobby, American boys his passion.

"Chase, I'm delighted," Niccolo said, embracing him.

I was introduced and Niccolo offered us tea, or something stronger. He spoke in a convincing American accent. We went into a sitting room off the library. On the wall over the sofa was the Caravaggio—a young Bacchus with lyre, fruit and flowers in sharp chiaroscuro.

"From the artist's earlier period, of course," Niccolo said. "Before his troubles began. . . ."

Tea was brought in, on a tray with thirty objects for three people, and Niccolo asked if I would be mother. I had no idea what he meant and gave him a perfectly stupid look.

"Pour, Peter," Chase said, and Niccolo smiled.

"So," he began, "What are you boys doing in Florence, besides breaking hearts and stopping traffic?"

"I should have thought that was quite enough," Chase replied smoothly. We went on lightly in this vein until Chase got up and crossed to a chest of drawers between the windows. "What an interesting commode," he said. "Chippendale, isn't it?"

"I have often hoped," Niccolo replied.

Chase got down to look under it, then stood up and ran his fingertips gently over the marquetry. "I've seen one like it somewhere."

Niccolo did not seem particularly interested, or perhaps he was nonplussed by the genteel cast of the conversation. "You must come back one day and go over the whole place." He turned

34

to me. "And you, my dear. What are your interests?" He handed me his empty cup. Filling it, someone in me like the young Emily Dickinson replied, "I would like to be a writer."

Taking back the cup he said, "And who are your favorites?"

I said Forster, Genet.

"Really! Antiques and literature. You boys surprise me no end."

In the street outside Chase announced, "The commode of course, like the painting, is a fake."

"How do you know that?"

"Peter, this is the city of fakes. They fake everything here, from furniture to orgasm."

"Didn't you enjoy all that?"

"Virgiliano is rich but he's old," Chase replied. "He's tall but he's thin. . . . He's too polite and condescending. *'And you, my dear. . . .'* He was, however, foiled by two perfect young ladies."

The boy Lorenzo, Zá-zá's nephew, was fifteen, and that winter sixteen—old enough now to help in the dining room. And we thought it a mercy that Rashid had been thus spared; for Lorenzo was living art. Hardly any of us, male or female, took our eyes from him as he came and went. Zá-zá herself favored him like an idol, called him *bello,* smoothing his hair and petting his cheek—as the rest of us would have done, given the chance. We watched him the way women watch a beautiful child who is not theirs, exchanging glances and shaking our heads.

Lorenzo was big for his age, broad and sturdy-looking, with coal-black curly hair and the glorious eyes and lashes of an actress. He was shaped, apparently on the strength of the odd soccer game, like a young gymnast, with the line of a lyre down his back and a perfect, high, melon-shaped ass. It was easy to think of the rest of him in terms of fruit—firm, fresh, pickable, tasty—or perhaps of flowers, including the idea of fragrance and the subtlety of delicate, translucent coloring. He seemed never to speak aloud, only occasionally whispering in reply to whatever Zá-zá said to him, which suggested that the disposition we knew so little about was yielding and sweet. Or sometimes it seemed that his beauty, like a debt, must be otherwise repaid—with young meanness or dense stupidity, or untenable narcissism—balancing the riches he had been given with necessities withheld. It was impossible to tell, for if any of us said a word to him he blushed or affected not to understand. Chase said Zá-zá had warned Lorenzo off all of us, filling his head with tales of our strangeness and corruption. In any event, he avoided us. "She's sure we'll eat him," Chase speculated. "And she's right. The boy supersedes the genre."

Chase's own good looks mildly anesthetized him to youth and physical perfection in others—that is, beauty without the telling bits and pieces of idiosyncracy. For Chase, the signature of sex was written with a less meticulous hand. Desire should be, in his phrase, "vividly natural," meaning unrefined, filled with passionate flaws, the smells and smudges of sex, exaggerations, even the aberrations of a deep, continually unrequited yearning that never abated and was never appeased. The easy delectation of young beauty did not appeal to him, although after his own rape something in the idea of the innocent child's defilement— at the hands of a true sadist perhaps—momentarily piqued his interest; as would the rape of a nun, in which the mockery of vows is poured like a sauce over the hot dish of outrage. While I might have daydreamed of Lorenzo's smooth olive skin, Chase allowed himself to picture for a moment, in the abstract, the frightened eyes of an animal caught in the teeth of a trap.

But all of this was idle speculation. We would as soon have tried to drag down Zá-zá herself. The point was that in the case of Lorenzo we thought it pretty merely to think about.

One day Zá-zá put before me at lunch a plate containing twice the amount of pasta everyone else had been given. Chase and Margi looked at their plates and then at mine. The same thing happened at dinner and again at lunch the following day. Zá-zá always came around with seconds, so that these enormous portions arrived with the force of a message.

"Per il principe," Zá-zá said with a chuckle as she set one of them before me. It was not at first clear that the plates were coming from Lorenzo. After a few days of this, I asked why I was being fattened up.

"Buh, I don't know," Zá-zá replied. "Ask Lorenzo. He fills the plates. Is it too much?"

"He's trying to tell you he likes you," Margi volunteered somewhat ingenuously when Zá-zá had left the table; and then, thinking again, she added, "But if you touch a hair on his head I will personally call the police."

"A young Tadzio, if ever I saw one," Chase remarked. "The young of this species devour their suitors, like spiders."

And then, after a few more days, the portions of food returned to normal. Lorenzo had disappeared. When we asked where he was, Zá-zá replied offhandedly that he had returned to school.

Quite sweetly and bravely, since she had not been required to do it, Margi invited Chase and me to her wedding and to the reception afterward at the villa of her new in-laws, near Fiesole. The wedding could be described as an apotheosis, the transformation of an ordinary blonde American beauty into the queen of Italian wedded bliss, ever after a goddess of marital attainment and legitimacy. The groom, who bore the title of baronet, was the sunny, easy-going and affable result of his mother's capacity to interpret facial expressions in her first-born, thereby obviating the need for actual tears and cries of need, and in the end obviating all need itself; so that Marco in life had seldom thought he absolutely had to have anything in particular—except lately: a beautiful girl to make love to on a regular basis. He had seen and selected Margi on the bus to Fiesole. Had she in any way resisted him, Marco was not the type to have pursued her. Fortunately she had perceived this from the beginning, and had adapted becomingly to a role of trusting acquiescence, masking her true nature of quiet but fierce ambition. Not that she didn't love Marco; she loved his malleability and easiness. *She* wanted enough for both of them; and besides, why should Marco be needful when he was in possession of so much? The villa might have come, stone by stone, from Beverly Hills—pool, cabaña, garden and all. She would one day be a countess. If, for now, her mother-in-law was firmly, rather suffocatingly, in charge, it was understood—rather as a prenuptial agreement with Marco—that they would spend a good deal of time traveling. All this for a cheerleading captain from White Plains.

A glacial white tent had been erected in the garden. All was elegance. Margi's parents, used to country-club life back home, thought themselves well prepared but slightly outclassed, which in a way only made them happier for their daughter. Margi's father had not realized that eye-talians could get so fancy. Her mother felt smug about her family pearls. Margi and Marco browsed from table to table, grazing socially. The bride carried a white satin bag the size of a small pillowcase into which guests stuffed checks and lire worth twenty thousand dollars. The tops of Margi's milky breasts attracted great admiration. It was thought her Italian was coming along. She need not have worried; soon she would be dreaming in it.

Perhaps not coincidentally, Count Virgiliano, an old family friend, was seated at our table. One now understood the finite boundaries of Florentine society, although he seemed surprised to see us.

"What a treat!" Niccolo declared, shaking our hands. And under his breath he added, "Breeders in full cry. Be careful you're not eaten with the cake." He rolled his eyes and flicked an imaginary mustache.

Apparently Chase and I, simply by attending this legitimizing event, had ourselves gained stature, for immediately Niccolo invited us to his country house for the weekend, which he had not brought himself to do previously. We said yes and Chase asked where it was.

"About an hour from Florence, near Arezzo," Niccolo replied. "I'll send a car for you the Friday at five."

Margi and Marco appeared. We rose and Niccolo kissed her hand.

Precisely at five on Friday Zá-zá knocked on Chase's door and said a man in a uniform and cap had arrived. We approved of the car from the window. The driver was entirely sympathetic. In the back seat Chase slowly removed imaginary gloves, finger by finger, meaning the car was his, the chauffeur was his, all of it was his.

We drove east up the valley along the Arno, veered off, came back to it, left it again, returned, while the river itself got smaller and larger and smaller again, none of it being equal to the stretch that ran through Florence. Then it disappeared altogether and we rose up into hilly country dotted with vineyards and silvery olive trees that glinted orange as the sun got lower. Chase asked how long *il conte* had had this house and the driver replied, "Three hundred years."

It was a cross between a castle and a manor, rather like a fortified villa, with a high stone wall across the front. As we came up the gravel drive I counted fourteen windows in a row across the front and four full stories, not including dormers in the attic. Virgiliano appeared with three collie dogs in a froth.

"What fun!" he declared and shook our hands. *"Giù! Giù!"* he said to the dogs, and gave one of them a swat. "Welcome to La Favola!" The driver got out and took our bags and Niccolo led us into the villa, into a large vaulted foyer peopled with suits of armor, the white stucco walls lined with swords, lances and breastplates, dirks and axes, in meticulous fan-shaped arrangements. Cannonballs had been piled here and there on the floor—the petrified droppings of war. In one corner a full-sized cannon was aimed at the imaginary hills of an ancient battle site, or directly at the front door, depending on your view. In another corner an enormous staircase rose up, clad in a bright crimson runner with shiny brass fittings, as in a Grand Hotel. Upstairs we turned into a wide hall the length of a bowling alley and Niccolo said, "Now, I've given Chase the Bishop's Room—this one . . ." We walked further down the hall. "And, er, Peter, the Green Room—this one. But you may switch, or share one room, or choose others if you wish." The Bishop's Room seemed the most distinguished.

"He wants us in separate rooms," Chase said when Niccolo had left us to settle in and freshen up, "so that he can make his midnight calls at will. Divide and fornicate." He went to the ten-foot-high window and pushed it open, turned, and declared, "One might have hoped for a little something in the way of art on the walls of the principal guest room, but the furniture isn't hideous."

Igor, the butler, waiting patiently at the bottom of the stairs, showed us into a *salotto* off the foyer, where we found Niccolo talking to a tiny old woman. Niccolo's mother lived upstairs. Chase stepped forward and actually kissed her hand. With great embarrassment I did the same. Her hand was the size and consistency of a chicken wing wearing an enormous amethyst ring.

"What sweet, polite boys," the old lady said in Italian, in a voice that sounded as if it was coming out of a telephone. "I don't suppose either of them speaks the language."

"*Sì, mama,*" Niccolo answered in a tone neither of us had heard before. "They speak it perfectly well."

We had both been studying Italian for months, I with a tutor, Chase on his own. In fact he understood it as well as I, but spoke with an atrocious accent.

There was sherry. The old lady wanted to know which of us was Anna's boy. Suddenly she said, "You're not lovers, are you?"

"Mother!" Niccolo exclaimed. "Of course they're not. What a question."

"We are merely friends, Contessa," Chase said smoothly.

"Ah, well. *Meno male*. Niccolo sometimes. . . ."

"Mother, please." He turned to us. "My mother," he said in English, "is something of a tease. She says exactly what comes into her head."

"Speak Italian or I'm going upstairs," she threatened. Wordlessly she held out her empty glass. "So," she took up the conversational thread, unpopular as it had been, "you're not lovers. What are you then, since you're obviously something? Artists?"

Chase said, "I am a university student, and Peter is a writer."

She turned in her chair, from the hips, as if from the waist up she was all one piece, which she might well have been. "A writer," she repeated dubiously, as though he had said a fortune teller or an acrobat. She peered at me like Maria Ouspenskaya—*"Forgive me, my dear, but here is the question of age. . . ."*

She looked back to Chase. "I so miss your poor grandmother —*di buon'anima."*

Chase said, "So do I, Contessa," and Niccolo said, "Chase is a furniture expert. He has already authenticated a commode for us in the city, in the Caravaggio room."

"Has he?" She looked at him. "In the what room?"

"In the city, Mother. The Caravaggio room."

"Oh, yes, I know that room. . . . You go through the library."

Niccolo said quietly, "She's tired." But rather brightly she said to Chase, "We have a few things here, too. Do you know about furniture from the Russian Imperial court?"

Chase pulled his shoulders back and said, "Yes, of course."

"Then tomorrow you will come to my apartment and see some of *my* things. Don't let the trash in this room put you off." She made a dismissive gesture. "Where has Niccolo put you?"

"Chase is in the Bishop's Room, and Peter is in the—"

"The Bishop's Room," she said. "That's right. The Bishop was actually Urban XII. In the old days they called it the Pope's Room, but I put a stop to that."

A woman in white, wearing a white snood, appeared in the

doorway and approached the contessa's chair. *"Pronto,* Principessa," the nurse said and helped her to rise. A cane was produced. Niccolo's mother was not much taller standing up than she had been sitting down. We rose with her and she said, *"A domani, e buona notte a tutti."* Niccolo leaned down and kissed her cheeks, Chase made a little bow; and slowly, as if teaching her to walk again, the nurse led her from the room.

"I thought we'd get that over with right away," Niccolo said. "Mother likes to meet whoever comes to La Favola. They are the only people she sees."

"The nurse called her Principessa," Chase said with a hush of respect in his voice.

"Mother was born Princess Odischalchi, although she does not use the title. You will hear the servants call her Principessa."

"She is magnificent," Chase said reverently.

"Yes. She was a lady-in-waiting to Maria José, the last Queen. She lives here quietly."

A moment later we went in to dinner.

In the middle of the night I heard Chase cry out. I went into the hall and listened for a moment by his door. Virgiliano was saying he was sorry, and Chase said, "Sorry! You pig! Get out!" But then things quieted down and Niccolo did not come out. I went back to bed, heard no more and fell asleep. In the morning I listened again at Chase's door, then knocked and he called out, *"Favorisca."*

As I came in he said, "Now I know how the pope got hers."

"Was it awful?"

"Awful doesn't do it justice."

"How about saying no?" I suggested.

He looked at me. "Peter, this is life. You do not say no to life."

The idea apparently was that Chase had spent the night with a dead pope. "Then don't complain about it," I said.

42

"You don't understand. There being no equivalent for this idea in New Jersey, it is not possible that you understand."

"What idea?"

"He—Niccolo—is not what I had in mind. But I am exactly what *he* had in mind. In other words, if you can't have your fantasy, *be* the fantasy—for someone else."

"Be adored, you mean."

"There is that, yes," he said, and lifted his arm. "Don't touch me today, I'm holy."

"Chase, what about the act itself? The fuck. Don't you care about that? Don't you enjoy it?"

"Yes," he replied, "but certain meals are tastier than others. I mean, really."

"You mean, it's like eating . . ."

"Peter, in some quarters, it *is* eating."

We spent the afternoon by the pool. This lay alongside a Turkish folly done up like a *hareem,* piled with striped silk cushions beneath wrap-around murals of a desert oasis on the wall. I dove into the pool from the back of a turtle fountain that gushed water out of its mouth. Chase sprinkled lemon juice on his hair to make it lighter. Niccolo took pictures for his scrapbook, principally of Chase, but also of me. After one such shot, he lowered the camera and said, "You know, Peter, the sunburn suits you." And Chase looked at me and smiled knowingly and Niccolo took another picture, this time, I later saw, capturing a look of sudden realization on my face.

That night he did not come through the door to my room, but out from behind a bookcase in the corner that creaked open like the gates of doom.

"A secret panel," I said in great excitement and turned on the lights. Niccolo closed the bookcase behind him.

"Open it again, please," I said. "Where does it lead?"

"It leads all over the villa," he replied. "This way and that."

"Take me through it."

He came over and put his hand on my shoulder. "Better to wait until daylight. In the dark you can't see where you're going. . . . Are you quite comfortable in here?"

I drew back and his hand dropped away. "Did you build that or was it here?"

"Oh, it was here. We even have a dungeon in the cellar. You must ask Chase to tell you about it."

Chase had said nothing about a dungeon. "Did he go down there with you?" I inquired.

"Yes. Would you like to see it?"

I said I didn't think so, then remembered what Chase had said about saying no to life, and said all right. He went over and pushed a dowel at the side of the bookcase, which clicked open. The scent of dank stone and dust came through the opening. Just inside, Niccolo took up a candle he had left there. The illuminated space resembled the wings of an old theatre backstage —even to ropes and counterweights to work the scenery, and doors. The walls of the passage, as we walked along in a dusty white bubble of candlelight, were sometimes stone—the outer wall of the villa—and sometimes wood lathing that oozed hardened mortar like foam. Here and there stark rectangular shapes were delineated in white paint, to show if not glow in the dark. These were the backs of movable panels into various rooms, marked in Italian: *Camera verde. Camera del papa. Picc. salotto.* etc. We descended steep, rough-hewn steps in a tight spiral to another level where a narrow stone hallway led off in the pitch dark. We spiraled further down, a considerable distance, into an enormous room at the bottom. A single light bulb hung from a wire at the center of a vault twenty-five feet high.

"Is this it?" I asked, looking for the torture racks and iron maidens.

"This is the lower cellar. The dungeon is through there." He pointed into the corner. Bats swooped and squeaked in our faces. We went stooped through a tiny doorway and down a few more steps. Niccolo flicked a switch, revealing a small space crammed with leather and metal objects. A table stood in the middle over which straps, loops and cuffs hung from the rafters. Straw littered the floor. A wooden rack with open-spoke wheels and ship-sized hawsers was up-ended like a tilt-top table; rings in the stone wall, thumbscrews lying about, a small brazier now cold, metal shapes with screws, objects not immediately recognizable—everything was oiled and dustless. Another glaring light bulb gave the little room a pained and evil attitude, an atmosphere equivalent to small, pitiful cries heard at a distance.

"Well, what do you think of it?" he asked.

I was appalled, though of course unwilling to say so. Our attenuated, pathetic aristocrat had suddenly become the master of a working dungeon, presented as nothing more than the accumulated paraphernalia of an eccentric but benign hobby, like the restoration of old cars, or an unexpected personal tick, like dressing up in women's clothes—which anyway Niccolo also enjoyed doing, one learned. It seemed his old-fashioned, almost anachronistic air, epitomized in his aged mother, had here like a sleeve been pulled inside out. A diorama of cruelty and torture, thrust into the arena of modern sex, made both the dungeon and the sex seem timeless, and Niccolo himself appear sinister and perhaps fascinating—no longer the rich old queen, but an intimate, perhaps superior, partner with great, potent sexual power.

"Take me back," I said.

"Yes, of course," he replied immediately, with a half-smile on his angular face. "Although we might discuss it."

I shook my head.

"One should not say no to life," he quoted.

"You were listening."

"Listening and watching," he replied calmly.

45

"What a little playhouse this is," I said, as if this were horrible and derisive.

"At any rate, no one can see or hear us. You might put on that mask." He indicated a black rag on the table.

"Did Chase put it on?"

He didn't answer and I started out the door.

". . . something of an American prig." He turned and pulled the heavy door closed with a single delicate click. "You would not be hurt." Some small, lingering notion—of being a disappointing guest—momentarily outweighed the guest's disappointment. We climbed the spiral stairs in the gloom and dark. With, I thought, a good-natured pat on the shoulder, he said good night and I came back through the bookcase into my room.

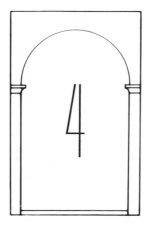

I awoke when Chase came through the door followed by Igor with my breakfast tray. Chase flicked the curtains at the window, came over to the tray beside my bed and as in the pensione helped himself to a *panino*.

"Sleep well?" he inquired. "Strange, medieval dreams?"

"You might have told me," I said sleepily.

"Told you what? That the basement closely resembles the Tower of London?"

I looked around. "He's listening, you know."

"He's gone to town." Chase was casual. "I saw him leave." He flopped down on the bed. "What happened? Did you love it?"

"What did he say?"

"Only that he came through the bookcase and you asked to see the passageways, and when you saw the dungeon you suddenly turned into a sadistic fiend. . . . Niccolo's convinced all Americans would just as soon beat you up—like Germans."

"But a dungeon," I remarked, pouring my coffee.

"Think of yourself and Lorenzo down there," he said, "and tell me you wouldn't be interested."

"Lorenzo?"

". . . Or one of your little street-finds. Anyone but Niccolo." He turned toward the bookcase. "Sorry, dear, if you're listening."

When I had dressed, Igor knocked on the door with a request that Chase call on la principessa. An hour later, flushed with excitement and incredulity, he found me by the pool.

"You are not going to grasp this, I know," he said tentatively. "It's a baroque idea."

I said nothing. Chase put great store in the relationship between excitement and unbelievability, the one proportionate to the other. In my case this was complicated by naiveté.

"Either the principessa has gone off completely," he began, "or it's the chance of a lifetime."

"Chance for what?"

"She wants me to marry her niece."

"Her niece Ralph," I said. "She *has* gone off."

He looked at me. "Yes. . . . But it's all quite logical. Niccolo won't marry, even to please her, so she has this scheme. She's looking for someone to adopt; that is, for Niccolo to adopt—who will then marry her niece and have children and save the ranch."

"And *you* are the best she can come up with . . . ?"

"She does not, apparently, have a lot to choose from. She says Niccolo likes them young and stupid."

"And would it be too illogical to pick an Italian?"

"He won't have anything to do with Italians. She never meets any."

"I came in," he began, "and she had *granità* and pastries and she said, 'You're thin, like my son,' which launched her into a speech about Niccolo being the last of the Virgilianos—about how it was, quite simply, the end for them and their world, and

---

48

the greatest disappointment of her life that her only son was homosexual. . . . The furniture is stunning—a full suite made for Catherine the Great; the Imperial Seal, and on the walls amazing Futurists and Italian Impressionists and Tibetan prayer rugs and Etruscan bits, and icons, and it's all fabulous. Any museum in the world would take it just as it is, Miss Helena included . . ."

"Stuffed, in a sitting position."

"She says I could come and go after the child was conceived. I could go back to school, travel, whatever I like, and only stay here on weekends—until. . . . The girl is an obscure princess with no money—her brother's daughter."

". . . You would become Helena's adopted son."

"Niccolo's."

"Can you be adopted with live parents? Or had you forgotten?"

"It's the old Roman deal of declaring one's heir. It can be anyone. No restrictions."

"Get it in writing," I suggested.

"You think I should do it?"

"I don't know. It's too bizarre."

"I'm to think about it and tell her next week. . . . That's why she asked if we were lovers. She said, 'What wife would want two of you here?' "

On Monday it was all ridiculous, on Tuesday entirely possible, on Wednesday definite, on Thursday absurd again. On Friday morning, when Chase awakened after a night in the streets and park, he said, "This is absurd. Maybe I should do it."

We had told no one, but talked all week long of nothing else. We made lists. It would be one life in exchange for another; one open and unknown, the other respectable, secure, enticing, even glamourous, with all the assurances of family.

Chase said, "You know, if it turned out to be Not Possible, I could simply leave."

———————

Later he said, "There is the part about babies. I would actually have to fuck someone in her poo-poo." Then he mused, "I could come in a jar and they could inseminate her like a cow," which seemed temporarily to solve the sexual misgivings. On Friday we said nothing about it until lunch. Toward the end I asked, "What the hell are you going to do? Igor will be here in three hours." And Chase said, "Not another word," and went to his room.

I went down to the amputees' bar and sat regarding all the cripples and freaks, the bewildered tourists who wandered in but did not linger, the beefy bartender whose canny, observant wife manned the cash register, the barefoot gypsy with her filthy baby who came in, saw the cripples, and quickly left, giving everyone the evil eye. I made myself think I was Chase and must decide in that moment whether or not to accept the Virgiliano offer.

Yes: Here was the legacy of a great family and its history; palaces, servants, titled in-laws and offspring; richness also of experience, a complete and utter change.

No: A masochist for a nominal guardian; a life not of one's own devising; pretending to be—if not becoming—something and someone else; giving up whatever and whoever one might otherwise have done and been.

It was clear then that the reasons for accepting were in a realm different from the reasons for refusing. One might do it for material gain or curiosity, or not do it to be true to oneself. While thinking that I would not have accepted, I could not be sure that if the question were explained to Chase in these terms he wouldn't simply wonder if the stakes were high enough.

Then Chase himself came through the red and blue plastic streamers from the street; I told him what I had been thinking, because it seemed my duty as his friend to warn him of the moral danger he faced, as if he were selling his soul.

"Look," he said impatiently, "it's no different from any other bride proposal. And if it's a question of selling one's soul, I sold that years ago. In fact I gave it away."

"Then what are you going to do?"

"It's Donna Helena. After Grandmère, I simply cannot say no to an old lady. I'm going to try it."

"But what about your own life?" I said, truly surprised and looking at my watch to see if time remained for him to change his mind again.

"This *is* my life," he protested. "Who else's life is it? I'm sure they'll agree to a trial period. If not, I will graciously decline."

In the end, when Igor came at five o'clock, Chase went with him back to La Favola.

On Sunday he telephoned the Bardolini to say that Niccolo and he would be returning to town and would I come to dinner on Monday. I asked him about keeping his room at the pensione and he said, "I'm certainly not going to give it up. Think of it as Lola Montcz's empty wagon, following Liszt's at a distance."

Monday evening, after an appreciable walk behind Igor, I was shown into Chase's room—rooms. Chase was sitting in a chair by the window, smoking a cigarette and gazing at the gardens below.

"May I simply say, number five?" he whispered, kissing me on both cheeks.

"Just this once," I replied, looking about the room. Besides being enormous, which was easy in Florence, it was lovely. "Do the walls have ears here too?" I asked dubiously.

"Niccolo swears not, but who knows?" he replied. "It seems they confine that sort of thing to La Favola on weekends."

He showed me through the rest. "Have you ever seen such a bed? It's like sleeping in a big hat." The bed, of flounces and fringe, was easily fifteen feet tall. We went back into the sitting room and drank champagne. I asked about the adoption. "It's on," he said. "I will be about twelfth in line for the Italian throne." He had spent most of the weekend in long talks with Niccolo's mother. Donna Helena was telling him everything she could remember—the intrigues, the accomplishments, the scandals, the characters. She showed him photographs, gave him notes on behavior. She hated his clothes. His accent was unacceptable. His hair was too long. He was, however, good at table.

Soon he had established a routine that unfolded pleasantly day by day, in a succession of Italian lessons, suit fittings, the opera, dinner out with Niccolo—living at the Bardolini during the week, with weekends at La Favola. Adoption proceedings were begun immediately and went along quickly because Donna Helena so felt the dwindling of time. Chase would become Chase Walker Virgiliano about the time he got engaged—in the spring. Along with the name would come an allowance of one thousand dollars a month, beginning immediately, which at the marriage would be increased to five thousand. One hundred thousand dollars, deposited in a Swiss account, would be paid at the birth of the first child, male or female, and for every child of the marriage thereafter. With the money Chase had already inherited from Grandmère—fifty thousand at his twenty-first birthday, just passed, and another fifty to come in his thirties—he was, as he said, "one of the richest women in the world." He said Donna Helena would not hear of his jerking off into a jar or dusting her niece like crops. "You cannot imagine the circumlocutions required to explain all of *that* to her in Italian. She assumed I was joking and thought it in the worst possible taste."

During the week he lived much as he had before the Virgilianos. On evenings he didn't spend with Niccolo, we would cruise the park. Or Chase would go out alone, having rushed home to change after a night at the opera. Occasionally I saw him and Niccolo in Piazza Repubblica after dinner, and at these times, witnessing the public act—the distinguished, gray-haired aristocrat and his ravishing purchase—you could see the power, the theatrical success of the two of them together: Niccolo's height, thinness and wealth, and Chase's youth and beauty. You saw, for an instant, an allusion to the great dynastic matches of the past —one state marrying another, one nation taking another into its bed, one power merging with its complement to form an alliance. The reference they made, sitting together at an outdoor café before two little cups of coffee and a lighted candle wavering in the breeze, was not to other male couples but to great glittery matches like Diamond Jim Brady and Lillian Russell, chin up and tits out, proud of her jewels; or Edward VII and Lillie Langtry, the most glamourous quadruped ever. Together they took on a power squared by their connection to each other.

At the end of November John Kennedy was assassinated. Zá-zá came into the dining room and said tentatively, *"C'e qual'cosa che non va in America.* They've shot your president." It seemed everyone thought it was a conspiracy involving the same people who had poisoned Pope John XXIII. The tears streaming down my face, I ran along the river at night and thought that if we went back to New York we would all be killed.

Chase had not realized, nor was it explained to him until rather later, that to become Niccolo's heir he must also become an Italian citizen. This meant being liable to the military until the age of twenty-seven for a mandatory two years of service. This risk he refused to take, and the whole thing was nearly called off. Then Donna Helena, or Niccolo, was able to secure a theoretical, and preferential, exemption—as a Virgiliano—on falsified medical grounds. Chase had intended after school to declare his homosexuality to stay out of the American military; this Italian medical excuse, which claimed a faulty heart ("It's not faulty," he said, "it's missing") seemed at least as effective, and perhaps less trouble, than an embarrassing sexual declaration. When he was given proof that the exemption was valid he agreed to continue, and in March, after signing many documents, he became Chase Virgiliano, legal if not titular heir to the Thirteenth Count of Arezzo.
    Also in March he met his future wife, Olympia Odischalchi, at a dinner party to which I was invited, held at La Favola so that

Donna Helena could preside. Olympia, the daughter of Helena's brother Rudolfo, was seventeen, lithe, blonde, and pretty. She fell in love with Chase immediately, having been bred for centuries and in a million tiny ways for this event: marriage to a foreign prince. The surprise that Chase was handsome so unnerved her that she wept, briefly, apparently in relief. Chase and I pitied her extravagantly. She knew nothing about sex, Niccolo said, except that women had babies and someone would eventually come along and give her one. To the idea of homosexuality, Niccolo said, she was beyond ignorance, into oblivion. Chase remarked that if Miss Olympia should come upon two men fellating each other she would assume they had been in a swimming accident and were trying to save each other's lives with extreme medical procedures.

Chase thought her childlike, and she, intuitive as a geisha, therefore became as a child in response. It was fascinating to watch her turn from the automatic class sophistication of her manner with everyone else and face him with the simple, patient, vulnerability of the young girl to her adored uncle or father, seldom taking her eyes from him, delighted by him as by the intricacies and nuances of a magic act or subtle landscape. The combination of innate sophistication and childlike affect resulted in a charged and attentive silence, punctuated with receptive sounds; the rapt gaze alternating with a demure looking away. Her mother had instructed her at the age of three in the art of the fan; she knew that a brusque tap of the closed fan meant no, definitely no.

Subsequently she and Chase met again, never alone, except once so that he could ask for her hand.

"If only it were just the hand," he said ruefully.

Chase's family, the Walkers, knew nothing of any of it; no one did. It made rather a long list of things his family knew nothing about. But the American Embassy, in the course of verifying his records, notified the Walkers of his change in citizenship, and a letter combining bewilderment and outrage arrived from New York. Could it be true? Could he possibly want to become an Italian? Had he lost his mind? Chase wrote back announcing his decision to marry and inviting his parents to the wedding. He intimated that through the love of a beautiful young woman, and practically a friend of the family, the true and natural desires of his heart had been released, restored, refurbished, redecorated, redeemed. They were to disregard all previous telephone calls and luncheons to the contrary. Becoming an Italian citizen, he wrote, was nothing more than a requirement of the bride's family—rather like becoming a Catholic—which, weren't they relieved? was in this case not necessary. He left out the part about becoming a Virgiliano, choosing to emphasize instead the social appeal of marrying an Odischalchi. Dubious but appeased, the Walkers replied that they would attend.

After the engagement, Donna Helena said Chase was free to go, to travel or do whatever he wished, as long as he returned to Florence in June for the wedding. Through a series of coincidences involving a Harvard friend in Spain, he decided to go there for two months, after first thinking of Greece, and in the beginning of April, after telling Zá-zá we would return in early June, he left for Spain and I went with him.

We took the train to Naples and embarked on the *Cristoforo Colombo*. As the ship paused by Gibraltar we stepped into a launch at dawn and were conveyed, through a bright roiling mist, to Algeciras. It was the moment for the Costa del Sol, particularly Torremolinos. All the excitement centered on a lovely beach that lay untouched at the bottom of a steep cliff, and a new bar run by a young English woman named Sheila. Sheila and her mother had been acquitted of the murder of Sheila's husband in London and they had left England forever. In Torremolinos fate blew out the right rear tire. Sheila stepped down, shaded her eyes and looked around: here lay an attractive little fishing town, undiscovered, on the road to Marbella. "This will do, Mother," she said, and they settled in Torremolinos.

The bar they opened thrived from the beginning. Sheila hired cute, short bartenders selected from among the fishermen on the beach. She put one of them in charge of music, which was free and constant, making him the first—at least, the first Spanish—deejay of the modern era. The other little bartenders, four of them, like mice, made percussive instruments out of bottle caps strung on wire, pot covers, the steam jet of the coffee machine.

We lived at first with Chase's Harvard friend, but discovering him to be pathological in too many areas—including food, sex *and* clothes—we found a furnished room with kitchen near Sheila's bar. Out came the three-piece cream-colored gabardine suits for the promenade and bullfights. This costume so confused the crowd, in their shirt sleeves and sandals, they took us for celebrities. We had only to keep our mouths shut. At first I enjoyed the bullfights. At first one did. I wondered about the bulls, the grace of dying; had read of the beast in the crowd being exorcised. Young Americans in the sixties sought out bullfights, not exactly the way one sought out the Leaning Tower of Pisa or the Mona Lisa—to say one had seen them, or even to feel one had seen them—but to qualify, as in an initiation; to see if one could pass Hemingway's little test of machismo and gore. One afternoon suddenly I realized it was *me* out there in the tight suit and black pumps; not the bull, but the man. I wondered what was *wrong* with these people, and put my head in my lap. Chase said, "Peter? What is it?" And I woke on my back in a little white room with a matronly woman standing over me, offering a glass of cognac and saying, "This one's coming around."

The beach lay at the bottom of a nearly vertical cliff, down a narrow donkey path that zigzagged through the rocks and was frankly dangerous. Later a room-sized elevator was built to haul tourists up and down, but this was before numerous accidents had led to that. The descent and climb from the beach each day had its trials and rewards, the trials being obvious. As rewards were stunning views of the sea, which from that height tilted up the sky like a blackboard, and a sense, as you went down or up, of passing backward and forward in time—past caves and huts that had in one form or another been there for centuries and were still occupied; and the cliff itself, which, having been heaved up from the ocean floor, was stratified with the layers of every age back to the Pliocene, including every camp fire ever lighted, every bone ever cooked, every hardened donkey turd. Halfway down the cliff, where a little plateau jutted out like a shelf, was a graveyard. Through a black iron gate eight feet square you saw clusters of grave markers on a quarter-acre of very uneven ground. To one side was a small stone hut where the caretaker-grave-digger lived—a man of about forty, vigorous, dark, powerfully built—who might or might not be visible through the gate as we passed. This was the game that got us up and down the cliff each day—a point for Chase if we saw him, a point for me if we didn't.

When on occasion I came up from the beach alone, I fanta-sized that the gravedigger would see me at the gate and invite me in. With these men, the fishermen especially, you had only to make yourself obvious. They would either politely pretend not to notice or smile and immediately begin to make love. I don't think it was for them so much a question of sex with a male or female, as it was sex with youth, or simply sex. Youth attracted them. This seemed clear because I was not as handsome as Chase, and yet he didn't seem ever to have an advantage over me; they reacted to both of us in the same way. It was something general that appealed to them—not angelic looks or height or coloring but an idea: that we were young.

One day the gravedigger *was* standing by the gate as I came up. I froze, as if before a coiled snake. He was opening the gate for the imminent arrival of a funeral cortege. I looked at him with the directness, the brazenness of a biblical whore—did he want it or not? Not seemed inconceivable. He gestured for me to enter and led me toward the hut. Nearby was a freshly dug grave, awaiting the cortege, its pile of dirt lying beside it like an extra blanket. I jumped down into it and we stood pressed against the wall of the grave, my eyes an inch above ground level, the tilted sea looming up like sky over our heads.

"Love and Death!" Chase shrieked when I told him about it. "Have you no shame? Can you conceive of the taboos you have *trampled?*"

"It was simply to get out of sight," I replied, "and that stifling hut was not going to be possible"—for inevitably, I had begun to talk like him.

"You are doomed," Chase said in a deep theatrical voice. "You mock death, you even mock sex and love. You are flaunting life and tempting fate . . . In a grave, darling, I love it."

Thereafter we had another new contest: to fuck in unlikely places. Chase came back one afternoon and said he had done it in a confessional in the church. He also had the gravedigger, but inside the hut. He did it in the town square in the tall grass in broad daylight; in the back of a crowded bus standing beside me in a crush of soldiers, his face immobile but red.

"Well, there's another hundred thousand down the drain," he remarked as we got off the bus and he straightened his clothes.

One afternoon, very excited, he returned to say he had just had a bull dedicated to him in the Plaza de Toros in Malaga. "Both ears *and* a tail!" A man he had met in a pissoir the night before was a well-known bullfighter.

"Can you in the least imagine? He saw me in the stands, tipped his little hat and bowed. Everyone turned. It was thrilling! Then, afterward, covered with bull's blood and a week's laundry stuffed in his pants, he passed me *this!*" Chase pulled a bloody tail out of a piece of newspaper and held it up. "I will carry it on my wedding day."

We returned to Florence in the middle of June, and on the twenty-eighth Chase and Olympia were married in the Duomo, in a ceremony delicately poised between glamour and discretion. However, an archbishop married them, and the reception afterward at Palazzo Virgiliano was sumptuous and smartly attended. By now the scheme to save the Virgilianos was common knowledge, it seemed everyone was perfectly willing to go along, if not for the family itself, then for the idea of family. The degree to which the Virgilianos were prepared to counterfeit and extend heredity, over this admittedly difficult patch, was matched by everybody's hope that they would manage it, that Chase would rise to the occasion, that the little Odischalchi girl would conceive, and that the Virgilianos, in this slightly altered but acceptably legal state, would continue on through the generations, refreshed.

Meanwhile, Zá-zá had given me my old room. Chase and Olympia went off to Lake Como to see what they could do, and I lingered, for only one reason: Lorenzo. In Spain I had conceived the notion of a grand passion for the boy. I imagined that with school out he would once again take up his duties in the dining room, which he did. The enormous plates of food again arrived at my now solitary table, placed before me by Lorenzo himself, with a slight smile. The dark down of a mustache had appeared on his upper lip, further setting off his gray eyes. He was taller and more manly, though still a boy, his skin olive and thick with youth, yet delicately colored and satin-smooth, his cheeks high and rose-colored, his lips full and pouting, his lashes long as wings. He enchanted me as had no one I had seen that year, or at any other time of my life. The thought that it was time for me to leave and that I would never see him again—at least not as the two of us were then—and that I would never touch him, seemed an injustice, a punishment in itself.

When we are young the impossibility of what we want does not occur to us. We place ourselves in the way of a thing happening and assume it will happen. The great talent of youth is this unencumbered expectation. I simply looked at Lorenzo with the force of wanting him and imagined he must answer this feeling with his own. That it did not seem to happen this way—at lunch or dinner, or passing in the ingresso—did not mean it could not or would not. In the meantime I interpreted his glances, his smile, his boisterousness as he came to know me better; the more comfortable he appeared, the faster my heart raced, the more my blood beat in my temples when he smiled or brushed by in the hall.

At night I lay in bed imagining the short walk to his room on the other side of the pensione. Once or twice, in the darkened halls, I threaded my way to his door so that lying in my bed, I would—like the myopic Rosa—know every turn and stick of furniture that led to his presence. One afternoon, in the fierce excitement of a man surrendering to passion, I stole into his empty room and buried my face in his pillow, nearly swooning over the scent of his skin and hair, which thereafter I was able to identify whenever he came near.

Unlike Chase, I had nothing to show for my year in Florence except fragments that had come to nothing, and one day in a fit of frustration and disgust, I ripped them all to pieces and burned them in the stove in my room. Gone. It seemed then that with no evidence of ever having been in Florence, the logical thing to do was leave.

I told Zá-zá I was leaving. *"Mi dispiace,"* she said with cursory surprise but no real sign of regret, or so I thought; for in my great interest in Lorenzo, scrupulously disguised, his aunt had taken on the aspect of watchdog and guardian who, had she ever imagined my interest in the boy, would have thrown me out far more angrily than she had Rashid.

"I will miss you all," I said.

"We will miss you, too, Piero," she said smiling. "Especially Lorenzo."

"He will?" I was incredulous that I had in any way evoked a response in the boy, and grateful to her for informing me of it.

"He looks up to you," she said. "He too wants to travel and see things, like you do. *Il gran viaggatore.*"

I waited anxiously for lunch so that I could tell Lorenzo to come visit me in America. I said I would be happy to see him. He looked at me strangely; perhaps even at his age he had seen the imbalance and impropriety of such a suggestion.

"When are you leaving?" he asked.

"Tomorrow."

"Not tonight?"

"No, tomorrow morning. Why?" I asked.

"I want to tell you something," he said and went about serving the food.

After the meal I lingered outside the dining room, confused and fascinated that he should have anything to say to me. But he carried the tray of dirty dishes past me and disappeared toward the kitchen. I waited a while, and when he did not come back I went down for coffee, thinking he meant to tell me at dinner.

But at dinner he said nothing, except at the last minute he leaned over and said, "I'll see you later. Later tonight."

I went for a walk through the city, even stopping in at the pissoir in Piazza Repubblica, not for sex but as a check-stop on the circuit, as if saying goodbye to old friends. I sat for a while on the Ponte Vecchio and on the bench in the Loggia in Piazza della Signoria, ritually; one last time at each favorite perch. At several points along this walk I might have involved myself with someone, but declined, saving myself, in my mind, for the impossible tryst with Lorenzo. For the fact that I was leaving and might never return had taken on the aspect of an escape, escape from Lorenzo's protectors. I thought that if Lorenzo put himself alone in my presence, if only to say a benign goodbye, I would have him; in any event, would try. It was my departure that would make this possible. A boy will do practically anything once.

I came back early and went to my room and waited. He must come, I thought. I willed him to knock on my door. Only knock, and I would do the rest.

Instead he simply walked through the door and closed it behind him, showing in his care to be silent, in the fact that he was barefoot and so had come soundlessly through the halls, the knowledge that no one must know he was there.

"*Ciao,*" he whispered. "What are you doing?"

"I was waiting for you," I said. "I wondered if you were coming."

"I had to wait until they went to bed, until after she checks on me every night."

"What if she checks again?" I asked.

"She won't," Lorenzo said, smiling, "but if she does, I put pillows under the sheet."

I doubted I had ever heard anything more thrilling. Not only had Lorenzo deceived everyone to be with me, but he had come, in a way, on free time, having left an effigy of himself as hostage, having left one kind of body behind and come to me in another, secretly. Just in arriving he had given himself to me.

"Make yourself comfortable," I said, knowing exactly how to act from the movies. But he was already walking about the room investigating, pausing here and there, picking up things and laying them down again. Occasionally he would identify something, saying, "This is your typewriter," or "This is your passport," which he opened and examined closely.

"You said you wanted to tell me something," I began.

"Yes." He paused and smiled at me, always a devastation,

the more so now, under the circumstances. Though I was five or six years older and counted myself, in comparison, mature and worldly—an educated, traveled, now somewhat jaded American to his provincial schoolboy—it was Lorenzo who seemed in control, serene and confident, and I who felt, in the seductive half-light I had carefully devised, a near-panic of confusion and longing. He simply looked at me and continued to smile.

"You are returning to America?" he said finally, delaying his question or statement even further, so that I began to think he was perhaps teasing me, or unable to bring himself to say what it was he wanted.

"Yes, I am. But I wish I could stay."

"Well, why don't you?" he said.

"My family expects me," I replied. To this he said nothing but only nodded his head, in perfect understanding of the needs and commands of family.

There was a silence. I had begun to sense, in these moments, the addition of an extra ingredient between us—something that rose up in him to meet, if not entirely match, my feelings: a response. Either that, or Lorenzo had it in mind to ask a favor and felt awkward doing so.

"Are you going to say what you wanted to tell me?" I asked, choosing to be direct.

Again he smiled, looking down at the floor, then smugly up at me. "Can't you guess?" he said.

"Maybe I can," I replied, smiling back, realizing there would have to be a game with one so young, to make it possible; and I thought that in playing this game we might manage, in ritual merriment, to tack right up beside each other. I asked a safe but leading question. "Does it have to do with you and me?" Rather than you *or* me.

"Yes," he replied, firing from the hip.

"Something you want to say . . . or do?" I asked.

"Do."

"I'll be glad to do whatever you like," I said. "Anything at all."

Who knows how long this banter would have gone on if his own body hadn't betrayed him. He grabbed himself with his hand to show me he was excited. Instinctively I did the same, to reassure him. I locked the door, and wordlessly we removed our clothes.

Lorenzo revealed his treasures negligently, one after another, with the oblivion of indescribable wealth, and naked he hopped onto my bed. I sat on the edge for a moment regarding him, then lay down beside him, caressing him and kissing his shoulder.

It was the experience I had never had as a boy with another boy—youth and youth. We made love to each other several times, taking turns as if at bat, as if still playing a game in which first he and then I stepped up and loved. Chase would call it prehistoric sex, when two people take off their clothes and get into bed. In the twenty years since that night I have slept with hundreds of men. But in that long numerical count I never felt what I did for Lorenzo, that single night, the last night of the year I discovered myself.

•

I didn't see Chase for two years after his marriage to Olympia Odischalchi. However I have his letters, which I imagine so improve on life as lived, both in import and emphasis, that the need for actual history fades. In any event the facts are few. At Lake Como, on the honeymoon apparently, Olympia conceived. I have a letter about this trip, preserved despite Chase's request to burn it: 'I simply can't get over the feeling she's been mutilated.'

Triumphant, Olympia retired to Villa La Favola and the exquisite care and counseling of Donna Helena. In September 1964 Chase returned to Cambridge for his final year at Harvard. In February of '65 a blond boy child was born—Niccolino Virgiliano, Fourteenth Count of Arezzo, the crowning achievement of Donna Helena's old age. This event so pleased and relieved the old lady she made Chase the extra gift of six million lire, and Chase, who had flown in for the ceremonious *accouchement*, sent half this amount to me in New York, together with a letter that said, in part:

> You can't imagine the delirium. Helena is awed, as are we all, by the resemblance between herself and the child—for she long ago began to look like a newborn. Niccolino, her most distant relation, has her eyes, her at times toothless, crooked smile, the same abrupt, jerky movements of the hands. She wants him with her always, in case she should die—at which time, she insists, her soul will merge with his. Either way the child will have a crowded life. You never saw such fuss over the *least* fart . . . Concerning the enclosed, you may find these new bills too small for placemats, in which case I wish you would spend them on something like a trip to Rio.

As for *how* Olympia conceived, the letters only allude. In the first I received, in New York a month after leaving Lorenzo, Chase wrote:

> I was hopeless at night, but every man in the world wakes up with a piss hard-on in the morning, and it's rather easy then, if I can control my fantasies and just sleepily do it. To this end I have collected a sweet array of pornography, none of which she will even glim. You know my tastes. Please send along a heir-raising shot.

This I did, receiving back the comment: 'The very odor of Times Square lifts from the pages. I so miss New York, I miss the third balcony of the Lyric Theatre at midnight. I miss the crotch of an unknown, unknowable Transit cop, I miss toying with the man who comes to read the meter. I miss passion!'

After the child was born, Chase, while welcome, was less sought after by the Virgilianos. They did not press him to visit, nor, when he was there, to stay. According to his letters he made three trips to Florence the year Lino was born, and just one the year after. His relationships to Niccolo and Olympia evolved into a kind of siblingship in which the talk was easy, glib, sophisticated and emotionless. Niccolo went on unchanged, vestigially youthful, still somewhere and somehow the child, as long as his mother lived.

In 1965 Chase wrote that one day in May Donna Helena took a close look at Lino, reached out to pinch the succulent flesh of the baby's fat upper arm and said, "Nothing to worry about here." She gave a long, peaceful sigh, relaxed completely and closed her eyes. When she awakened she would not or could not respond to anything that was said to her. A few days later, aged eighty-two, she died in her sleep.

The year after Florence—1964—is rather lost, lost in the way I felt, lost in what I did with it. I dreamed of Lorenzo, and like a lover stranded by war lived on the memories of my last night with him. I dreamed that the years would pass and he would mature; he would catch up and set off to find me, as haunted as I over the years by that single night. In the meantime purity was required. I held myself in sacred aloofness, vestal reserve. I could remember his face only in the ecstasy of sex, alone, when his young gray eyes, smug with sexual power, regarded me for an instant and disappeared. I was twenty-three, Lorenzo seventeen.

It was the moment before Vietnam. In Florence that winter I had been called up for an Army physical, endured at the American military base in Livorno. Now, back in New York, I learned I had been exempted for minor medical reasons—reasons that would not have obtained later on, when the war escalated. The examining doctor was homosexual and had offered at the conclusion of the physical to excuse me for sexual favors. Properly and stupidly I refused. But perhaps he let me off anyway, for there was nothing wrong with me. In New York I thought I might study and then teach English. But someone pointed out that a writer, if not alone, should be among other writers rather than teachers —in a workshop. I therefore sent off thirty pages of high twaddle to the best workshop, which then was in the Midwest, and a few months later was accepted.

Periodically, I wrote Signora Zá-zá a card at the Bardolini, primarily as an excuse to include my fond regards for Lorenzo. In a hagiography I discovered his *onomastico*, his name day, which in Italy is more important than a birthday. St. Lorenzo, July 21. Boldly I sent him a card marking the day. In Iowa, through the frigid winter, he had warmed me. I would come around the corner in the early morning on my way to class and see the temperature sign over the bank: week after week it read minus twenty degrees, and I would say to myself, "Lorenzo."

It was to be with him that I began a novel about Florence —never finished—to create for myself what I couldn't have, to meet him at my desk each day and be with him for hours. But like his image in memory, after the initial and obvious elation, he faded. And in the book Lorenzo flicks in and out, here and there, a fond oblique illusion always out of focus. I could not make him a center of the novel—for the same reason I couldn't remember his face: because I hadn't known him at all. Instead, I made a construction in which my small idea of him would live. He was attached to this construction like an emblem, each brief mention of him encoding my true feelings and desires, which in seeing him appear were momentarily clear to me. Although I couldn't say it, this was what I wanted—Lorenzo—even if I wasn't sure what Lorenzo was or represented. In the novel he is the equivalent of the JMJ the nuns used to write at the top of the blackboard— for Jesus, Mary and Joseph. Now, looking back, he is the angel of youth and health, whom I had slept with one night and whom, sadly and at a distance, I so longed to see again.

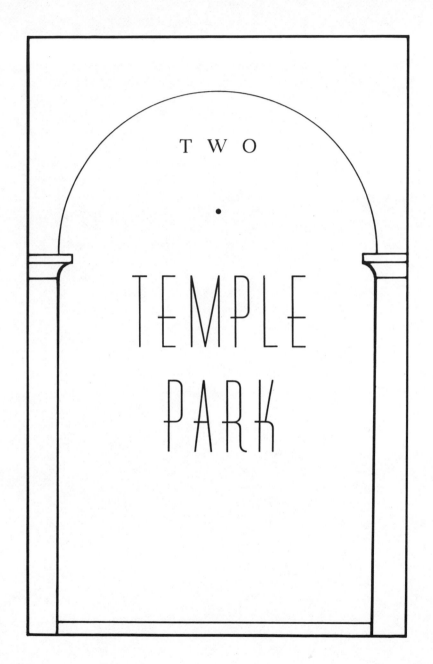

TWO

·

TEMPLE
PARK

I promise and swear that I will not write, print, stamp, stain, hew, cut, carve, indent, paint or ingrave it [Masonic Secrets] on anything moveable or immoveable, binding myself under no less penalty than to have my throat cut across, my tongue torn out by the roots, and my body buried in the rough sands of the sea at low water mark, where the tide ebbs and flows twice in twenty-four hours; so help me God, and keep me steadfast in the dire performance of the same.

—*The Masonic Oath*

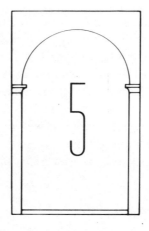

'I'o tell the story it is necessary to jump back a hundred years, to New York City in 1857, to the time of an ancestor of Chase Walker—his great-great-great-grandfather Orvil Starkweather, and to begin with a brief history of Central Park, and something about the Masons.

In 1844 the American poet William Cullen Bryant called for a park to be created in the center of Manhattan, before all available land was lost to development. In 1850, after both mayoral candidates made it a promise of the campaign, a Common Council purchased necessary but "unprepossessing" land from various owners for five million dollars. The next year a competition was declared by the First Board of Park Commissioners, assisted by a committee that included Bryant and Washington Irving. Thirty-three designs were submitted for consideration by the Board. Frederick Law Olmsted and his partner Calvert Vaux called their entry *Greensward*, a simple uncluttered plan calling for a picturesque landscape of glade, copse, water and rock outcropping. Greensward varied chiefly from the other designs in its revolutionary treatment of four required park transverses. Sinking them in troughs below the park obviated disturbance of the pastoral mood. If only for this innovation Greensward deserved to win.

It was for another of its features, however, that the design was chosen—a feature Olmsted himself added secretly, in an agreement with a member of the first Park Commission. This feature remained utterly hidden from everyone, including Calvert Vaux.

When the idea for Central Park took hold in the city, it was natural, and in a way automatic, that one or more of the men on the First Board of Park Commissioners should be Freemasons. From George Washington and the Founding Fathers on down, many of the most influential figures in the country had been Brothers of the Craft. In the matter of Greensward and Central Park, one of the Commissioners was also Grand Master of the New York Lodges: Orvil Starkweather, Chase's ancestor. It was Starkweather who wanted the secret feature added to the winning plan. In a private meeting with Olmstead, Starkweather explained that award of the commission to design the park would depend on an agreement between them. If Olmsted would make one addition to Greensward, and agree to keep it forever secret, horticultural and civic fame would be his.

By 1860, as for much of the previous hundred years, success in the United States in most spheres except religion and art was possible through this extensive, by now rather public, old-boy circuit of endless complexity, of cooperation and unquestioned loyalty—the Brotherhood of the Antient, Free and Accepted Order of Masons. Every county and city of size in the East had its Blue Lodge or Odd Fellows Hall. The abiding rule of the Masons was brotherhood, support and friendship. In America in 1857 a Freemason would trust with his life any man who displayed the Masonic emblem. In the end, as an example of its ubiquity in the society, elements of this emblem even turned up, faintly disguised, in the Great Seal of the United States.

Olmsted was thus invited to an interview at Commissioner Starkweather's house on East Eleventh Street. Egbert Vielé, the park's first surveyor—and Olmsted and Vaux's main competitor for the commission—had earlier proved obtuse and uncooperative in a similar meeting with Starkweather. Olmsted had recently published a book on Abolition that was widely admired, and Washington Irving himself had put him up as first Park Superintendent, a job for which, ironically, the Commission thought Olmsted too literary. Only Orvil Starkweather's power with the other Commissioners had seen him through. Olmsted was thirty-five, Starkweather fifty-four. Except for Orvil's financial and corporeal heft, the two men were similar, especially in the focus of their intent. Frederick was wildly ambitious, with the specific if vague desire to change and improve American life. He did not possess Orvil's cynicism, but certainly thought he knew why he was there; he had seen Starkweather's influence with the other Commissioners and sensed, as an animal senses water, that in a moment the direction of his life might change.

Orvil outlined the situation. "I believe you'll favor what I am about to say, once you've heard it," he said. "I'm confident of it. But first, before going on, may I ask you, sir, if you are a Brother of the Craft?"

This was the moment. Frederick felt something pass through him. "Yes," he replied. ". . . that is, I was, at school. The Scottish Rite in Brooklyn. But I have not kept up with it, I'm afraid."

"Nevertheless!" Orvil declared, enormously pleased. "You will solemnly agree, then, as a Freemason sworn to the Craft, to the total secrecy of this discussion and of the idea that comes out of it, under the usual oaths, for as long as you live."

"Yes, sir, I do," Frederick replied formally.

"And so help you God."

"So help me God."

"Good. It all depends on you," Orvil said. "I knew you wouldn't fail us." He opened a drawer in his desk with a key and removed a single sheet of paper. This he handed wordlessly to Frederick. On the paper was drawn a simple diagram of a building to be built underground. Across the top was written TEMPLE PARK.

Frederick regarded the drawing. It showed an underground space perceived in cross section. All of it was below grade, a rectangle lying in the ground, half again as long as it was wide and tall, in two stories, with two large ceremonial rooms above and five smaller chambers below, connected at one end by a spiral stairway —all of it simply but competently drawn by an architect. That which showed above ground, aside from five air vents like smoke-stacks, was merely the top of a spiral staircase. Below grade these stairs changed at a landing to a proper, even a monumental descent, into the first of the two large rooms. This first room, a foyer or porch, was, according to specifications, thirty feet high and forty feet across. The second room was taller and circular and sixty feet across.

"What," Olmsted said, "is Temple Park?"

"The Central Park," Starkweather replied. "Your Central Park. Temple Park is our name for part of it. Your park, my temple," he said, and smiled. "You and I, Mr Olmsted, will build the finest Masonic temple in this country—in the world. It will be our principal temple. It will be, in a way, our cathedral."

Olmsted stared a moment and said, "But may I ask, sir, why in the park? Why under the ground? Why not on the street, where people can see it—and admire it?"

"It's to be a *secret* lodge," Starkweather said, with surprise and something like sudden doubt in his voice. "You *are* capable of building such a thing, I presume? That is, under the ground and in total secrecy."

76

Olmsted examined the drawing further, then looked up again at Starkweather. "Yes. It's quite straightforward," he said, sensing—since he had already agreed—that Starkweather would prefer directness to caution. "Only these air vents and the staircase show above ground. . . . However, the implications are difficult in the extreme. Building it is one thing; even maintaining it. But having access in secret in a public park—this is the great problem. That is, if it absolutely must remain secret." Frederick paused.

"My dear sir," Starkweather said impatiently, as if this were the last time he would take the trouble, and perhaps further risk, to explain it. "Secret is the point."

Olmsted said that he saw.

"We will come and go only at night. I leave the exact location to you. Think about it carefully and present a plan—at your convenience, but within the next two months."

Olmsted did not know that the Board already had practically decided to award the commission to his Greensward, and that he needn't have agreed to Starkweather's extortion, although there existed the possibility that under Starkweather's powerful veto, Greensward, like Egbert Vielé's similar plan, might not win. Moreover, nearly everyone submitting a viable plan had been approached by private interests wanting additions to the park in return for money or favors. Throughout the park's construction, Olmsted himself would be plagued by them. Starkweather's offer seemed the most likely way to insure—if insurance was necessary —the award itself.

Orvil offered Frederick his hand, ending the interview. "I congratulate you, sir," he said. "You will, I am sure, construct a beautiful park, and a magnificent temple. You may take the drawing. I have a tracing."

As the first Landscape Architect—the term was invented for him —Frederick Law Olmsted was minimally interested in interior spaces, in buildings or temples, in their contents or function. His theory of gardening—the manipulation of flora and spaces on a large scale—broke with traditional arrangements of the outdoors into formal, roomlike patterns of elegant predictability, patterns that made you think, as in the precisely ordered gardens of Europe, of the great Indoors.

Still, the problem presented to him by Commissioner Starkweather—besides representing the career opportunity of his life—was in itself intriguing. It was the sort of thing his partner Calvert Vaux thrived on: the quest for form and function within the context of site requirements. To achieve the best solution he was tempted to present the architectural problem to Calvert, if only in a theoretical way; but did not. Instead he retired to his office with Starkweather's drawing and the complete plans for Greensward.

Three obvious problems attached to the idea of Temple Park had already occurred to him: choice of site, feasibility and secrecy of construction, and secrecy of continued access and maintenance. How to build a large underground structure, reaching some sixty or seventy feet into the ground—requiring the removal of thousands of tons of earth, and perhaps a quantity of the ubiquitous schist underlying most of the city—without the knowledge of either the public, the general park crew, the other Commissioners, or Calvert Vaux himself? How to hide not only the construction but its cost? How to effect the entry and exit of fifty or a hundred men and more, in and out of Central Park at night, without attracting attention?

And the biggest question: Why? Why the secret temple, when there already existed a small but perfectly good Lodge on lower Broadway? If secrecy was indeed automatic, even mandatory, with the Masons, why in the park? As Park Superintendent appointed by the Board, as an employee, Olmsted expected to take orders; as a practical man he was unsurprised at the private exercise of influence and power; this was the way the city, every city, was governed and run. But it seemed clear, should they be discovered in this hopelessly parochial scheme, in a clandestine and apparently illegal act within the greatest public project in America, that they and he would be ruined, perhaps imprisoned. A secret Masonic temple buried in the ground beneath Central Park seemed, especially in the political climate of the day, the height of folly.

The Anti-Mason Party, formed in 1826 to stem the pervasive, ever-growing influence of the Masons in politics, had thrived until the mid-forties. Within the Brotherhood this period was referred to as the "Persecution." Not until the Civil War would they reclaim respectability, with reports that captured Mason soldiers on both sides received special treatment at the hands of their Mason captors. For now, it seemed to Olmsted, the scheme was a mad, misdirected waste of money and effort by people who should have known better.

Nevertheless. He had agreed; and his future depended on the success of his solution. He spread the map of the proposed park before him.

Certain things were immediately obvious. The five air vents and the entrance—the spiral stair—could be hidden only in a building, with, for instance, the vents disguised as chimneys. Since Greensward had already been submitted, he would have to choose a building already in the plans.

Also, traffic through the park at night would go unnoticed, would in fact be permitted, only on the four transverse roads. Of these one was featureless, a trough of white stone cut through the proposed greenery at Ninety-sixth Street. No buildings. Olmsted imagined the Brothers arriving by carriage. Only the poor walked —not to mention the hour, and the distance uptown. But if a carriage could enter the park unobtrusively at night, it could not, along with so many other carriages, simply drop its passengers in the middle of a muddy transverse, especially men of the type and class who were Masons. Not only the location of the temple but the safety and identities of its Initiates must be protected. It would be necessary for the building to give directly onto the street.

By simple and immediate deduction this eliminated another of the transverses, the one at Sixty-sixth Street, which offered nothing really suitable. That left those at Seventy-ninth and Eighty-sixth. Olmsted examined each.

With a leap of respect for Calvert Vaux, whom he otherwise disliked, Olmsted saw that his partner had unwittingly solved the first problem. There on the Eighty-sixth Street transverse, already planned, was the answer: a proposed livery stable—complete with multiple sets of double doors—right on the street, with copious chimneys and vents; with, even, skylights for sentinels. Here was the only place in the park where carriages would logically come and go, taking on and discharging passengers at all hours. In addition Olmsted observed that curves in the road, and even an overpass for the Park Drive, concealed the eastern and western reaches of the transverse—not that it mattered.

In the following days Olmsted searched for an alternative site, both in the plans and in the park itself. But nothing could match the proposed Stable and Carriage House as a solution; and always he returned to the Eighty-sixth Street transverse, at present a long dusty lane just north of Belvedere Basin. He had the ground resurveyed to determine where the schist stopped. This took some weeks. Finally, a week or so short of Starkweather's deadline, he called again on the Commissioner at his home on Eleventh Street.

Olmsted was by now fully acquainted with the problems and ramifications of Temple Park, as well as deeply intimidated by the amount of work facing him in the general construction of Greensward, and he still half-thought to change Starkweather's mind or to convince him to put the temple elsewhere; perhaps even to refurbish or replace the existing Lodge on Broadway.

On the other hand, the scheme was so daring and imaginative, a child's game for wealthy men—romantic, illegal, exciting and hardly real, obsessive and thoroughly Masonic, so thoroughly the idea of men without women—that Frederick, hanging back, felt drawn into it. Orvil sat in his enormous favorite chair, with such wings it seemed more a stuffed bird than a chair, a tiny glass of sherry in his hand rather incidentally, along with a half-smoked cigar. His dark gimlet eyes sparkled from the fire, a thin smile on his lips. With now and then a glimpse into the grate, he regarded Olmsted pleasantly, perhaps expectantly, not saying a word. It was thought, among the other Commissioners, that nothing so unnerved them all at their meetings as one of Starkweather's pregnant silences.

Frederick had brought with him a reduced version of the master sheet for Greensward, an overlay of the livery stable complex and a set of developed blueprints for the underground temple, including elevations for the proposed Carriage House and Forge. He looked and felt like a man selling window shades, at the time popular. He finished his sherry quickly so that Starkweather might at least ask if he wanted more.

Instead the Commissioner gestured to a drinks table in the corner. In this way, Frederick forgot his indecision and thought only of telling his host what he had come up with, ingeniously, for Starkweather's game.

"Is it true then," the Commissioner said at last, "that you've found a way?"

"Yes, I believe so," Frederick replied, rather anxious now to perform. He looked around the big room for a suitable surface on which to display the plans. A cherrywood table glimmered in the corner, shining like caramel. "May I?" he asked, and went over to it.

Unfurling the long master sheet for Greensward, he anchored it with bronze objects from a collection of animal miniatures nearby: a pig sat on the site of the Plaza Hotel, a little horse in Columbus Circle, a dog in the Harlem Meer, and a silver frog, standing on its hind legs in a kind of leap, held down the north-western corner.

"A very noble plan," Orvil muttered politely, looking it over.

Frederick began with a statement of the three obvious problems—choice of site, secrecy of construction and secrecy of access and maintenance. In turn he eliminated Ninety-sixth Street, and then Seventy-ninth and Sixty-sixth, zeroing in dramatically on Eighty-sixth and the Stable complex. He unrolled a copy of the drawing Starkweather had given him, which Frederick himself had enlarged, together with a matching overlay of the Carriage House.

"You will notice," he said, "that this part of the Stable-as-planned fits perfectly over the Temple, with either a slight shift of the chimneys or of the Temple vents.

"If you will picture it, sir," Frederick began. "A carriage appears, here, coming in from Fifth Avenue. At a prearranged signal, let us say an amber light displayed by the coachman, a sentinel in the skylight, here, orders this first set of double doors to be opened. The carriage enters here, proceeding right into the building. Or, coming through the underpass from the West Side, it enters through the third set, here. In either case, the carriage disappears directly into the building, discharges its passengers and comes out again a moment later, through these center doors, here. In this way two carriages can enter and unload at once. Indeed, the building is long enough to accommodate four or five carriages simultaneously, perhaps even more if necessary. I propose that the entire livery concession be entrusted only to members of the Brotherhood. Otherwise the scheme is not possible.

"Once inside the Carriage House," Olmstead continued, "the Brothers—dry on rainy nights, and unseen at all times—then pass through an otherwise locked door into a small room at the western end of the building, disguised as a storeroom, and unlocked only on the nights of Lodge meetings. The Tiler of course will oversee all of this, standing here, taking the roll as

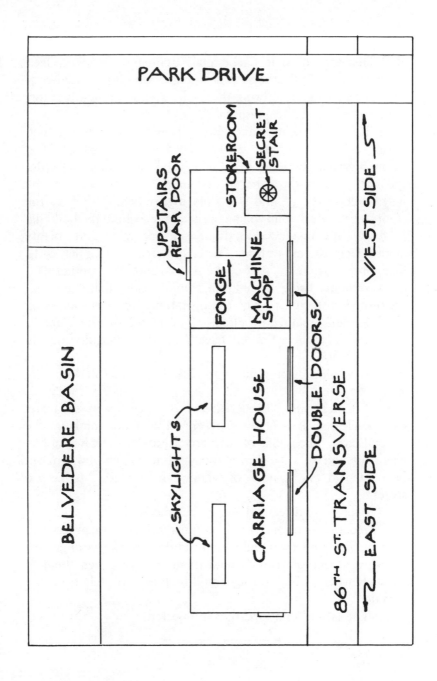

PARK DRIVE

BELVEDERE BASIN

UPSTAIRS REAR DOOR

STOREROOM

SECRET STAIR

SKYLIGHTS

FORGE

MACHINE SHOP

CARRIAGE HOUSE

DOUBLE DOORS

86TH ST. TRANSVERSE

WEST SIDE

EAST SIDE

members arrive, assisted by the Marshal and sentinels. I propose also that a stagecoach or coaches make a circuit of the city collecting certain of the Brothers, so as to cut down on the number of carriages arriving, or to bring those who do not, on that evening, have a carriage at their disposal.

"If, on the other hand, Brothers wish to come on foot, having perhaps entered the park elsewhere—say perhaps here, below Belvedere Basin, or here, along the Drive—they may enter the machine shop through a small door, at the back, where as you may perceive the ground is a story higher behind than in the front. A great deal of fill will be needed here, behind the building, to obscure it from view along the Basin. But we will have plenty of that from the excavation. There is, moreover, so much earth being moved from one part of the park to another, together with great amounts being brought in from outside, that I am not concerned with that part of the operation. No, it is something else." Frederick paused for effect. "It is the schist. The Manhattan schist, it is called. We will have to blast, and the blasting will attract attention."

"It would not be difficult to clear the area," Starkweather suggested.

"Yes, to be sure," Frederick replied. "The area would in any case be cleared. It is of the park crew that I was thinking, the general crew. Thousands of men are already at work in the Department, and we will be hiring thousands more, few of whom can be trusted at much, none of whom can be trusted to keep a secret."

"I see," Orvil seemed to say, but did not.

Frederick went on. "I plan to use a series of special crews to work on Temple Park. I will handpick fifteen or twenty engineers to excavate, and afterwards send them away or assign them to work elsewhere. Perhaps they could be hired privately from the outside."

"The latter," Starkweather interjected.

"After that, we will bring in a second crew, and then a third, and so on—none of them thinking they are building anything more than a large overflow cistern for Belvedere Basin. A last crew, comprised of Initiates, will finish the work, including modifications to the Carriage House and Forge, the chimneys, and the little storage room containing the secret entrance. From that point on, everyone employed there must be a Brother, with our Tiler in charge.

"As for the Temple itself, it will be constructed of the same rough-hewn white stone we are using to line the transverses. We will simply add to the supply already ordered for the cuts. Other materiel will be diverted from constructions elsewhere in the park." He paused again.

"Ah, well," Orvil began, placing his pudgy arm on Frederick's shoulder. "What a choice you were for this endeavor, sir. The solution is brilliant, brilliant! It's logical, simple, practical, and yet daring. I congratulate you. And, I think I can safely say, this will certainly assure you your next—that is, I believe, your final degree in the Brotherhood."

"I am honored," Frederick replied graciously, although he had never moved beyond the lower degrees of Freemasonry, and hardly cared to. It had all been something he had joined automatically at school.

"Yes, indeed," Orvil murmured.

"The problem above all others that we face," Olmsted said, returning to facts, "is the cost. It will be expensive, especially with outside engineers for the excavation and the huge amounts of stone for the walls and staircases. It will be difficult to pay for and more difficult to hide. Mr Green," he continued, referring to Andrew Haskell Green, the Comptroller of the Park, a notorious skinflint who could create panic on the crews just to save a penny, and who ruled Central Park like a despot—"Mr Green is in fact our biggest problem."

"I will handle Mr Green," the Commissioner said briefly.

85

He drew himself up. "It is, I hope, understood that Temple Park will be paid for entirely out of Brotherhood funds. I want it clear, Mr Olmsted, in addition, that we are to build the finest-looking Masonic interior in America. We are to face the rock walls with marble. I want columns and friezes. I will send you special men when you're ready for them . . . After your men have finished, *my* men will finish—with, let us say, the final touches."

Olmsted had been able to go just so far in his enthusiasm for the actual Temple to be built underground. It was the concealing of it, the accounting for it, that had interested him. He would sooner have gone back to clearing and planting and was relieved to know that, all of it being beyond him, none of it was his final responsibility. He would create the space, unfinished, in the ground, and Starkweather would fill it.

"What would you like me to do now?" Frederick inquired.

"You may hire your engineers immediately, if you wish."

"Some other problems," Olmsted said cautiously. "My partner, Calvert Vaux, who designed the Stable complex. . . . It would be impossible to make modifications in his plans without his knowledge and approval. I don't suppose—"

A look from Starkweather killed this idea utterly.

"There is also the schist," Olmsted said, "and the blasting. He will want to know why we are going down so deep."

"I'll arrange to detain Mr Vaux elsewhere on the days, even the weeks you are blasting," Starkweather mused. "So many of his buildings are going up, he can not oversee them all quite so carefully."

"But Commissioner. The park's construction is planned in stages, just to avoid that sort of thing. The Stables are not due to go up for some years."

Starkweather allowed himself to be amazed. "Oh no, no, no, that will not do," he exclaimed. He looked suddenly overripe, like fruit in the heat. "Won't do, won't do," he repeated. He drew in a deep breath and stared at the plans.

"I have thought, however," Olmsted said slowly, "due to public demand and the unexpected popularity of the park, even as it stands, that construction of a livery for pleasure riding could be moved up, and started in a period in the nearer future—that is, when the Drive is completed, and of course after the cistern is built."

"Mr Olmsted, sir," Commissioner Starkweather suddenly resumed his hearty, clubby mode, coming up beside Frederick and draping a bulky arm along his shoulders. "What a mind for solutions, sir! I congratulate myself on choosing such a person. Excellent! Excellent! And then you and I will decide later on the precise moment. . . ."

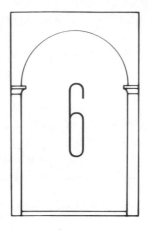

Nothing excited Orvil Starkweather like secrecy, as a tool and for its own sake. Any project that depended on secrecy for success took on glamour in his eyes and brought out the best in him. As he carefully laid out the elements of an elegant scheme or strategy, he thought of the sudden effect it would have on his friends and enemies; and the anticipation of surprise, carefully and ingeniously arranged, to him was as sweet in the making as, in the end, triumph itself.

He was the sort of man who cannot be comfortable unless given control, even of life's most banal situations. With efficiency and skill he had so arranged his existence that very little of it ever escaped his manipulation. His reputation as a generous man came from a compulsion to seize the bill for any service he had received, or simply witnessed—a restaurant check for thirty people, for example, or the divination and fulfillment of some implied whim on the part of a guest or companion. He gave copiously to charity and culture—all for control. He would often, and only to satisfy this neurosis, take the reins of his carriage from its stoic coachman, and when alone inveterately sat up front with him, not from any sense of camaraderie or self-effacement, but to choose the streets, to give constant adjustments of etiquette, and exhortations to move in the wild, muddy, cacophonous traffic.

To everyone but his delicate wife Dorothea, Orvil had the impeccable reputation of a devoted and faithful husband. In fact he was indifferent to women—including Mrs Starkweather, who had other compensations—and did not allow himself to be touched in this regard. Sex had long since been tamed, subdued, diverted into other channels. In the impersonal manner of a necessary biological experiment, he had fathered two children, afterwards transmuting these rare bodily urges into more profitable activities—his careers as stockbroker, banker, landlord, philanthropist and clubman—all of which benefited from passions and intensities other men squandered in their personal lives.

As Grand Master of the influential New York Masons, and after a few judges and senators, Orvil Starkweather was arguably the most powerful obscure person in the East. The combination of wealth, position and secrecy—a childlike but exciting element of fraternal secrecy—within an organization that boasted a half-dozen robber barons and high-level politicians—all of them sworn to blind allegiance—gave Orvil an unbeatable edge in his machinations; this during an era in New York when, as now, power brokers thrived, but without the least shred of personal conviction beyond that which commanded them, at all costs, to succeed. In the office of Grand Master, which gave him a shadow cabinet to rival that of any opposition government, he had ignored and then overridden the usual Brotherhood rule of yearly succession, and in 1857—at the time of his pact with Frederick Olmsted—had already been in full power for three years. No one thought of replacing him, and from this point on in the New York Lodge, the office of Worshipful Master was held for years on end by any who cared or managed to keep the job.

Like Venus in the surf, Orvil in 1852 had appeared suddenly on the floor of the New York Exchange, full-blown, with a carefully arranged deal of such scope and force that the holders of the richest copper claim in the country lost title. The copper stock, now Orvil's, rose dramatically; within a year he was ineffably rich.

No one knew a thing about him; nor, beyond a name for driving ambition and the qualms of a hooded executioner, would he ever be known. He was not demonstrably a crook. He did nothing overtly illegal. He was instead, you might say, shark-like, feeding on the unprotected limbs of other people's fortunes. He had failed quietly several times in metals. Steel was spoken for, sterling a British monopoly. Of the base metals, really only copper was left, and by 1857 Orvil Starkweather was effectively copper.

In the meantime he had with care placed himself socially, this being largely a matter of wife, tailor, horses and carriage, address, clubs, charity donations and constructive attention to important men, whom from the beginning he had sought out. It was to meet more of them that he allowed himself to be drawn into the Masons.

One was not asked to join; instead, one was presented and, with the right sponsors, accepted—especially during the period between 1825 and 1850, known as the Persecution. The Anti-Mason Movement had been remarkably effective. It decimated the Brotherhood; by 1830 New York membership had plummeted from twenty thousand to three thousand. Upwardly mobile wives had learned that the Masons were not respectable; they were secret and fraternal and segregationist. In the North the Anti-Mason Movement formed an alliance with the Abolitionists, who listened to the Catholics. Wasn't it, they wondered, all Zionist in the end? It was markedly ironic, certainly, that

Olmsted, a great Abolitionist authority, should be selected to build the Temple.

On the floor of the Exchange Orvil discovered the connection between the Masons and the ruling elite of New York. Certain names recurred. He realized he saw the most important men in the city rather more at the Broadway Lodge, and their representatives at the Exchange. It seemed clear that the way to advancement in one realm was through the other.

Ordinarily the Masonic process was a long, careful business conducted in a generational time scale. In Freemasonry thirty-three years was the mystical duration of the life of every Initiate who attained Mastership. But with the exigencies of the Persecution, these symbolic time requirements were waived or reduced. Within three years of his induction Orvil had attained the "hour of high twelve," meaning he had achieved the required mystical age of twelve—seven years of Apprenticeship and five years of Fellowcraft—and in 1853 he became a Master Mason.

He gave himself over to the workings of the Lodge and was recruited and used in minor offices and committees, all the while accumulating information and powerful friends. Sometime after his final Investiture he realized that this normal if accelerated progress through proper channels would not take him far enough. He desired the office of Worshipful Master—leader of the Blue Lodge—which in the case of New York City brought with it the title of Grand Master of every Lodge in the state, in his day numbering over three hundred. Too many influential men stood between him and this high office for it ever to be his in any automatic, eventual or relatively natural way.

Meanwhile, his eminence at the Exchange gave him leverage in the Brotherhood. After the general elections at the end of 1854 he was appointed Deputy Marshal by the new Grand Master, James MacNaughton—an important honor, considering his recent full Mastership and the traditional incestuousness of Masonic leadership. As Deputy Marshal he was given access to the complete membership roster; among other things it was his duty to inform the members of Lodge meetings and to keep records of their attendance and absence.

When Orvil had understood that everything in the Craft was ritualized and ordered, he was able to discern the outlines of an inner group in the New York City Lodge. As a matter of normal evolution and adaptation to the Persecution, Lodges throughout the country had been closed and consolidated. The effect on the New York City Lodge had been a retrenchment of leadership. Under threat of extinction—all the more serious because of the harrowing financial and political implications of a general Masonic failure—the leaders of the New York Lodge had formed a secret committee of cooperation among themselves: a Cabal. They would use their individual and collective influence on the city and state levels to ward off the Anti-Mason Party threat; not as a conspiracy, but as the representatives of a body under attack.

This inner group of Brothers, numbering not surprisingly thirty-three men, held power by means of a secret agreement to control all offices and membership in the Lodge. Within an organization founded on and steeped in secrecy, they themselves met and functioned as a secret ruling body. Men in this inner group had all reached their maturity and were in some cases being replaced by their sons at the time Orvil was made Deputy Marshal. He was not one of them; he had not been chosen at an early age and brought along through the system. If anything, Orvil made the Cabal nervous by the unremitting intensity of his ambition. It was hoped that this fringe position of Deputy Marshal would satisfy him for a time.

The Cabal achieved anonymity by adapting itself to the structure of the Lodge. The single change they instituted was the rigging of general elections. Instead of the Grand Master being chosen by the membership in yearly elections, he was selected secretly and nominated by the New York City Lodge at the convention. Official nominees were always victorious. All other officers were then appointed by the new Grand Master. The New York Lodges operated under this system from about 1838 until after the Civil War, when membership again became unwieldy and inner secrecy at last broke down. By then as well the motives of the Cabal had been thoroughly obscured and corrupted. Safety from the Anti-Mason Movement had been replaced by the expediency of the profit motive, with the Cabal degenerating into nothing more than a common and highly successful capitalist conspiracy.

When Orvil discovered its existence, the New York Masonic Cabal was in full cry. They might even have grown careless and over-confident from success. Certain members of the group may have naively got the impression that Orvil, as Deputy Marshal and constantly on the scene, was one of them, or about to be. And something in Starkweather—an instinct for choosing the right way through a situation even when that situation was not clear to him—made him see the traces, and most especially the effects, of the Cabal. At the Exchange he noticed that whenever a stunning deal was made by a broker who happened to be an influential Brother, other Brothers were also involved, sharing in the profits. They stuck together. They quite clearly helped one another. This was to be expected; but was it not perhaps untoward that these little stock deals sometimes included as many as twenty Brothers, proxy upon proxy, forming a phalanx of power and cooperation that swept all competition aside? One such deal even caught Orvil unawares, arousing his ire along with his suspicions. Taking up this thread of information—a contract for the manufacture and supply of mining equipment for base metals—he discovered a tangled skein of deals and ventures that included, over and over, the same thirty-three men. Their holdings and fortunes overlapped inextricably. Together they practically controlled a half dozen industries. What one needed another would supply. It was as much to become a part of this investment trust and share in its power as to get to the top of the Masonic heap that Orvil struggled to learn all he could about these men and their business connections.

He spent months at it. He hired detectives, chosen for their unscrupulousness and pushy ways. Assiduously he courted those of the Cabal who might, and did, yield information and indiscretions under the influence of drink. He made lists and charts, collected documents, bribed clerks, hired away assistants and secretaries. In the end he assembled a dossier on every member and had come to understand its methods and effects, its implications and potential, rather better than did any of the Cabal, most especially better than the current Grand Master, James Mac-Naughton. What MacNaughton lacked, what the group itself lacked, was what Orvil labored to achieve: an overview. The Cabal by its nature could not help succeeding; it was already powerful. But it needed someone like Orvil to take it further, to a level of national influence.

Finally, using the special stationery of the Grand Master's office, easily purloined, Orvil ordered the Cabal to convene—all of them except MacNaughton himself, under whose name the meeting was called. This unscheduled meeting was understood to be a strict command of the Grand Master to discuss an important matter, and the entire Cabal attended.

These were the last days of the old Lodge, a small rather Gothic building on Broadway and Duane Street in lower Manhattan. The room to which the Tiler directed the Brothers as they arrived signaled the seriousness of the occasion. It resembled a small provincial theatre or opera house—tall, ornate, Germanic, lugubriously dark and constructed completely of wood, so that its occupation by more than a few people set it to knocking and popping like fire. It was necessary for anyone addressing a meeting in this room to speak up.

Having tapped on MacNaughton's door, the Tiler shouted, "Brothers, the Master!" as a signal that all were present and the doors sealed. The din of thirty-two men settling into old wooden chairs sounded like the fusillade of a distant battle. Orvil Starkweather presented himself at a podium on the dais.

Many exchanged looks of shock and incredulity that the Cabal had been assembled in the presence of an outsider. The Grand Secretary, second in command, rose to his feet and demanded to know the meaning of "this outrage, sir!" Another officer, the Marshal, who like everyone else had assumed the meeting to be at the command of the Master, also rose with a shout. Perhaps he felt some responsibility for his Deputy. "Starkweather!" he demanded, "What the hell is going on?"

"The meeting will come to order," Orvil announced blandly, practically under his breath, so that no one heard him in the uproar. He repeated the order more loudly, to no response; then a third time, nearly at the top of his voice. "The meeting will come to order!"

"How dare you, sir!" the Grand Secretary said, and began pushing his way through the row of chairs to leave. "This meeting is illegal and I will have no part of it. Get out of my way!"

Without a word Orvil walked to the side of the dais where a large blackboard on wheels was kept for the visual demonstrations that Lodge meetings occasionally required. He pulled the blackboard to the center of the dais and turned it around.

A silence fell. On the blackboard Orvil had written the names of every company, stock, and tentacle of the Cabal, some of it so buried or obscure or esoteric as to be unknown even to some of the lesser members themselves. Stocks in railroads, utilities, banks, steel, real estate, metals, insurance, shipping, construction, publishing—plus other companies and listings whose names gave no clue to their category—had been chalked in neat little block letters, names on one side, figures on the other. At the bottom of the column of figures a total number of shares was equated with a sum of money. A box was drawn around this figure to make it stand out.

In the ensuing prolonged silence, punctuated by the creaking wood and short explosive remarks, Orvil put his hands in his pockets and perused the crowd.

One by one they finished reading what was on the blackboard and turned to look, with new eyes rather, at Orvil.

"As perhaps some of you in the back can't make out the addition," he said, "I will read out the total. You boys together are worth something like two hundred million."

The Grand Secretary, a tall straight man in a tailcoat who had stopped at the end of the row to look at the blackboard, now came forward. He approached the dais and looked up at Orvil.

"Where's MacNaughton?" he asked quietly.

Orvil looked down. "Master MacNaughton has retired," he said. "Let us say, semi-retired."

The two men stared at each other, the Secretary glaring. Then turning like litmus from purple to pink, acid to sweet in a moment, the Secretary glanced again at the blackboard and said, "I see."

It simply had never occurred to any of them that this could happen, that someone might pierce the secrecy and put it all together. Hidden, they were invulnerable; exposed, for all their networks of influence, the Cabal was absurdly powerless. To expose this unprincipled, if not plainly illegal, conspiracy was to destroy it utterly. They would all lose their shirts, and the Grand Secretary, looking up and now calm, suddenly knew it. "I see," he said again.

"I thought you might," Orvil remarked simply, and the Secretary returned to his chair and sat down.

The Cabal had two choices: either to make Orvil the new Grand Master or to kill him. Too much was at stake to risk anything in between. Nor would Orvil himself have put it any other way. The drastic nature of this alternative to his election—

murder—was the final ingredient of his scheme. These men were not the murdering type. And the alternative brought with it a kind of dowry, which Orvil now offered them—in the form of his huge copper holdings and extensive portfolio—together with a talent for administration and manipulation amounting to genius. Added to this was the underlying fact that the present Grand Master, MacNaughton, for all his connections and the limitless resources of the Cabal, had so far lost rather than gained financial ground for the group. He had been chosen for his willingness to take direction, together with his magisterial—they would say, Masonic—manner: he looked like a Grand Master and had great personal style. Great personal style however is often a camouflage for incompetence, and so it was with MacNaughton. It seemed now to everyone that this hideous breach of security was somehow the result of MacNaughton's financial clumsiness.

The thirty-two men, all seated and subdued, looked up expectantly at Orvil. Before their eyes in an instant their little realm, powerful if small, had changed hands. They had just witnessed a palace coup, and this short, corpulent man, whom all of them respected but none particularly liked, was apparently their new king.

Orvil savored the moment. How omnipotent knowledge was, he thought—the knowledge of others' wrongdoing and mistakes, the power, the force of cleverness in league with secrecy.

"Gentlemen," he said with the smile of a midwife. "I cannot, in all candor, withhold from you my joy in presiding over this gathering tonight. And I want to reassure each of you that your hopes and desires for the Brotherhood, and for yourselves, are also mine. I am to the Craft solemnly sworn, above all else. . . ."

Starkweather paused. "I am honored to be here," he said, "and sympathetic to the sense of shock, even outrage, that you all must feel. But it is time to face change. You were hardly able to hold your own against MacNaughton's mistakes. Whilst we all revere him as a friend and companion, several crucial . . . misjudgments on his part—in the matter of Kennecott, for example, or the Matideconk Mills deal—should alone have cost him the Mastership. And several others. . . .

"But he may stay, in a ceremonial capacity. I do not want a title or an office beyond the fact that in the minds of the Brothers here present, I am your true Worshipful Master.

"As you can see," he went on, gesturing to the blackboard. "I know what there is to know about us. There is great potential here. Dramatic possibilities. But they have not been carried far enough. An organization like this—not the Brotherhood, but the Cabal—cannot be run by committee, and under MacNaughton that's what you have been doing. I don't want to run the Brotherhood; MacNaughton may do that. I will run the Cabal.

"Furthermore, we can be useful in a Nation in the midst of troubled times. We are needed. Our strength as a group gives added power to the Northern economy. Our gains are Union gains."

Some of the Brothers were nodding their heads in agreement and exchanging looks. No one had ever pointed out before that the accumulation of great wealth was patriotic. This struck them as wonderful—the connection between personal gain and national pride was an exhilarating idea. Here was a man, they thought, who saw the big picture.

The agreement worked out that night between Orvil and the officers, most especially with the Grand Secretary, Giles Springer, had its complexities. In effect, the Mastership would alternate between Orvil and MacNaughton, but without MacNaughton's participation in the vital plans of the Cabal. Orvil understood what MacNaughton or even Springer had not fully realized: that the power of the group lay in its leader's ability to act quickly and autonomously, using the combined influence and resources of all the members. These thirty-two men were individually powerful; together they virtually controlled New York City and Albany until the advent of the Tweed machine ten years later. It could be argued that the Cabal contributed to an atmosphere in which the Tweed event became possible, even inevitable.

Orvil, as phantom Master, was now the instrument of the Cabal, invested with the power and deference of the group—the king and his barons. Of all their leaders he was the most autocratic, and thus the most successful. That he practically kidnapped the Cabal gave him what previous Grand Masters had never truly earned: obedience. He never, in the years he led them, either as the phantom or real Grand Master, asked their permission to do anything. And so it was with the project he called Temple Park.

The descendancy from Orvil Starkweather to Chase Walker proceeded in this way:

Orvil had married Dorothea Patton Shaw of Brooklyn in 1835. Their elder son, Franklyn Starkweather (1840–1903), married Jane Stevens Grinnell of Brooklyn Heights. Their only child, Evelyn Starkweather (1866–1929), married Edward Chase of New York and Sharon, Connecticut. Evelyn, who had been a spoiled and imperious woman, died of profound shock and a bad heart two days after the Crash. Her daughter, Anne Starkweather Chase (1882–1959), who thus inherited the remnants of the Starkweather fortune, was Chase's Grandmère. She married John Walker of Stonington, Connecticut in 1908 and their son, William Starkweather Walker (b. 1909–), who became a patent lawyer and inventor, married Juliet Tate, an English actress. Chase, their oldest son, was born in 1943 in Manhattan.

Orvil Starkweather   m. 1835   Dorothea Patton Shaw
—————┬—————
Franklyn Starkweather   m. 1861   Jane Stevens Grinnell
—————┬—————
Evelyn Starkweather   m. 1886   Edward Chase
—————┬—————
Anne Starkweather Chase (Grandmère)   m. 1908   John Walker
—————┬—————
William Starkweather Walker   m. 1939   Juliet Tate
—————┬—————
Chase Walker (Virgiliano)   m. 1964   Princess Olympia Odischalchi
—————┬—————
Niccolino Virgiliano

The Starkweather line took its most unusual turn with the arranged marriage of Chase to Donna Olympia Odischalchi, seventeen, of Florence—part of an ersatz, complicated, but apparently legal maneuver to save the ancient but expiring Virgiliano line, and serving further to obscure the quite gone Starkweathers —a name that lived on, vestigially, in the offspring of Chase's younger brother, Stark.

The child Niccolino, called Lino, was raised by his mother in Florence, in the Virgiliano palace, with scant connection to his American father.

Chase meanwhile completed a final year at Harvard; then, pursuing an interest in horticulture and gardening, the summer after graduation took a job without pay at the Brooklyn Botanical Garden, as curator's assistant in the department of Plant Studies and Evolution. After one year he was made an assistant curator —a neat distinction, in that now he was paid a small amount of money for doing the same thing, potting seedlings and rummaging through the endless steamy greenhouses. An assistant curatorship was considered a young gentleman's job, stylish but poorly paid. You were not expected to be in it for the money. In fact throughout this period Chase lived on the residue of the Stark-weather fortune—the great copper mine and Orvil's fortune had been lost in the Crash, except for these bits from Grandmère—and hardly touched the stud fee from the Virgilianos. He moved into a small flat in the West Eighties not far from the Stable complex at Eighty-sixth Street. The Carriage House seemed then to be just another dilapidated, ill-used building from a gentler time—the darkening nineteenth century—about which less and less was known, and more imagined.

After two years in graduate school I went to New York in 1968 to teach. Then my first novel, about a sea voyage, was published and I used its slim profits to travel. Having thought constantly of Lorenzo, I returned immediately to Florence, to the Bardolini—to find him gone; although Signora Zá-zá said he appeared from time to time unannounced. He had joined the Merchant Marine to satisfy his thirst for travel. She rattled off the places her nephew had so far seen: China, Japan, Australia, California, Norway.

"Not New York?" I asked.

"Oh, sì, New York, yes," a reply that cut my heart. He had forgotten. But then how was he to find me?

"And where is he now?" I asked.

"Buh! *Chi sa?*" She raised her hands and shoulders in an enormous shrug. *"Non si sa mai."*

In the afternoon I telephoned Palazzo Virgiliano and asked for *il conte*. Niccolo came on the phone.

"Peter!" he said. "Are you here? How delightful! You must come at once, and stay for dinner. Are you alone? Shall I send a car? Olympia will be thrilled. You will not recognize Lino."

Lino, who was then seven, could not have been, however, more recognizable, being not only a *putto* one saw on ceilings everywhere, but at the same time a miniature of Chase—blond, delicately formed, with large blue eyes, rather grave. He was led in by the hand by Olympia, now twenty-three and still a child

herself until you looked closely. Here you sensed, amid the seren-
ity of young motherhood, an air of want and speculation. You
could see her other self as though peering through a mask she had
not yet discarded. Or so it seemed. We hardly knew each other.

Niccolo, gray to white, more angular, thinner, and just as
erect—a Quixote—had found in these two the true beneficiaries
of his life's intent; in, most especially, the child; for Niccolino,
Linetto, Linuccio was the object of all the most important motives of his heart: motherliness, male worship, dynastic dreams,
self-love, exquisiteness and benefaction; while the mother, *la prin-
cipessina,* in the great legitimizing act of giving birth, had herself
crossed over into the circle of his love. Added to this constant
satisfaction was the awareness, the palpable certainty of his dead
mother's ongoing approval, ghostlike and hovering, that things
had turned out so beautifully. All this was in the air.

"How is Chase?" Olympia asked immediately.

"He is very well and sends his love," I replied, and added,
"And this for Lino." I handed the child a small package, reaching
down to where he presented an attitude of charged seriousness at
the reception of something from a stranger. "This is from your
father," I said, as Chase had instructed me. It was a lapis ring.
Automatically Lino looked up at Niccolo.

"He does not yet understand . . . the circumstances,"
Olympia explained simply, in English. "We think it better not to
confuse him." Then, kneeling before her son, she said in Italian,
"This is from someone in America who loves you very much."

Lino nodded, immediately satisfied. What better reason for
a gift than that, even distantly, one was loved?

Later, alone, Niccolo said, "I miss the two of you so. What
fun! What excitement! Such coming and going. How is he? He
does not write to me. And the phone calls, when I am able to
reach him, seem at first to make him giddy, then regretful—or
guilty . . . so difficult.Is he well?"

"He loves what he's doing—at the Botanical, and appears to

be very good at it," I said, thinking to defend Chase. "He's well thought of, in what they call weeds."

Ever polite, Niccolo smiled. "Does he have anyone?" he asked. "Does he have a lover, a boyfriend?"

"None, and several. He doesn't settle long before something happens. Everything is simultaneous with Chase, though he feels things deeply, I think."

We had tea beneath the Caravaggio, my real reason for coming. Was that still how Lorenzo looked? With panic I often realized that I wouldn't know Lorenzo now even if I did see him; or perhaps I already had.

And me. "And you, Peter? What have you been doing? Writing, isn't it?"

After Florence, and then Venice, before I knew what I wanted, I abandoned my itinerary and went to Genoa, this being the largest port in Italy; for here I thought ships of the Merchant Marine must frequently call. It was romantic to allow myself such a frivolous motive for travel—the off-chance of finding a man I would never recognize—but also dangerously strange and then depressing; although the excitement of an encounter on the waterfront with a sailor who could have been Lorenzo if he chose served to stoke the Laurentian fires—a phrase Chase had used. On another whim I returned to Florence solely to obtain a photo-graph of Lorenzo at Zá-zá's. This spy-like and difficult assign-ment, to snatch his likeness, and in so doing to snatch his soul, was in the end accomplished not with guile, but by simple theft. I went into Zá-zá's room one afternoon when I heard them all in the kitchen, and removed a picture of him, one of several, from her mirror, in my nervousness hardly noticing, but afterwards keenly recollecting—as if having stolen a picture of the room itself—an image of barren disorder, so different from everyone else's room: a naked mattress, bedclothes strewn on the floor, bare walls and half-shuttered window, a scuffed-up rug and the vanity table and cheap cosmetics of a small-town spinster, all in disarray. Where was her finery? Where the history of her life?

The photograph of Lorenzo, cupped like a flame in my hands, showed him in his whites: bell-bottoms, middy and cap. He was sturdy, dark-eyed, smooth and smiling, looking somewhat older than his present twenty-four years, which meant the picture was recent. It seemed that in capturing this prize I had got all I could from traveling, even though the rearrangement had cost me France and Switzerland. Leaving my new address in New York with Zá-zá, I returned home.

Chase examined the stolen photograph, along with those of the Virgilianos entrusted to me by Olympia, and exclaimed, "Unless the camera lies, he's a young god. And look here, in the eyes —such eyes!—the eyes of an idol, yes. When you do find him, take my advice," he said, handing back the picture. "Don't look absolutely into his eyes . . . Listen to me. They are unfillable vessels."

I felt armed by this photograph and carried it everywhere. It gave me the feeling of a connection of power between us, from which I sipped occasional electric charges. I scarcely had to look at it to see his face which on its own bobbed up and mingled with the Caravaggio: blue-black hair, the wide evenness in the eyes, winged, succulent lips drawn over the same white as the cap and blouse; and with the slightest blur in focus, due to the velocity of his beauty. "All you can do is watch out," Chase concluded.

Nor was I oblivious to the trap I was setting for myself. The dim recollection of our only night together had taken on the force of legend; in the imprecision of memory, that night itself was love. I doubted either of us could live up to such expectations—all of them mine, none of them his. I was aware also that while Lorenzo was real, my vision of him wasn't; and that while handsome, he could not be so impossibly perfect. Should he ever approach these standards—one did see such people sometimes in the streets—I was doomed. Should he not, then—then what?

In the meantime Chase made gentle references to widow-hood and the purity of emotional restraint. With this, also, he himself could identify; during this period he was unable or at least unwilling to fall in love; or, at the very most, only lightly and seldom.

But like me, he wanted to. He had idealized this state until its achievement was a physical, emotional, even a spiritual im-probability. The difference was that no pure and specific object like Lorenzo stood in Chase's way. People were constantly fling-ing themselves at him. I never knew anyone to receive such offers of admiration, lust and partnership. He was the icon of so many. The Virgiliano offer, I now saw, was not grossly unusual; what was strange was his acceptance of it. In New York he would probably have declined, as I saw him decline a handsome proposition from the leader of a sizable religion, or the opportunity to preside over a grand ménage in Bermuda. These offers were invariably charm-ing and flattering, but their execution might be boring, perhaps humiliating. They implied he was desirable, but acceptance meant surrender to someone else's idea of him, and this he would do only temporarily, one night or a few weeks at a time. Perhaps because of his son Lino he thought that each acceptance might bring some new unwanted responsibility.

In New York we went everywhere. We might begin at a smart dinner party in the East Side triplex of a Harvard friend, and then rush back to Chase's flat for clothes more suited to the West Village—a pattern developed in Florence and imposed on New York. It was the early seventies and we were children at play in the fields of social change. We came in for some local harassment from street toughs and occasionally, at a distance, from the police, but the world at large was unaware of our sort of life. It was a period without consequences, except to ourselves. We did as we pleased, with a feeling of invention—things other people would never imagine doing—within, it seemed, the interstices of real life. Our existence was like a building with many doors, different doors. Once inside, it was the same for everyone.

As part of an exchange training program, Chase twice spent six months in London during the mid-seventies, attached to the Royal Horticultural Society and studying the great gardens of England. During each of these visits he saw Lino in Florence; on the second occasion, when the boy was eleven, Chase explained to him over coffee and an ice cream in Piazza Repubblica that they were father and son. Lino thought Chase by far the most glamourous person he knew and was thrilled. To the child Niccolo had come to seem more like an aunt than a father. That his mother was a princess was enough to spare him the insecurities attendant on this sudden revelation, and there emerged in him that which his Italian grandmother had most feared: a passion for all things American.

Chase wrote of the joys of motherhood. Beneath the glibness he was awed, and unprepared for the emotions Lino evoked in him: pride; intimidation; love of course; fierce identification. "You cannot in the least imagine," he wrote, "what it is like to see your own child being you—again and before your eyes."

Chase had so dreaded the declaration of his homosexuality to his parents—one of life's great absurd encounters—that the declaration of fatherhood to a beautiful boy child had a pleasant compensatory ring to him, as earlier it had to the Walkers, who had not expected perpetuity from this quarter. Chase felt neatly bracketed by Lino, wedged snugly between one sort of family and another, neither of which pressed him to behave familially.

In London, also on the second trip, he met a Norwegian diplomat who lived in Eaton Square like the ghost of Henry James. The diplomat, a cultural attaché, heard a crash one evening in the street and rushed out to find Chase lying on his back some distance from the entanglement of a jeep and a huge black motorcycle. Chase, unhurt, looked up at the diplomat and his dinner guests—all in black tie and evening gowns—mistaking them for a heavenly reception committee, which in a way they were. In this part of his life he was fortunate even in the accidents that befell him—if, by now, it was also clear that while life's accidents would continue to occur, the good luck to survive them, even to benefit from them, was limited and dwindling.

He gave up the cycle and moved into Eaton Square. The bike, a 750 BMW, had been an expensive, dangerous prop representing one half, approximately, of his personality and needs—the sexual, theatrical, ritualistic, private half, the half he so actively and compulsively cultivated, and which was balanced, in the other half, by all that someone else would have perceived in him as mannerly, refined and educated. The diplomat was dazzled by the combination, but could in the end only appeal to the second, nonsexual half, there being literally nothing in himself that was rough or in the least sinister. As with Niccolo years before, and it seemed a hundred other times, the sexual aspect quickly diminished and disappeared, leaving friendship intact—friendship being, as Chase had quoted to me once, 'Love without His Wings.' The diplomat was close to sixty and it had all been, nearly, a moot point. But aside from the breakfasts in bed, the butler, the superb food, plus tea and drinks with half the Royal Horticultural Society, the great attraction here for Chase was the diplomat's own love of gardening and his house in the country—specifically, the acres of manicured park that encircled it. It could be said that the continuity and time frame of their friendship was established by Chase's desire to see his herbaceous borders mature. This was the reason, he claimed, why serious gardeners often lived to a great age: because they so needed to see the seasonal outcome of their obsessive labors.

From this point on, I think Chase chose his friends for this one reason above others: their access to a garden. A man with a garden was as attractive to him as a handsome biker or a New York leather icon. Eventually the two aspects absolutely merged in him—sex and gardening—although this took time. But even then, in New York in the late seventies, he would describe a weekend of sex and spring planting with a dreamy, lusty air.

In 1978 Chase took the second half of Grandmère's bequest —fifty thousand dollars—added it to the leftover Virgiliano money, and bought a country house of his own. He found it in New York State in the middle of nowhere, in a valley given over completely to farming by families that had been there since the early nineteenth century. The house and forty acres cost sixty thousand, and over several years he spent another thirty on improvements. Like all the houses in the valley it was a simple, clapboard Greek Revival with pilasters at the four corners and a covered porch across the front. A dining room and kitchen lay to one side of the hall and a long parlor with fireplace to the other, with, upstairs, three bedrooms and a bath. It had also a root cellar below, a separate garage, and a tool shed in the back. At the front along the road four enormous trees, intended for shade in summer and as a windbreak in the winter, had long since matured—proof of the fine unselfishness of the past.

The house lay close to the bottom of the valley, at the base of a steep hill that constituted most of the forty acres. In front, across the road, the valley's trough dipped further down and flattened out in a patchwork of alfalfa, strawberries and corn belonging to the farm opposite, rising up the other side in a gentle sweep to the crests of several hills and high meadows. We would sit on the porch and watch a long line of black and white cows seep slowly down the hill in the evening, to occasional lowing complaints that came across with the scent of milk and manure; and in the morning, when the bells around some of their necks rang out more clearly, they would climb back up out of a cottony mist that covered the valley floor. At the top the early light caught a swath of gold hay beside a trapezoid of emerald grass, beside another of a darker color—all of it far enough away to seem to shift and change with the eye, as it did with the seasons. Chase kept rockers on the porch and we would sit out and rock and admire the good, decent industry of farmers—knowing that little of it but the crops had changed in decades, except for the enormous change we ourselves represented. And Chase would say, "Here we are, as we will end up: side by side, rocking back and forth on the nursing-home porch. Yes, with nothing but our memories."

It was his first house, and all he had learned—from Grand-mère in Connecticut, from the many gardens he had managed or dabbled in, from Niccolo and the Botanical—he applied here. It was a small establishment run like a large one, but with none of the obvious pitfalls and pretensions. Halfway up the hill behind the house a stand of birch trees and undergrowth had been left to mark the division between two meadows; it lay like a thin dash parallel to the house. Chase cut a gap through it at the point above a pair of French doors in the parlor, so that looking out, you saw through it to a patch of sky at the top of the hill—an abbreviated but effective allée; not an adding to but a taking away. On the lower slope beside the house he constructed a square sunken garden in which he planted only blue and white flowers, leaving the lower side open so that the morning fog and mist dripped out of it in theatrical creeping vapors. He designed a series of plantings that would quickly mature. His roses were serious; his borders expensive intellectual gambles. Inside, the house was made comfortable, even stylish, using the local vernac-ular—quilts, simple furniture, rag rugs, old turkey carpets—to which he added a sense of scale and position that made one arriving houseguest declare, "Ah, the abode of an important cottage queen."

His was a talent for manipulation, for the rearrangement of what was present and available. To this, especially outdoors, he added piece by piece the components of a specific, articulated vision; not so much a creation of what he imagined as the reproduction of what he remembered, imposed on the hilly simplicities of a New England farm. To him, Grandmère was likely to walk through the door at any moment, expecting a familiar lunch or a traditional tea. Indeed, in making himself comfortable there Chase, in the abstract, prepared the house for an invasion of all his ancestors, right back to Orvil. In the garden, dividing his day lilies, he thought of them all as hovering and pleased.

The Walkers came to visit. The procession of tableaux and events through the weekend seemed to them so familiar and evocative as to keep William Walker in a state halfway between pleasant nostalgia and anxiety. Grandmère's day china, long in storage and to Chase but a souvenir of the age, was to his father the artifact of his own youth, not in the abstract but real, with all its happy-sad, lost allusions. Was this his son's house or his own dead past? And Juliet Walker, raised in Wales, thought she saw through the guestroom window a corner of the garden where she had herself been young. Through the window, for a moment, she saw the life she had subsequently not led in England—not that she missed it, or ever regretted it, but there it was.

The two of them had been utterly bewildered by their son —Juliet from the moment over lunch in the Central Park Zoo when Chase told her he was homosexual, and William from shortly after that, when he entered his son's room without knocking and found Chase lying on top of a schoolboy friend. All right, he thought; the boy is a deviate, but such a thing at home was unthinkable, and rude. And although they had attended the wedding, they only half-understood the adoption and change of citizenship—as an extraordinary social opportunity—and though they understood that a grandson existed in Italy, after whom they inquired politely, the entire business with the Italians was not real to them. Now, from their other sons, they had local grandchildren, one of them even named Juliet. No need to imagine here; no need to wonder. They seemed extremely fond of me, and it was obvious for years that they took Chase and me for lovers, an impression of which, in the conversational no-man's land of sex, they were never disabused. Perhaps this suited everyone. I was thus dealt with as a cross between a son-in-law and a houseguest, and shown the affection of a distant relation, privy to much, if not all. I found them always decent and well behaved, so adaptive and intelligent they seemed ideal parents—but for me, not Chase. The things I admired in them—polite caution and consideration, refinement, sophistication—Chase saw in a different light, as hesitancy, indifference to others, self-sufficiency. He thought the priorities of their lives wrong, and they his; although with the passing years they all seemed to soften toward each other, as they were themselves softened, like butter left out, by life.

Juliet Tate had been a pretty young actress in London's West End. She had big blue eyes, made bigger by thick glasses that got thicker, and short white hair that got whiter, as she aged. She had what she called a dicky heart, and was often out of breath. Her mother had died finally of the same sort of thing, but only in her eighties, so that this was not a great worry, if she took care. William Starkweather Walker loved her with a love unmatched elsewhere in the family, and whenever they were in range of each other they automatically touched. In an airplane, taking off, he invariably took her hand and said, "It's been wonderful." However his four children should turn out, or where, and whatever happened with the invention into which he had poured himself for twenty-five years, Juliet was his life. If it all worked, it was for her; if it didn't, having her made up for it.

William's invention was a kind of window. It had come to him in a flash sometime in the fifties, and he had spent the ensuing decades trying to understand its workings and implications. The window did not open in a conventional way; it swiveled, either horizontally or vertically, on pins. It consisted of two panes of sealed glass between which long filaments or strips were aligned in rows like venetian blinds. Within the glass the filaments, thinner than foil, could be opened and closed with, I suppose, an electrical switch. It was all a question of fluctuating parabolas, torque and surface tension. On my first visit to the Walker apartment after the year in Florence, Mr Walker showed me an early model he had made. He flipped a switch, and soundlessly the tiny louvers aligned themselves in a closed position, then opened.

"Every day a new problem," William said, and Chase looked at me over his father's shoulder.

Later Chase said, "My father's too much of a gentleman to do what's required. He writes polite letters of inquiry to Pittsburgh Plate and Glass, and they think he's crazy."

I said it seemed like a good idea.

"Oh, it is," Chase replied. "He's taken over a hundred patents on it already."

"So?"

"So, he can't get anyone to listen. He's got to be more aggressive, more ruthless."

"In the meantime," I pointed out, "at least no one can steal the idea—with all those patents."

I thought Mr Walker tremendously brave, to condense all of his energies, hopes, goals into one idea, into a single magnificent ongoing gamble, playing high, in a repeated doubling of his losses year after year. Even by the late seventies, when the invention had improved but still hadn't been adopted, William said to me, "This has gone on so long, but it's close now. It's ready. I've solved all the problems. I've taken one hundred and sixty-five patents on it. Practically anyone can understand its implications. The world is catching up. I mean to change the face of architecture. I can see it."

How wonderful, I thought. A fine finish to the Starkweather saga—a kind of circle, like a romance, from ambition to great wealth through ruination and back now again to wealth, across the generations, all losses recouped in a great high gamble of the mind. William looked forward to complete vindication, more important to him than the royalties, which were sure to be huge.

Thirty years of oblique, confusing choices, the endless list of problems, the ongoing impracticality of belief—all at last made right.

•

Gradually I had given up my dreams of Lorenzo. Certain things still made me think automatically of him. I can't say why, but often, in the shower, standing in the stream of water with soap in my hair and my eyes closed, I would think: Lorenzo. And sometimes at night, after years of imagining him before drifting off to sleep, occasionally the thought of where he was and what he might be doing had a calming, soporific effect. I would picture some distant part of the world where the two of us were alone, alien together amid strangers, on a beach, in a café. But now I thought of him less. I seldom looked at his photograph because it had come to represent something irretrievably lost; not Lorenzo but the picture itself was a symbol of everything I could not have, including, apparently, love.

Then in '79 I went back to Italy. Fifteen years had passed. He was then thirty-two and I thirty-seven. For no other reason than to find out where he was, I stopped in Florence and registered at the Bardolini. Signora Zá-zá was pleased to see me, as she was pleased to see all her old-time guests. She often waited up at night in the ingresso because someone from the past was due in late.

I arrived in the afternoon, well after lunch. My old room, Zá-zá apologized, was in use, and I was given another. At the door she waved the big iron key in admonishment not to lose it; then, laughing her uproarious laugh, she walked away down the hall. Oh yes, the laugh said, he knows all about it.

It was the end of April, a time in Florence when the air is ineffably sweet, fragrant with coffee and wood smoke. The light late in the day was a bizarre pinkish-gold revolving slowly like flame. At the western end of the river small clouds funneled down the sky in blazing, lurid colors: red, orange, turquoise—the colors of speed and change—all of it frozen and charged and symmetrical as if magnetized in a field of light. Now, with the awe of spectacle, I felt a hitch of nostalgia. To the history of Florence was added my own youth, making it all the more affecting. In the square where Savonarola was burned, I had met the artist. On the bridge where Dante first saw Beatrice, I had watched a hundred sunsets. All through these reverberant streets Chase and I had hunted men.

As on the last day fifteen years before, I made a circuit of the city, stopping at my favorite spots—the arcade in Piazza Repubblica, the Loggia, the Ponte Vecchio—all of them, but for the tourists, changeless and everlasting, and altered now only by a personal connection. And at dinner that evening, alone at table, my head whirling with memories, as Zá-zá put a plate before me I casually inquired after her nephew.

"He's very well," she said. "He's in the kitchen."

So might she have said he was under the table. She delivered two plates of food nearby and returned to the sideboard for more.

"He's not in the Merchant Marine anymore?" I asked, stunned.

She looked at the guests to be served next, matching their needs with particular portions. She knew who would leave food untouched and who liked more.

"No, no, he stopped that years ago. *Adesso, fa antiquario.* He has a shop. *E molto bravo.*" Then she added, *"E poi, si è sposato. C'ha due figli."*

Antiques, married, two sons: a caress, followed by a body blow and two sharp slaps. I felt my face reddening in disappointment and surprise—at my own ongoing, profound foolishness, at the mythology of loving someone for fifteen years who had no idea of my feelings, or even recollected my existence; who had only been beautiful. I wondered about all the people I had refused purely on the chance I might some day have Lorenzo again.

I know well the feeling that came over me for the rest of the meal. It was passivity and release: a kind of trust or surrender in which your own wishes, while taken into consideration, are not quite observed, or not closely observed. I sat in the ingresso for an hour or so, while the dining room emptied and guests either returned to their rooms or went out for the evening. I knew nothing, expected nothing. My mind and heart were blank. My presence in the ingresso—as opposed to the two alternatives of waiting in my room or going to the kitchen—went halfway between reticence and action, the former being stupid, the latter dangerous. He would not knock on my door, I felt, and I did not wish to encounter him, after all this time, in the presence of his attentive relatives. I waited. It grew quiet. If I did not see him tonight I might go to his antiques shop in the morning. One of the others would tell me where to find it. I needn't ask Zá-zá.

Then I heard his step in the passage—not that I recognized it, but I heard Zá-zá at the end of the hall and around a corner, say something that included my name. He came into the ingresso, saw me and stopped.

"Piero?" he said.

I stood up and awkwardly we half embraced, half shook each other's hand. He was fully a man, as if disguised. He said, "I would not have known you, with that beard."

He on the other hand looked exactly like the photograph I had stolen, if perhaps more substantial. He was only slightly shorter than I, but of a greater bulk, broad across the shoulders, with thick curly black hair, smooth olive skin, and a mustache that seemed to make his gray eyes swim and melt.

"Let's go," he said. "We'll have a drink."

We went out the door and started down the hundred steps to the street. I took his arm, as one does there, but meaning the touch to represent every intimacy either of us might remember.

The descending steps turned at three or four landings; halfway down, where one of the lights had burned out, we passed through a pocket of near darkness. I stopped him and we embraced again, and in the dark he allowed me to kiss him. It felt as sweet as any moment in life, and I thought, This is the prize for long devotion.

Walking along the river, my mind raced with possibilities. I wanted to take him to bed, to take him away with me. I wondered if either of these two miracles would satisfy me. The embrace and kiss in the stairwell had released in me a feeling of romantic hopelessness, of doom. I had seized him as a declaration of passion, as a wordless statement of years of love, meaning it to evoke and revivify our single night together so many years before. But in the night air the kiss itself, only minutes gone, seemed instead to fade, and with it the earlier memory, as if neither had really happened. We stopped at a café and had a cognac, then another. How much of the history of my love for him would he find flattering, how much of it obsessive? I took out the photograph. He had no memory of it and asked how I had got it. I told him.

"You were here?" he asked.

"Yes, of course. I came looking for you."

"As I went looking for you," he said.

I was incredulous.

"In New York," he went on. "I looked, but there were too many Conrads. None of them was you."

"What would have happened if you had found me?" I asked.

"I don't know. I was only looking." He smiled.

It had been 1972 or '73; he didn't remember exactly. He had been everywhere for years. "Later I went back again, and again I tried. It was never you."

"But now it is, Lorenzo." It would not have been possible to say all this in English. In Italian it was not so bad. "All these years later," I said. "You were so young. I did not think you'd remember."

"I remember everything about it. I thought about it for so long. It helped me to get out, to get away."

"But now you're back . . . married. With two sons."

He smiled and took out his wallet, removed several photos and handed them to me. His wife in a portrait picture, in a dark sweater and pearls, like a high-school yearbook picture, and his two sons, about four and six, cute little boys with bright eyes and shy smiles. He said their names affectionately.

"It's the way here," he said.

"What do you mean?"

"It simply happens. One is swept along. It's natural. Automatic."

"You mean marriage?"

"I mean all of it. The other is not possible in such a small place . . . when there is family. It was different when I was traveling."

"And you have nothing to do with men?" I asked.

"No, Piero, nothing . . . only thoughts."

"You mean desires," I said.

"Desideri, sì."

"Will you spend the night with me, Renzo?"

He looked at me a moment. "No," he said, "I cannot. I'm expected. And then, it wouldn't be possible at the pensione. That was all right when I was a child, but now it's too dangerous, too—"

"Yes, I know. You're right."

"Come to my shop tomorrow. We'll talk. Borgo San Frediano, *cinquanta.* After lunch. . . . And now," he signaled for the waiter, "I must go." He took out some money and gave it to the waiter, waving away the change.

"I think I'll sit here a while longer," I said. "Do you live far?"

"Up the valley a few miles. My car is nearby. Goodnight. *Sogni d'oro.* I'll see you tomorrow." He held out his hand and I stood up to hug him.

"You don't know," I said into his ear. "You have no idea how much I have loved you all these years."

He walked away down the street along the river. At the first bridge he waved as he crossed to the other side.

I sat there a while longer, over a third cognac, remembering what had been said between us. He had remembered and thought of me. He had allowed that night to change his life, as had I. Perhaps this was not strictly true, but mildly true; true enough. I had, he said, helped him to get out of Florence, to get away.

Come to my shop . . . *sogni d'oro.*

I thought of sleep only as a means of making the hours pass more quickly, but it would not come. I lay in my bed as I had lain a thousand nights, thinking of him. Now it was the real Lorenzo's face I saw, clearly and vividly, as if he lay beside me on the pillow. Longing for him, exultant and hopeful and happy to be within range, still the years of thinking of him at night put me finally to sleep, and in the next moment Zá-zá came through the door with the breakfast tray, very conscious of the ritual performed for an old friend and guest. *"Che bella giornata!"* she exclaimed, pushing open the shutters.

I thought Renzo might have invited me to meet him for lunch, rather than asking me to come to his shop afterward. But I understood the invitation better when I arrived and saw the steel street shutter pulled halfway down. He intended to close the shop, perhaps with us inside.

I leaned down and called his name, then stood up again, looking up and down the near-empty street. Lorenzo appeared and raised the shutter high enough for me to enter; then with an enormous clatter he rolled it down to the ground. He closed the door and locked it, and switched on the overhead light.

"Piero," he said, turning toward me.

He smelled of wood and resin and something else, like

lemon. We held each other. Then he stepped back and looked at me, his hands on my shoulders.

"Let me see, Piero. Last night did not seem real." He smiled. I thought of Chase's warning not to look absolutely into his eyes, but like a man who thinks he can fly, I threw myself trustingly over the edge. It was a look between two people raptly engaged in sex, or the look a mother exchanges with her nursing baby— a steady, deep, knowledgeable stare in which nothing is feared, all is admitted, confirmed, and given away.

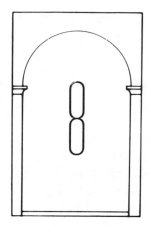

We lay in a bed in a little room at the back of the shop. At one point someone rapped on the steel shutter outside and called Lorenzo's name. It was a woman. She called again and went away.

"My wife," he whispered, and kissed me.

"What will she think?" I asked him.

"That I went off somewhere, for a coffee or something. She won't think anything. Why should she?"

Our lovemaking was as it had been fixed fifteen years before. We did everything equally to each other with such precision and ease and passion as to restore the faded details of memory. Physically he had matured along every line of promise shown in the boy of sixteen, and beyond, with a full, dark, smooth, generous body. His shoulders and arms had been developed rather more than was natural, by work in the Merchant Marine and athletics, particularly those muscles you would use if arms were wings—the biceps, the trapezius, the latissimus dorsi—with a beautiful vestigial tapering to the forearms and fingers, as to a single feather. His skin, a smooth, light honey color, darkened in the creases of his arms and thighs, in his genitals and the cleft of his buttocks, into a slightly darker shade, like a shadow. This also colored his eyelids, giving them naturally the effect Rashid had sought to achieve with kohl, setting off his eyes like the velvet of a jeweler's cloth. They were almond-shaped, with the outer corners slightly higher and faunish. Their color changed within a spectrum from gray to pale blue, which included a kind of green, like teal, and even lavender, depending on the colors around his face. He had kept the long lashes of his earliest youth, due I think to the general luxuriance of his skin and hair, which was a thick, curly blue black that fell onto his forehead and over his ears, and which he allowed to grow in ringlets across the back of his neck.

His sex was fitted out with the same richness, fullness and surprise as the rest of him, with also a charge running through it, like a current. It grew the way a balloon grows, in all directions, getting heavier and larger than seemed at first likely, then even possible. He had learned over the years, I imagined, to be very calm about all this. It made me think of a very fast car driven by a person in no great hurry.

We dressed, without having spoken of what was to come next—that evening, the next day, or ever. I was at the disadvantage of one whose feelings were more intense than his—for I could hardly keep from touching him, from admiring and praising him—and could think of nothing to say that made sense, or was not aggressive or possessive. Instead I walked about the shop looking at the furniture and objects he had collected for sale.

He came up beside me and indicated the few things he had not chosen and did not approve of.

"*La moglie,*" he said flatly. The wife. These things lacked purity and austerity. "But they will sell," he added. "Her things always sell."

He opened the door and pulled up the steel shutter. Daylight flooded the shop. Suddenly people were walking by. Someone stopped and looked in the window, at a prie-dieu, two candlesticks, a bright peach-colored azalea in a terracotta vase. This person looked up and into the shop, at the two young men standing inside. I saw the sudden conclusion in his eyes before he looked reflexively back at the azalea and was gone.

"I had better go, Lorenzo."

"Would you like a coffee first?" He smiled a soft, sweet smile, glancing over my shoulder to check that no one in the street could see the expression on his face.

The impossibility of it all fell in on me in that moment, standing with the world of people at my back through the shop window, and our remote world behind him in the little room where we had made love. His was a settled, complicated life and I would not fit easily into it, or be easily explained.

"Will you leave everything and come away with me, to America?" I asked, as suddenly as I thought of it.

"You're joking," he said, as he would have had to.

I looked at him and shook my head slowly, no.

"When?" he asked, not needing to know when but stalling for time.

"Tonight. Now. I'll get my things and we'll take a train to Rome, then fly to New York. All you need is your passport, your papers."

"But . . . my clothes, my children," he said helplessly.

If he had said anything else—his wife, his shop . . . but he had not. "Can't you stay in Florence awhile, Piero? Can you not give it a little time?"

"Yes, of course," I said. "You're right. I'll see you later."

"Ciao," he called as I went through the door into the street. "I'll call you later at the pensione."

I went back to the Bardolini and packed my things. Signora Zá-Zá was momentarily surprised at what seemed like a grossly sudden departure, and asked if something had happened. I made some excuse about family.

In my mind I pretended I was meeting Lorenzo at the train station. On the train I told myself it was better this way, to leave before impossibility turned everything to resentment and recrimination, to rejection and exile. Better to settle immediately for exile. On the train and then in a room at the mandatory dreary hotel near the Rome station, I went through all his imagined protestations. I had come into his world, not he into mine. He had no idea what my life was like or if he would fit into it. I was free and single; he had a wife and children, a shop to run. I gave up nothing, he would give up everything. What would he do in New York? He couldn't speak English. He had no green card. . . .

Against the purest abstractions of love would be hurled, like wet laundry, the cold realities of daily circumstance. But I was tired of the successive, inevitable disappointments of pretense; I did not care, after this taste of real love, to return to the abstract; I could not sacrifice another fifteen years to the idea of a person I still hardly knew, and only worshipped, unreasonably, for his physical perfection. I saw suddenly, in one of the clean but badly lighted rooms for which Italy's hotels are famous, that my pride and unreasoning impulsiveness would cost me the only chance I had with Lorenzo. It *was* more logical for me to stay in Florence with him—living on the fringes of his life, at least for now—than for him to give up everything precipitously and come away with me. And while I was sure he could make a living as a photographer's model, this would bring other problems to the situation, and was anyway just an idea.

As quickly and impulsively as I had decided to leave Florence, I left Rome and returned, although not to the Bardolini. I chose instead a cheap hotel in Via Faenza that Chase had used in the old days for affairs that required privacy. Its owners, unlike Zá-Zá, were not vigilant or concerned with who came and went.

At dinnertime of the second evening after I had seen him in his shop, I telephoned Lorenzo at the Bardolini.

When I announced myself he was quietly angry. "What happened? Where did you go? Zá-Zá said you checked out and left. I thought you had gone."

"I did. I came back."

"Could you just go away like that, without saying anything? Without giving me a chance?"

"A chance to what, Lorenzo?"

"Listen," he said after a pause. "We're in the middle of dinner here. Meet me afterwards—at that café. You know the one."

I got there early and had several cognacs to relax. I felt a sense of relief that I had come back, victimized not only by circumstance but by my own stupidity and impulsiveness. However, in running away, I had cut the knots of frustration and helplessness that bound me: I had acted, even if it had come to nothing.

Lorenzo sat down, ordered a coffee and looked at me. "I understand why you did it, Piero," he said. Did he really? "I suppose the whole thing is frightening. But to leave before anything at all has happened, this must be wrong. You will stay so we can see how we feel, and then we'll decide what to do."

I said nothing. None of this seemed new.

"*Non ti pare?*" he said. The waiter brought his coffee. I saw myself in Lorenzo's arms. Two days had gone by, two wasted days in trains. However, my sudden departure and absence seemed to have served another, unforeseen purpose: from Lorenzo's point of view I was not yet firmly held to him. I might still bolt. This must be unusual to a person with his looks, if in him, as a beauty, complacency was a danger.

But now the city lights glinted off his black hair and gray eyes. I felt a fool for having risked missing even this glimpse of him. Reading my thoughts he ran his tongue lightly over his lips and smiled, contriving a sparkle to his eyes that was mesmerizing. Here, on the sexual level, once it had begun again, both of us knew precisely how to behave.

"Where did you go?" he asked.

"Roma."

"You were going home?"

"I thought I was. I couldn't go."

"*Meno male.*"

"I love you," I said.

"It doesn't mean anything to say those words. They must be demonstrated."

"But I've never said them before, to anyone. I don't say them lightly now."

After a moment he said, "I don't know you well enough to see what you really mean when you say even something like that. Anyway, I've heard it before, when all it meant was 'fuck me'."

"It means that too," I said, "even if you think it shouldn't."

Back at the hotel in Via Faenza we lay in a big *letto matrimoniale,* our bodies inhabited by one pair of angels after another. They passed through us, lingering to swoon at the physical simplicities. We drifted off. Through the night others arrived for more. In the early morning, when the light started through the shutters and I heard the first Lambretta, I looked at us and felt at the pinnacle of my life.

"You love me," he said into my ear—as anyone else would say, I love you: the one being in him so close a step to the other as to be the same thing.

It had been my fear that after the first time in his shop, Lorenzo would consider our lovemaking in terms of whoever else he had slept with, and that in this I would be reduced to a name, a foreign name at that, on a long list. This fear had made me force the issue so suddenly and bolt to Rome. Watching him dress to leave soon after dawn, I let all this fall away. I wanted nothing. Even his leaving would be something to consider while I slept, wallowing in the scent he left behind.

"What will you tell la moglie?" I asked softly. We never said her name. She was an abstraction.

"That I slept at the pensione. I often do."

"She's not jealous?"

"No. She has never had reason to be. I never go with women and she wouldn't think of men. She's very—"

"Overwhelmed," I said. I saw myself inviting her to lunch at the Florentine equivalent of the Plaza: her shock at the news, immediate acquiescence to all demands, a certain red-faced horror beneath a big black hat. La moglie.

In the next week we saw each other every day, either in the afternoon at his shop or at night in the hotel. Hotel is too generous a word for what was clearly a whorehouse, most of its rooms rented by the hour, with a tremendous coming and going. I made them give me a room at the top and back so that we weren't constantly awakened by the cries and groans of men about to come, by drunken tricks trying the wrong door, by enraged prostitutes, male and female.

When we weren't together I slept, or walked around Florence in something of a daze, trying to work on a story or fragment —never getting anywhere, but passing the time until I could be with Lorenzo again. The money from the publication of another novel, on which I had planned to live for some time in New York, was already running low, before I even got home. I had enough for another few weeks, or less if I didn't return to the Bardolini. But I could not think about what this meant.

At the end of the week Renzo said he had promised la moglie to spend the weekend at her family's house in the country; he had made this promise some weeks before and could not get out of it. He didn't say so, but it seemed he too needed a few days of rest, away from what was for us both, but for him especially, a pace and schedule that would exhaust a twenty-year-old. And I'm sure he wanted to decide how to arrange these two diverging parts of his life: la moglie and *l'Americano.*

And I must myself decide—to go home, with him, which seemed improbable, or alone. I had no money, no means to make any, no suitable place to live, and except for Lorenzo would not have stayed another day where I was. On Saturday morning, at loose ends, depressed, doubtful, and for once profoundly bored, I decided to lay the whole thing at the feet of someone else— choosing Niccolo Virgiliano for his aged wisdom and general suitability. I called him up. His voice was unchanged and enthusiastic. "Peter, how lovely. Are you back? Time plays such evil tricks."

I said something had brought me back and I wanted to talk to him about it.

"Is it Chase?" he asked, one would have thought fearfully. I said no, it was personal, and asked to come over. He invited me to lunch in an hour.

The big portone of Palazzo Virgiliano was open for the day and through the gate I saw into its lovely emerald garden which merged, as in a trick of mirrors, with the huge Boboli beyond. Beneath swags of trees, the great park receded in sunlit stages. I rang the bell and Igor came down and let me in, sweetly smiling and murmuring welcome. The wide stream of American youth had dwindled to a few maturing faces, of which clearly mine was one.

We went all the way to the top in the little mahogany elevator, walked down a long white corridor with a line of tall arched windows to one side; at the end we came out into a large open loggia built like a temple porch with widely spaced Doric pillars, and filled with palms and wistaria in full bloom. It was the moment for the loggia. Dappled sunlight fell on Niccolo, seated in a wicker chair and dressed in a blue seersucker suit and tie, as crisp and fresh as a haberdasher's ad. He pushed himself slowly to his feet.

"My dear," he said, *"dai mi un baccio."*

The gardens rose up the hill to a pergola at the top of the Boboli, beneath a silvery blue sky. I said it was beautiful.

"Ah, sì." He reached over and patted my hand. "Of everyone you had the sweetest nature." When I blushed he added, "There, you see? Now what will you have for an aperitif?" As Igor slipped off to get it I asked Niccolo how he was feeling.

"Never ask that of the aged," he replied with a small laugh. "Every day some new calamity, a new ache to be accounted for and explained away. But I have a few good years left. My poor mother—*di buon'anima*—you saw how she went on and on. I will do the same, though not as cleverly, I fear."

I said I thought of her often.

"She is with me constantly now, more and more. . . . But tell me, Peter. How are you getting on? I have read your book, and I must say I'm proud of you. I've given it to a friend in publishing here. Perhaps something can be done about the translation."

I thanked him and he said, "Nonsense. . . . And what now? Are you writing another?"

I said my hands were full at the moment with something else. "Which is why I called. I need some advice."

"Advice! From me? In the old days I gave the worst advice imaginable. I was famous for it. People were ruined by my bad advice. I once told someone to sell *all* his Coca-Cola stock—"

"This is not business," I said. "It's love."

"Oh, well, I see. That's different. No one knows more about love than I. . . . Peter in love—with an Italian, no doubt—with, God help you, a Florentine—who only knows about love from Dante, and *then,* only from what is said about it . . . *Nevero?*"

"I'm afraid so."

"First," the old man enthused, "you must tell me what he looks like. You will put me in the picture."

"He is the most beautiful man in Florence," I said immediately.

"O Dio," Niccolo exclaimed.

"He's thirty-two and married."

"My instinct is clear," Niccolo said suddenly. "Leave immediately. Go home and get on with your life. This affair will ruin you."

"Leave him?"

"Get away now, while you can."

"I tried that," I said. "I went to Rome to fly home. I couldn't do it. I came back."

"Then you are doomed, my dear. Doomed to love." We sat quietly, listening to the birds in the garden trees. Somewhere in the middle distance a woman asked an incomprehensible question, in anger, to which the answer could not be heard. "Well," he said, standing up. "Let's go down to lunch, and we'll talk more . . . of your dilemma. You may be doomed, but first comes a period of bliss."

I said I was living that now. "Yes," he peered at me. "I noticed it in your eyes. In a woman it's the sign of pregnancy."

We went down the long icy-white corridor. Stepping into the elevator he said, "I have tried to think where we should have our lunch—"

"Are we going out?" I was disappointed; the only difficulty left in living in Florence was achieving privacy. But he said, "No, I mean here in the house. We have a hundred places to dine in Palazzo Virgiliano, as you can imagine . . . Then it came to me —the Caravaggio room."

We came down into the library and through it to the sitting room. "That's what Lorenzo looks like," I said, indicating the youth in the painting, having waited until this moment to make the declaration.

"Non mi dire."

"Almost exactly, although older now and, if you can believe it, more beautiful."

"That would be the effect of his being real," Niccolo said rapturously.

"And the eyes are gray, not black."

"Gray!" he whispered.

"The same hair, the same angelic face, the touch of mischief, of cruelty; the mouth, the translucent skin. It's your fault I fell in love with him."

"Mine!" He smiled. "How is that?"

"It was after seeing the Caravaggio that I noticed the resemblance. Something took hold after that . . . I don't know why or how. That was fifteen years ago. His aunt owns the pensione I lived in, with Chase."

"Signora Zá-zá."

"After all these years, I came back. And now—"

"Yes, and now?"

"Now I don't know. It's complicated."

"Have you made love?" he asked.

"We have been making love all week in a hotel in Via Faenza."

He gave a small cry. "Making love with my Caravaggio! Oh my dear . . . There will, of course, be hell to pay."

A table was laid in the corner. We sat down to it and Igor wheeled in a white-skirted cart filled with silver chafing dishes, with several choices for each course. Niccolo took a little soup and then a spoonful of rice. But I saw pasta and veal, a soufflé and salad. I had a little of each, to please him. We spoke of Olympia and Lino, who were at the moment in the country at La Favola.

"Since we're speaking of love," Niccolo said, "let me say I loved Chase. I still love him, with a special part of my aged heart. If only he would come to see me now and again, as you do. Apart from that, it's wrong the way he treats Olympia and Lino. They are, after all, his wife and son."

"Not really," I said, perhaps rudely, but it's what Chase would have said and I did not wish to be disloyal. They had not made Chase feel welcome when Lino was small.

"I believe Lino resents the fact that his father shows so little interest in him," Niccolo went on.

"And Olympia?" I felt invited to learn all I could, so as to tell Chase later.

"She does not speak well of him. I do what I can to make her understand, but it's no use. She wants a husband. And of course there is no divorce for a person like Olympia. It is she, I'm afraid, who has turned the boy against his father."

"Does Chase know this?"

"I have only just realized myself that she harbors this grudge. To speak plainly, Olympia needs a man. And she won't take a lover. She's turning into a bitter old maid, drying up like a lemon. Peter, she needs what everyone needs from time to time. If only she'd let me arrange something. It would be so simple, a phone call away, really. But no. She's very religious lately. The drier she gets, the holier she feels. Only Chase can save her, and she knows he won't. She hates him for that."

We agreed this was awful.

"And now the major question of the day," he said, pushing his chair back from the table. "Where will we have coffee? *Il gran salotto? Il giardino?* A little sunlight, perhaps . . ."

"Yes, that would be nice."

". . . to warm these old bones."

Niccolo murmured instructions to Igor and by the time we got outside a tray had been placed in a sunlit bower, on a little white table amid the green of plants in bloom—orchids, lilies, fuchsia, palms, more wistaria, a trickling fountain. Madness to think of taking coffee elsewhere.

"Now tell me more about . . . about Lorenzo," Niccolo said

when we had settled in. I said I had loved him since he was sixteen, but did not know if he loved me.

"The beautiful sometimes can only be loved," he said. "They cannot lose themselves in the need for someone else, as others can. They see it happening all around them, in their own lives. They know what it is, but cannot feel it themselves. It is never enough."

We drank our coffee and listened to the garden. Niccolo dropped off for a few minutes and was awakened when Igor came out with a telephone saying it was Donna Olympia on the line. Hearing from him that I was there she invited me to dine one night of the following week. Niccolo said, "She has a favor to ask."

I said I'd be delighted, calculating the hours it would keep me from Lorenzo.

"We can be sure it concerns Chase," he mused. "Most intriguing."

We set the dinner for Tuesday at eight-thirty. I got the idea it would be an occasion to which I might be encouraged to wear something anachronistic, if that was not inconvenient. Olympia, it seemed, made rather a lot of these few evenings she entertained. Soon afterward I thanked Niccolo and said goodbye.

"How sweet of you to come, my dear. I'm afraid I haven't helped you much. But it's good to know one is not completely a stranger in a strange land."

Later, when the shops opened, I went to one near the Duomo and rented dinner clothes for Tuesday's event, thinking it would please Miss Olympia. It's what Chase would have done, and the evening would go that much better for the effort.

On Monday morning I called Lorenzo at the shop and we met for lunch. Over the weekend his skin had been darkened by the sun, the deeper honey color serving to lighten his eyes further, as if something—an inner shade of gray—had been removed, allowing me to see deeper into him, or so it seemed. He looked at me as a woman would in a new hat, expecting comment and approval but not directly asking for it.

"You look wonderful," I said, happy and comfortable giving praise. I felt great sympathy suddenly for la moglie, whose picture —of an attractive but usual sort of woman—I had seen the first night. She must think of herself as the invisible lady, if also the quite envied. I saw now why she was not jealous. To be jealous of such a phenomenon was pointless and could end only in confusion. It was, finally, a question of self-possession and free will. Perhaps she had come to see that in Lorenzo admiration was not looked for, but simply missed when it didn't come—if it didn't come. Or perhaps she took pleasure, as did I, in the public association of herself with this treasure, as if she were wearing a sable coat or a fabulous jewel. For after looking at Lorenzo, people would look at me, then again at him with the thought of themselves in my place.

How arbitrary, it suddenly seemed, that *I* should be sitting there with him, and not someone else, anyone at all. In my mind perhaps I felt qualified to be there—qualified by the years I had spent loving him; but what about in *his* mind? Why should it be me?

Perhaps with him, too, it was simply a question of having known me before the world threw itself at his feet. Perhaps he saw me, because of this, as an exception, as he must see la moglie as an exception—she because he had arbitrarily chosen her, and then because she had borne him two sons; myself because of the connection and recollection of that single episode of his youth, and mine, which fifteen years later was still inexplicably and ineradicably important to us both. While from me must come immediate surrender to him whenever our lives should intersect, for if Lorenzo needed and deserved admiration, I needed to give these things; like a believer denied the ecstasy of faith, I had too long been deprived the object of my love, the idol of my praise, the vessel into which I would, if allowed, pour myself completely. If only, I thought, the connection on his side could be as strong. I wondered how I might induce this same obsession in him, that he might in the end need me as I needed him.

After lunch we retired to the hotel in Via Faenza to make love time and again, each event as if the last. We took from and gave to each other with a generosity I had never seen or felt before —a prodigious gift of physical bounty that left me gasping. Each time I felt stronger and more beautiful, as if, could we only do it enough, we would at some indeterminate point in the future actually become equals, or even change places—I becoming the angel, he the mortal supplicant who yields more than he can afford. What Lorenzo gave me, momentarily, in those long bouts of love was self-esteem, self-love, which I had never had in quantities. That he should turn to me, with those gray eyes and munificent flesh, and smile, filled me with peace and calm, which, in the presence of love, is love itself.

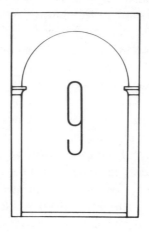

The following evening I again presented myself at Palazzo Virgiliano, for dinner with Olympia. She had changed. The child in her had been obliterated by the woman, and the woman herself was overdressed and made-up, as in some large compensation. Her hair, which I had remembered as being chestnut and long, was now a near-blond, cresting on the top of her head into a tall, single wave ever about to break. This must have taken someone all afternoon. She was wearing diamonds and a ballgown with long white gloves. Her most startling assertion, however, was her maquillage: she had whited out her face with, apparently, rice powder, like a geisha, her huge dark eyes floating in the featureless white. She looked clownlike or operatic, or jaded and even sinister, crowding beyond theatrics into parody.

Was all this extravagance, as Niccolo had said, simply flags of sexual distress? The lavishly applied and costly perfume, the powder and queer colors, the flamboyance—all the elements of the rare hothouse flower that depends for its survival on the attentions and ministrations of an even rarer bloom, an exotic nowhere to be found, or even expected—Chase; inducing a desperate evolution and further extravagance. I saw how kind Niccolo had been about her at lunch, and why he had taken the unusual step of suggesting I wear dinner clothes. Everyone, because of Olympia, had dressed to the teeth, and still she had overdone it. To overdo seemed the point.

I had not seen Margi from the Bardolini and her husband since their marriage fifteen years before. It seemed that in the meantime she and Olympia had become friends. Margi had plumped out but was still handsome and blond. She was friendly but restrained, demonstrating all lack of regret. Her father-in-law had died. She was now a countess.

"Peter," she said, taking both my hands in hers. Not to have kissed on both cheeks would have been a cruelty to Olympia, who hovered. Marco had kept his shape. We shook hands, appearing to have equal amounts of preconceptions about each other, though nothing to interfere. Olympia was relieved that Margi and I remembered each other, which she had rather doubted.

Also present were two very elderly ladies—sisters—with different titles and the same large nose. Niccolo, kissing their hands, said it brought tears to his eyes to see such dear, dear friends of his mother's again. "How wonderful of you both to come out."

"And on such short notice," one of them agreed. Fifty years before, owing to her frankness, Donna Rita had been the scourge of the Italian court. Since then she had gradually exchanged this habit for her sister Carlotta's shyness; now it was Rita who was repeatedly mortified in Carlotta's company.

"Niccolo," Carlotta went on in a piercing whisper, "would you tell us please what Olympia is got up as? It's only a dinner party. She looks like a Hollywood whore . . ."

"Carlotta!" her sister exclaimed.

"Non essere cattiva," Niccolo soothed. "It may be a bit . . . *esagerata,* but Olympia likes it."

". . . or even a man," Carlotta concluded.

It was true. Olympia had gone clear through the feminine in her costume and had emerged into the hard and faintly butch. More than a prostitute, she looked like a convincing transvestite. As Igor passed by with a tray of eight perfect hors d'oeuvres, Olympia took notice sympathetically of a decorative orchid at its center: a beautiful dead symbol of herself. She picked it off the tray and stuck it—one last hideous piece of decoration—in the cleavage of her satin gown.

"Do you still see Chase?" Margi asked me. Igor offered her the defoliated tray. Though briefly tempted, she knew better. This made, in fifteen years, her one thousandth tray of hors d'oeuvres.

I said that we saw each other often in New York.

"Furniture, isn't it?" she asked over the lip of her glass. How clear it seemed she had always known exactly what she wanted, out of Italy and Florence, or any situation she happened to find herself in. You could see in her eyes that she had never not known.

"Horticulture and gardening," I replied. "The Brooklyn Botanical."

"How lovely," she allowed, thinking it a suitably attenuated occupation, if one had to work, and an American man, of course, did; even one like Chase. "What could be more perfect for him? Are you staying at the Bardolini?" she went on. Soon it would be her turn to be interviewed.

I said no, a hotel.

Sensing a story, she asked why. She remembered poor Rashid being thrown out, and perhaps imagined or hoped for something similar. I wondered how she would arrange herself around the knowledge that little Lorenzo and I were lovers.

"It's rather noisy," I said. "It's not the same, you know."

"Well, nothing is," she agreed, bored. She and her husband,

as if by radar, turned simultaneously and gave each other a long look across the room.

Dinner seemed to be up to Niccolo, though I helped all I could, and Margi made an effort. Olympia, hardly present, twice got up from the table and abandoned us altogether; and I wondered—from her calm when she returned—if she weren't retiring to an anteroom for drugs. She certainly looked it, her eyes huge in the powdered face, darting about at the food, over our heads at the servants in skittish little glances, as if she would never find anything to please or reassure her. She ate nothing, drank a little champagne, smoked whenever she dared.

Lino, like a little ghost, joined us for dessert. How serious and blond and like Chase he was. The two old sisters looked at him as the only edible thing they'd seen all evening. When he made it clear that he did not like to be touched or fondled, they thought this all the more fitting and princely. This was the flower, the tender shoot of their dessicated civilization. Let it have its way in all things.

He was fourteen, one year younger than his father when, watching a parade in New York City, he was winked at and subsequently seduced for the first time.

We got to the end of the evening with Olympia making no allusion whatever to the ostensible point of it all. I had practically walked through the door when she called me back. The sisters had gone to their enormous palazzo in Via Cavour; Margi and Marco to Fiesole and the children. Even Niccolo had retired.

"Peter," she said nervously. "Would you like a drink?"

Igor had been sent away. She put a finger wonderingly to her lips, to think where one might find a drink at the moment. She led me dubiously into the salotto. "Olympia," I said, following behind. "What's the matter?"

She turned. "Nothing." She put out a hand to indicate a drinks table in the corner.

"What's troubling you? You've been nervous all evening."

She lighted a cigarette and blew smoke up at the ceiling. The ceiling itself caught her eye, as if she'd never noticed it before.

"Olympia," I said.

"Yes!" she snapped.

"Would you like me to leave?"

"No, of course not. . . . I simply don't know how to begin."

"Just say it."

"Very well. It's Chase."

"I know that. What about him?"

"Look," she said, turning and putting her hands on her hips. "I don't think you should be quite so sure of yourself. You don't know what's going on."

I said nothing, quite surprised. I poured out two cognacs and handed her one, waiting for her to go on.

"Would he come?" she asked disjointedly.

"I don't know," I replied.

"Will you ask him for me?"

"Yes, of course," I said. "But you could as easily ask him yourself. I'm not sure when I'm going home."

"Yes, I will. But I thought, if you asked him he might sooner come."

A big clock was ticking somewhere. The windows across the front were triple glazed, the heavy curtains closed. You could not otherwise, beyond the clock, hear anything.

"Do you think he would come?" she asked again, then added bitterly, "Oh, come or not come, what does it matter?"

"Why ask him then?"

She looked at me, her eyes in the powdered face open wide with amazement. "Because, I must do something. I want my husband." She let herself fall into the huge divan. "I know what you're thinking," she said. But I was a child then—innocent, naive, ignorant beyond words. I had no idea what Helena was up to. No idea about Chase. But we're mature now. Chase too was young and wild. Now . . . he might . . ." She stood up again, to walk about the room.

"But you see," she went on, roaming about, "in the eyes of the Church, and legally, we're man and wife—*and* child. Lino must mean something to him. His only son."

"I should think so, yes," I agreed. While she was lighting another cigarette I said, "Olympia, why are you made up like an oriental trollop?"

From depression she went instantly to shrieks of laughter, then back again suddenly to seriousness. "What utter shit this is."

"And the gown and the hair?"

"To make myself look as ridiculous and outrageous as I can," she said aggressively. "To annoy Niccolo."

"Is that all?" I pressed her.

"Why shouldn't I, if I feel like it?" she snapped. "It's my only vice. It makes me feel unreal."

"Unreal?"

"That's right. It completes the sense of invention. I want Niccolo and everyone to know I can do as I please, including making myself look . . . oriental." She laughed again. "I was so glad to see you tonight." She looked at me imploringly. "If only I could get Chase to come—just for a while. We could travel. All of us. We could take Lino and *sail* somewhere—Sicily, Greece, the Nile. Would you like that?"

"Me!" I said. "What have I got to do with it?"

"He would surely come if you did. And it *would* be wonderful—all of us on a yacht, a big white yacht going up the Nile. You could bring someone too."

"Olympia—"

She looked at me, quite clearly disliking me for hanging back with the facts, the improbabilities.

"What?"

"A trip up the Nile on a yacht is not a marriage. It will not solve your problems."

"It's a start!" she whispered.

I smiled and she relaxed momentarily. "Chase is not husband material," I said. "You know that."

"Perhaps he's changed. As I have. He's older now. Besides—"

"Besides what?"

". . . things he doesn't know," she said cryptically. "Things which when they are explained would change his mind."

"*What* things?"

She lifted her chin and stared at me, the princess and the American. "It's far more complicated than you think," she said warningly. "But if I'm to expect your help I suppose you should hear it. . . ."

Of the story she told me I remember these essentials. In the 1950s Niccolo's mother, Donna Helena, found herself marooned: a widow with a homosexual son whose continued refusal to marry matched and expressed his contempt for nature—his own and the world's. Helena's particular torture in life was to have borne this only child, although the torture was retrospective. For years it had been merely unfortunate; it had seemed at first that one child would do.

Helena's brother was Prince Rudolfo Odischalchi, the head of a formerly royal family of Hungary, now principally Italian. Across the years, through the grace of their longevity and position in European banking and commerce, and despite their constantly dwindling number, they had remained unutterably rich. But in choosing, from the Virgilianos, the remnant of a pack of wide-eyed humanists, Helena had not chosen well. She had instead married for love. Now, to save an impossible situation, she asked Rudolfo for help. Her son, Niccolo, would not marry, and that meant the end of them. She therefore wished to reincorporate her dying family back into the Odischalchi. To this end she had devised a plan.

The plan, though a good one, was complicated—so much so

that without the indulgence afforded by her own rank and the affection of her brother, one would have given it no chance of succeeding. It called for the use of Helena's niece—Rudolfo's elder daughter, Olympia. Rudolfo had two sons and two daughters. Might he not spare Helena one of them and do her, his only sister, this last kindness? Rudolfo, however, while sympathetic to his sister's dilemma, had to be convinced; and in the end it was not Helena but life itself that did the convincing.

Olympia's boyishness, more pronounced as she matured, was matched by a certain effeminacy in both her brothers. The eldest, inconveniently, died young; the other, although married for years, had not produced an heir. Suddenly Rudolfo himself stood in danger of a kind of extinction. Helena's plan took on new meaning; together this time they refined it further.

Helena had wanted Olympia for Niccolo. Once they were married, she would quietly arrange for the girl to be impregnated; who knew how? Privately she believed it was not heredity that mattered but tradition; these things could always be managed one way or another. For his part, Rudolfo was resolved to leave nothing to chance; he felt that Niccolo, having shown his true stripe, must be kept out of the matter completely, and he reserved for himself the right to choose the father of Olympia's child. This person, adopted legally into the Virgiliano clan, would then marry his daughter the princess and from her would beget an heir to both families, whose names would merge.

By the early sixties Rudolfo and Helena had reached an agreement and had even signed a most peculiar contract, although both had everything to gain by the deal. It would be necessary to wait—until Olympia had matured enough to marry, and until Rudolfo found a suitable man to breed her with.

"I was so young, Peter," Olympia said, lighting another cigarette.
"Helena said you were an obscure penniless princess."
"No. Except for a few odds and ends to my brother and

sister, I inherited everything—from my father, even from Helena. *That* is what I'm getting at. Until Lino comes of age, Chase is legally entitled to half of it. They of course neglected to tell him that."

"Wait," I interrupted her. "Why Chase? Why did your father choose Chase?"

"I don't know—except that it took years. He told me very little about it until the end. But he used genealogies and detectives, and pored over family trees and lists. Once he said that Chase was distantly related to the Odischalchi, but when I asked Chase himself he said it was nonsense."

"Helena told Chase she chose him out of Niccolo's weekend guests."

"Well, Helena knew Chase's grandmother in the old days. But it was my father who told her to invite him to La Favola, to make the offer."

"How could your father know Chase even existed?"

"I told you. Helena knew his grandmother."

I left this for a moment. "Niccolo said you simply need sex and won't take a lover."

"Niccolo," she replied, "is jealous. . . . How rude. He is just like his mother. He has *become* his mother. I watched it happen. But he wants Chase back just as much as I do."

"And why Chase?" I persisted. "Why didn't they choose someone who liked women, for instance?"

"They wanted whoever it was to *leave* afterward—which was not much of an arrangement for me—and who but a homosexual would agree to such a thing?" She said this without contempt or anger, although perhaps only for my sake.

Helena had counted on Chase wanting in the end to live his own life—since Niccolo had shown her that was what such people did. She had told him nothing of the real advantages to the Virgilianos, other than the promulgation of the line—that it was not simply their salvation she was engineering, but their apotheosis, the equal certainly of anything that had happened to them in the fifteenth century. And all from an old lady only doing her best to turn liabilities into assets.

From Chase's point of view, with all the Starkweather business—the legend of Orvil—great wealth had long been ephemeral, dreamlike and unobtainable. What money he had at the time actually gained from his marriage seemed to him quite generous of fate.

"He's never known the real possibilities here," Olympia said. "They were kept from him. If he knew, perhaps he'd come back."

"At least for a look," I agreed. "But why should anything be different now from what it was between you?"

"I'm in control now," she replied soberly. "My father and Helena are dead. Niccolo is old and feeble and has never had the stomach for this sort of thing. I know that after he met Chase he would have stopped the marriage if he could. He did delay it for a time. And if I weren't in control would I dress like this?"

"They wouldn't care, if they thought you were harmless," I suggested.

"There is no *they,* Peter. Tell him that."

The next day, with Lorenzo, I asked if we might spend the following weekend together—perhaps in Venice, or Siena, or somewhere by the sea—anywhere we could be alone and safe. He said he often went on weekend buying trips, sometimes without la moglie, and he would arrange something.

We drove through the lovely green countryside, the top down, the air and light fresh in our faces, through the small towns and mountains, the meadows and vineyards, the Tuscan springtime. I watched his square brown hand on the gearshift, a gold chain bracelet swinging lightly from the wrist, quite as enthralled by this tame, collared exotic as by the passing wonders, the *castelli* and clouds: Lorenzo's hand. It was the same as knowing I was eternally safe to know I might at any moment reach out and touch it; but not doing so. We spoke little in the windswept open car, with the roiling sky overhead and so much to see, pointing wordlessly to this and that, speaking only to the occasional direct possibility of a particular farm or vineyard one day belonging somehow to ourselves. We stopped for lunch in a town at random, in a *paesetto* beyond the big tunnel. The restaurant was called Il Cantagallo—the crowing rooster. This took on the meaning of the moment at dawn when your lover slips from your body and from your bed; from your life, eventually. I realized the whole weekend, most probably, would be filled with such portents.

We had chosen Porto Ercole where it was thought the rich were too sophisticated to be troubled by oddities. We lay half-asleep on the beach and he turned to me and said, "You're going to do something soon. I can tell."

I told him I had no money left and must go back to New York. He sat up and looked at the sea. "And then what?"

Quite suddenly I thought of Olympia's fantasy of sailing to Egypt with Chase, which now, far from seeming impossible, was clearly the answer not only to Olympia's problem but to my own. She had invited me to "bring someone." Anticipating the romance of sailing up the Nile with Lorenzo made me suddenly want us to go, quite as much as Olympia must. When I had explained the idea to him, Lorenzo said I was crazy.

"Completely crazy," he repeated.

I did not admit it was the height of folly to depend in any way on Olympia, or on Chase, or that much of her story might be untrue. Chase himself might now be involved with someone in New York, or unable to leave his job, or unwilling to see his strange estranged wife. But the fantasy was now feasible in my mind; and attractive, it seemed, to everyone—even Lorenzo, even Chase—for the fact of its temporary quality. This romantic, improbable cruise, lasting only a few weeks, would be a stopgap in all our lives; and afterward we could each return to whatever we had been doing.

Renzo and I had only to think that our imminent, now announced separation was not permanent to be able to construct the rest of the weekend—an interlude, like a piece of music or a story itself, with a continuation and development that would come to a satisfactory ending, either Sunday evening, or Monday morning if possible. And afterward, in the not distant future, would come more—perhaps on Olympia's yacht, perhaps elsewhere, but more. This meant he and I might now separate, but would find each other again.

Within a few hours the idea of two weeks on a yacht had gained merit. It would be worth arranging, worth putting yourself out for, and Lorenzo began to think of ways he might get away from Florence. Two weeks, he said, were out of the question; but perhaps a week, or ten days. I pointed out, in the way we embroider hopefully upon the impossible, that it would take time to get back and forth. We would want a few days at least to be on the yacht. We let ourselves daydream about it.

"I don't understand," he said. "Where will the yacht be?"

Somewhere in Italy, I thought. Or perhaps we would fly to Greece or Egypt to meet it. We went on like this intermittently for hours, after making love, during dinner, lazing on the beach all Sunday morning. By late Sunday we were discussing what one might wear.

"I think most of it will be done in white dinner jackets and linen suits," I said. "Olympia is very formal." Instead of putting him off, he found all sartorial requirements appealing. Lorenzo's eyes, brightened by the light and taking on the color of the sea and sky, as their reflected duplications, were softened and focused on the furthest view, straight off beyond the horizon. His gaze now contained everything I cared to have from him—love and attraction, pride and peace, the desire to be part of the glimpse.

I watched it fade from his face before he looked back. "Do you really think it will work, Piero?"

"Yes, I do." No, I didn't, but so wanted it to that I would try. "I'll speak to Olympia. But otherwise I'll come back to Italy as soon as I can."

We had made ourselves practically invisible at the hotel—an enormous palace-convent with a cloister in which, if it amused, you could have coffee where devout ladies had dedicated their lives to Christ. The purity of the architecture had been preserved; religion hung in the air overlain with commerce, as if the nuns themselves had opened a deluxe café. This gave the hotel tremendous respectability, in which perhaps we felt alien and vaguely, mildly threatened—two men *insieme* in a romantic setting favored by rich honeymooners. We stayed in the huge, high-ceilinged room and ate elsewhere. In the lobby nothing mattered if you were properly dressed.

We watched TV in bed, smoked hashish I had brought, and fell on each other. Later we could not sleep and hardly tried, but simply held each other for hours, until some small caress from one or the other got embroidered into something that gripped us for another hour. At dawn we drove back, in the lovely fresh repudiation of Monday morning, of other mornings he had left me in the hotel in Via Faenza; of the return to Florence and the facts; repudiation of the crowing roosters in all the still sleeping farmyards we speeded past.

Before leaving Italy I had to see Olympia once more, to be sure she was serious about pursuing Chase, about the idea of the cruise. She said of course she was serious. Had we gone through all of that for nothing? She got excited when I said I would myself like to be included—with a friend.

"You don't know him," I said, to give her the pronoun.

"Don't be too sure," she replied. "You're forgetting Igor and Elvira."

148

"Who is Elvira?"

"My maid," Olympia replied. "She was trained by Helena. His name is Lorenzo. He resembles our Caravaggio and has a wife and two sons, a shop in the city. His aunt Zá-Zá runs the Bardolini. . . ."

I could only stare at her.

"It's all Helena's doing. It goes on by itself, as part of the house, part of being in this family." She shrugged.

"I will help you with Chase," I said flatly, "if you will include Lorenzo in your invitation." I wanted it clear I could in no way afford such a luxurious mode of travel as floating one's own hotel to Egypt.

"Agreed," she said immediately, radiant with happiness. Without the rice powder, and infused with a bit of good news, she was again the attractive, serious, intelligent *donna di famiglia* she was raised to be, a woman who seems in life to have everything anyone could wish.

I saw Lorenzo once more before leaving and only briefly, in the street and in a bar. Afterward I thought this criminally stupid, but at the time it seemed we should leave things as they had been in Porto Ercole—complete and romantic, as against the seediness and squalor of Via Faenza. We arranged for a post office box, I gave him my telephone number and we established the days and hours he was to call. I gave him Olympia's number just in case. We discussed the possibilities for an excuse to la moglie, and the projected dates (September) of the cruise, and where and how and when, until everything practical had been said. All that remained was the devastation of parting. I began to cry and could not stop. Neither simple embarrassment, nor mortification at being in a confined public place, nor even Lorenzo's pleas and comforting could help me regain control. Suddenly I did not believe in the probability of a cruise to Egypt, or in Olympia, or Chase. Only this physical fact of parting was real. Nothing could mitigate or patch the crack it put in my life. We would never, I felt, see each other again—not as we were, not in this bliss of love and feeling, of understanding. Something would keep us apart. And whatever the separation—weeks, months, years—it was all the same, for something that each of us needed and received from the other would in the meantime disappear. All of this caused me to weep uncontrollably, and we went out in the street where I said a few incomprehensible phrases in Italian: "Better to slip away. Better just to go. . . ." and wandered away from him as in a huge crowd.

On the plane, in the aisle after boarding, I experienced another crying fit. The steward assumed I had been tragically orphaned and moved me into first class where these things were better understood. I found Chase in Manhattan two days later, having by then regained such faculties as did not touch on humor and optimism.

Chase said, "You'll see him again before you know it. In the meantime, can you tell me any of the dirty bits?"

I looked at him unbelievingly. "You are slime that crawls."

"It's the scene," he went on lightly, "in which the plain-talking secretary/friend enters the room and throws back the curtains of Drear. Sunlight floods the stage. The heroine sits up in bed, spreads her lovely legs and yawns. It's another day."

We drove immediately to the house in upstate New York, now called the Farm, although his land was cultivated by neighbors. Here, he said, I would be coddled and nursed and given the reassurance that only consultation with an expert in these matters could give, in an atmosphere of monastic contemplation and pastoral simplicity, far from the sexual temptations of *la città*.

During the drive up and in our first hours there, I spoke only of Lorenzo, of our time together; the whole love story poured out. Chase was entranced, and went about the house and in and out of the garden sighing and asking questions over and over.

"Did he *really* say he *actually* loved you? . . . Did you say Niccolo saw him?"

"No, only that Olympia knows from her maid."

"Elvira . . . Helena's maid. Very severe. Even Helena called her *la spia.*"

Chase wanted to know if Lorenzo's provinciality was manifest sexually.

"I would never call him provincial," I replied.

"Oh, wouldn't you?"

"You're forgetting the Merchant Marine. Many trips around the world."

"Don't tease." He was deadheading old blossoms and failed buds. "At tea you will again produce his photograph. Now that he no longer exists merely in the abstract."

But at tea I meant to discuss everything Niccolo and Olympia had enjoined me to tell. Over his second cup, on the porch, I said I would now tell him something not just important but central to his life. He said, "Oh well, then I'm glad it's the Darjeeling."

"Olympia would like to see you," I began.

"Olympia would like to eat me."

I paused. It was better to let him deliver his lines; otherwise he made no effort to follow.

"She would like to figure a way," he elaborated, "to dine on my brains and have me enjoy it."

"If so, I think she's found it."

"Oh? Has she grown a penis?" He sipped his tea.

I felt the way Olympia had, trying to explain a complicated situation to a person who thought he knew better. To capture his attention I went straight to the money. "Olympia is worth millions. As her husband you are entitled to half. I gather she is slightly richer than the Queen."

He said nothing and I went on. "Did you know that yours was the sperm in a practically royal marriage? Olympia was not

---

brought in to save the Virgilianos from extinction. *You* were brought in to save the Odischalchi. This was all cooked up by her father."

"Her father? But Helena—"

"Simply an enterprising old woman. What has happened is that through you the Virgiliano line has been transferred to the Odischalchi. Your son is Prince Odischalchi-Virgiliano and will inherit everything."

This was glamorous indeed. We sat and rocked and thought about it and watched the cows come down the hill. The sun had dropped behind the high hills in front. The only drawbacks to the Farm were short days and missed sunsets.

"Peter," he said finally, "as usual there are implications. Can we name them sensibly and not get carried away?"

We rocked quietly for another few moments.

"Is it like California law over there?" he asked. "Is the husband entitled to half?"

"Apparently; until Lino inherits it. I don't think it means you can simply walk in and steal her charge cards. It's more a question, I think, of her inviting you."

"And why now, after all these years?"

"She says because they're dead and it's just between you and her. You know, you were supposed to be divorced years ago. She forbade it."

"Forbade?" he repeated, for the sound of the word. "Why?"

"Because she loves you. She has never stopped loving you. She believes that with maturity you will both . . ."

Pouring a third cup, he said, "You are now to go back and start at the beginning. Tell me everything, every single thing, no matter how trivial. We have all weekend."

It took the weekend to sort it out. Chase was astounded at his naiveté, as we always are; at Helena's duplicity and cleverness, at Olympia's loyalty. He would come in from the garden, sweat on his brow, in large filthy gloves, and say, "What does she expect? What does she want?"

———

Looking up from the formation of a dough lattice for a cherry pie, I replied, "She wants you to come see her and Lino."

"What good will that do?"

"Actually, she wants us all to go up the Nile on a yacht."

"You sound like a waitress." We both laughed.

"How big a yacht?" He clutched his breast. " 'Egypt! I am dying!' " he quoted, and went back to his day lilies, which must, he said, be divided like squabbling children.

Later, outside, watching him a while, I said, "Chase, she's invited me and Lorenzo to come too. Unless you agree, I won't see him for . . . well, probably a year."

"When does she want us?" he asked, packing dirt around something and tilting his head to look at it.

"September—for as long as we like. Lorenzo can only get away for two weeks, at most. But we could stay longer."

"If it was only the money, I'd go," he said. "But to meet Lorenzo the Magnificent," he smiled beatifically. "How not?"

At another point he asked who else was coming.

"Lino and Niccolo, I think, and I guess Igor and Elvira."

"How intimate. Still, I think we'll want a yacht that sleeps twenty."

I said I thought he could make these decisions, since it was just an idea to her, to whom the main thing was making it attractive enough for him to be unable to refuse.

"She sounds desperate," he observed. "Why, after fifteen years, is she throwing yachts at me?"

"Don't be unkind. She loves you. This is all being done for you."

Driving back to the city, it was decided I would telephone Olympia and theoretically accept the invitation. Chase said September would be fine. He would postpone until then his upcoming vacation from the Botanical. His only regret was that he might then miss the turning of the leaves. To be on a ship in the fall of the year was, I must understand, the chief sacrifice a horticulturalist could be asked to make. Death in the plant kingdom was not to be lightly missed.

"But you could be back for that, by October, and bring Olympia and Lino with you."

"Olympia and Lino at the Farm!" he exclaimed. "They'd wonder where the ballroom is."

"Not true," I said. "They'd love it. Show them your life. You know, it's not so different from Olympia's."

"There's no room at the Farm for her entourage."

"You'd be crazy to bring anyone but them," I warned.

"She can't brush her own hair."

I said he could brush it for her, and do the cooking if she couldn't boil water, since he did most of it anyway. "And you never have to worry about a boy on a farm."

"Oh, I would love to see Lino there," he said wistfully, driving across the George Washington Bridge.

Olympia could be described as overjoyed at the news. I was even able to suggest that after the cruise she and Lino might be invited to America for a time, to Chase's farm.

"A farm?" she said ecstatically. "With cows?"

"Nearby," I said. "Other people do the farming." This she thought perfectly natural. This was tenant farming. These people were serfs.

"It's not at all grand, Olympia. It's a small farmhouse. No servants."

"Just the *donna di servizio*," she volunteered.

"No one."

"I see," she said from thousands of miles away.

"Chase wonders," I said, moving on, "how big a yacht you were considering."

"You may say it will be bigger than his farmhouse."

"And where will we meet it?"

"It's in Livorno, but I can send it anywhere he likes."

I said Livorno would be fine. We set a day for the cruise to begin—September 1, a Friday. Anyone who liked—meaning Lorenzo—could join us in Capri, or Messina, or Greece later on. She said she couldn't for the moment remember the name of the yacht.

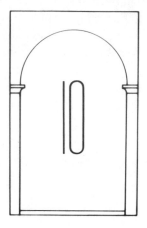

In August of 1859 Olmsted was thrown from a runaway carriage in Manhattan and broke his left leg in three places, very nearly a mortal wound. Thereafter this leg was two inches shorter than the other. A week later his newborn son died from cholera infantum. The profound depression induced by these two events, together with the task of building the park, and in which he was steadily falling behind, delayed the start of Temple Park.

Aside however from the intangibility of low spirits and the pressures of overwork, the greatest impediment to the secret project was Frederick's only superior in the construction of Central Park: Andrew Haskell Green, a member of the first Board of Commissioners and Comptroller of park funds. A handsome bachelor described as having the head of a Roman coin, Green was the great tight-ass of Central Park. On the basis of an absolute financial veto, he ruled the park and its development like a czar. It was Green who in 1863 finally drove the exasperated Olmsted from his job. By dint of the fact that Green had been given power to refuse payment for the smallest service, even to the removal of a tree or the cutting of a lawn, Olmsted's theoretical autonomy as Designer and Superintendent was virtually eliminated. He could do nothing without the written or expressed approval of the Comptroller. This was Orvil Starkweather's principal, indeed his only, failure. Orvil had thought to neutralize Green by paying for the secret work out of Brotherhood funds, but Green's relentless scrutiny of every activity and expenditure, down to the last dime for fertilizer, together with constant unannounced forays into every corner of the park, made even the preliminary work of excavation impossible, and Olmsted continually put off the groundbreaking.

The months went by. While Starkweather's impatience mounted, Frederick's depression deepened. Just when he felt most strongly the impulse to act with an artist's freedom, he found himself impeded by the autocratic Green, delaying or destroying weeks, even months of work. Because of a discrepancy on a bid to caulk a new bridge, Green delayed its opening to the public, all for the unaccountability of a few dollars in the bill. Meanwhile the public trampled new plantings at its approaches. The drafting of plans for work crews was halted for days when Green discovered an error in the price being paid for pencils. In the face of this constant harassment Frederick had all he could do to follow and meet the regular schedule of construction. Anything extra, in the expenditure of either time or money, was impossible.

Meanwhile Starkweather fumed. His grip on the Masons was firm, but could not last forever. He had been Worshipful Master for two years and MacNaughton for two more. He doubted he could manage more than another two terms, although there was always the possibility of installing a second puppet Master in NacNaughton's place.

Events matured toward the end of 1860. In April the Board

of Commissioners ordered Olmsted to present a detailed statement of all work proposed for the rest of the year, with estimates of cost and reasons for each piece. Because of pressures from Green, and the fact that he was obliged to rely more heavily than he should have on the judgment of engineers, Frederick's estimates were low. Then, by the end of the year, the work had not been completed and costs were greatly overrun. Olmsted found himself in the mortifying position of seeming to have failed in his duty. He saw also that because of Green this sort of thing would be endless; that, having to work under the worst conditions of personal harassment, he would inevitably fail. And so, without warning, he presented his resignation to the Board.

Just then a politically delicate move to extend the northern boundary of the park—from One hundred sixth to One hundred tenth Street—was before the legislature, and any hint of mismanagement would have doomed the measure. In addition, a Congressional subcommittee investigation of every aspect of the park's construction and supervision, and instituted by a disgruntled former Commissioner—had singled out Olmsted and Vaux for their professionalism and integrity. Instead of accepting his resignation, the Board, spearheaded by Orvil, invited Olmsted to state his grievances. Even Comptroller Green professed surprise. New promises were made, the resignation rescinded, and for a time Frederick was allowed to proceed in an atmosphere of comparative freedom. It was during the period that followed—March 1861 to the middle of 1863, when Olmsted, again harassed by the stingy Green, resigned and went to California—that Temple Park was at last secretly built.

Olmsted's plan was divided into two stages, the first open if not public, the second completely secret.

In Stage One a large hole was blasted through the underlying Manhattan schist just north of Belvedere Basin—now the Sheep Meadow—along the Eighty-sixth Street transverse, ostensibly in preparation for the construction of a run-off cistern for the Basin. The hole grew to one hundred ten feet long, sixty-five feet wide, and seventy feet deep. The necessity of such a large flood measure was not questioned, since the matter was never discussed. Theoretically the dangerous possibility did exist that in a sudden downpour, overflow from the Basin could flood the new trough-like transverse—and even today certain of these will fill up in minutes with a heavy rain. Construction of the cistern was not hidden, but disguised; its dimensions were officially minimized. Funds for the work not being required from the Board, estimates were not presented to the Comptroller's office. Also, by now over ten thousand men were at work in the park. Blasting and earth removal were a regular, even a ubiquitous, sight. The story of a flood culvert served for those few who chanced to see it and inquire. Meanwhile Starkweather financed an architectural tour of European capitals for Calvert Vaux, scheduled to correspond with Stage One. Comptroller Green, suitably if temporarily chastened by Olmsted's threatened resignation, had generously slackened the reins of control. He had been asked to discontinue his spying tactics of unannounced visits to construction sites, and then was kept busy elsewhere in the city for the few weeks of blasting and excavation. All work was done by an outside crew hired and paid for with diverted Masonic funds, or so Olmsted was told.

When the hole was dug, a second crew came in to lay the walls and floor with white granite blocks and mortar. This, like the excavation, took place behind a high wooden wall erected along the transverse, which itself was closed to traffic for the duration. With the rough work completed, a ceiling was fitted over the enormous space by yet a third and then a fourth crew. The roof, of steel crossbeams and mortar slabs, left the deep empty space divided into just two sections. The roof, below grade, was then covered with five feet of earth. Only the air vents, located below plates and planks in the ground, would later pierce the surface, corresponding to the chimneys and stacks of the Carriage House. These would be connected and opened in the final phase of construction.

Vaux returned from Europe to find that an enormous cistern had been dug without his knowledge or approval on the site of a complex he had keenly anticipated building. Why had he not been told? How would the water get from the Basin into the culvert? Was it really necessary?

Frederick said Vaux had been told about the project, but had forgotten. Soon after the secret agreement with Orvil, at the time of the award to Greensward in 1857, Olmsted had risked all by planting the suggestion of the need for a run-off cistern for Belvedere Basin. Yes, now Calvert did remember, but he had certainly never given his approval. Vaux from the beginning was defensive, even paranoid, about Frederick's greater public visibility. He felt, and he was right, that Olmsted was given more credit for the creation of the park. It made their partnership difficult, and in the end was the cause of its demise.

Frederick protested that while Vaux had been in Europe, out of contact, and owing to the popularity of the park, the possibility of the construction of the Stable complex had arisen, somewhat prematurely; to allow for proper scheduling, the cistern had to be started immediately. In any event, he pointed out, Vaux's Stable–Carriage House complex would in no way be affected.

The real danger was that Comptroller Green would discover the plot, would discover even the cover story of the cistern. Since all of it was being paid for with outside funds, hidden funds—with not a penny subject to Board approval, and with no park labor, without the knowledge of anyone but Olmsted and Starkweather—even the cistern story must be contained, if not kept secret. After the roof was put on and covered over, the danger of discovery was less vital, for then no one could know how large the excavation really was. And with no estimates or record of cost, no one would. Even Green, should he now somehow hear about the culvert, would think of it as a minor flood precaution.

That the thing was accomplished during the period of greatest activity in the construction of the park was in itself the shrewdest part of Olmsted's plan. It was a time of near chaos. One project looked like another, with all of it in a state of becoming. Due to the chronic unemployment caused by the financial panic of 1857, the entire work force was regularly and repeatedly fired and replaced, with a constant coming and going. Order alternated with apparent pandemonium. Comptroller Green minded the purse strings and oversaw the estimates with his well-known and over-scrupulous honesty. In the general confusion, anything that bypassed these controls went unnoticed. It was assumed that nothing could be done without money. It was never imagined that private funds would be used to add something to the park. And so, with limitless money paid out by Starkweather clandestinely to small, hand-picked crews, the first and dangerously public part of Temple Park was carried out undetected. When the high wooden wall along the Eighty-sixth Street transverse was removed and traffic reopened to the public, all that could be seen was a steep, graded site, rising to the Basin beyond, and ready for the much-talked-about, eagerly awaited Livery.

Only Frederick knew the true dimensions of the huge space below ground, and only he knew where to dig to gain access to it. The last operation—filling in the dirt over a small hole sealed with wooden planks—had been given to one man, a laborer brought in at the last minute from another project in the park, whom Frederick had chosen for his shyness and slow, methodical ways. The rest of a fifth crew had gone. Only the small black hole, like a double grave, remained in the gently graded ground. Frederick asked the laborer to cover and fill it in before he left and to mark it with a stick. The next day, alone on the site, Frederick removed the stick and carefully paced off the secret spot, using a certain irregular tree beyond the north wall of the transverse as a landmark, crossed by a certain other tree up by the Basin.

Nothing now in Orvil Starkweather's life was as important to him as Temple Park—not his family, money, position, the Masons, not even his own well-being. The Temple was the embodiment of all these things and more. It represented the mystery and magic of his own life, the power of his destiny, the secrecy of his inmost self, the measure of his influence, his force of will, his desire to prevail and to leave behind, as the pharaohs had done, a monument that would speak for him when he was gone. Secrecy—of the construction, and afterward of the existence of the Temple—was an aspect of the plan that pleased him deeply, but that was also essential. A secret must be secret. Even as a child he had been intrigued by the idea of a hidden room, a place in his father's house known only to him, given over to his sole use; a place so secret that it existed only in his mind; a place he looked for constantly, upstairs and down, twisting the hooks at the backs of closets, carefully prying up the floorboards in the attic, digging up paving stones in the cellar, always looking for a way in. The best he could manage, by way of approximations, were the attic eaves and the cellar coal bin—not exactly hidden, but not plainly utilized, although filthy and unsuitable for the clean, ethereal use of the imagination. Outside, in the woods, he built a tree fort, and then found a small cave that provided great solace for years. He hid things beneath rocks and in the hollow trunks of dead trees—things of no worth or importance except that, being hidden, they took on inordinate value to him.

Temple Park was the escalation of this obsession, befitting his wealth and power. It was the childlike idea of a rich man, which is the best combination for elaborate folly. Nothing stood in his way except convention, the unwitting Andrew Haskell Green and one or two civil laws. No one but Olmsted knew about it, not even the Masonic Cabal. In the end Orvil had decided to pay for it all privately, with his own money, making it to him an even purer idea and thus preserving its secrecy until the last possible moment. At night he dreamed of Temple Park, flashing gold in his mind. He awakened in the early mornings to write down the details he had dreamed. He believed he was the instrument of a power outside himself; else whence came these incessant, magnificent details?

Whenever possible and many times for no reason other than to pass by, he had his driver cross the park at Eighty-sixth Street. The coachman, unbidden, would slow the carriage to a walk. Beneath him; beneath the ground. Occasionally Orvil stopped and got down, walking the empty site, imagining the great space hidden below: the Temple unfinished.

Work on the Stable and Carriage House started in the spring of 1862, according to proper estimates—always the lowest—and paid for out of park funds. For the next eight months the huge space beneath it remained sealed. A flood culvert was noted on the working blueprints and plans, but not its dimensions. Using a sort of code to himself, Olmsted had indicated the placement of the Temple walls, air vents and entrance—five feet down and covered over. More or less clandestinely, Frederick, who otherwise always left the details of construction to Calvert Vaux, visited the Carriage House site at odd moments, especially in the initial stages, to determine the exact placement of its secondary walls for inner rooms.

The building itself came up divided into long, rather narrow spaces devoted to carriages and their repair. Toward the western end were a forge and a series of smaller rooms for carpentry, leather work, a harness room, a changing room, with a small storeroom at the far end. Up a narrow wooden stairway were another carpentry shop, a lavatory and a Parks Department dormitory. The front façade of the building was thirty feet high, the back half that, with the lower level built right into earth heaped from the excavation. A small, unprepossessing door from the upstairs carpentry shop opened directly onto the rear yard and the Basin nearby.

Of the two buildings going up, Vaux openly preferred the Stable, which was U-shaped and more sophisticated, and he reported there most mornings to oversee the day's details. He largely ignored the Carriage House on the other side of the paddock; to Vaux it was little more than a large garage, and he was interested only in its façade—of brickwork alternating with three sets of large double doors—and subsequently in the roof, like that of the Stable made of gray slate and fitted with several generous skylights.

Orvil had seen meanwhile to the award of the Livery concession to a suitable candidate. This man, the Lodge's new Tiler, or sergeant-at-arms, was made general manager of the whole endeavor, with the duty, over the next six months, of finding coachmen and hostlers, blacksmiths, wainwrights and stablemen—all of a sympathetic nature, meaning Masons. It had transpired that in the extensive membership of the combined New York Lodges, not one professional livery owner could be found to put the concession together. Instead, the new Tiler had been chosen on the strength of his experience as a horse trainer for August Belmont, in which occupation he was urged to continue. Through the simple expedient of posting a notice at the Lodge on lower Broadway, only Masons were interviewed and hired.

The Stable complex was finished in November, although not scheduled to open for business until the following spring. For now only a part of the Park's independent police force—under the direction of Olmsted—was quartered there, eight or ten horses in the Stable and their riders in a dormitory on the second floor. The Carriage House and Forge, in turnkey condition, was not yet in use, there being as yet no carriages to store, hire, or repair.

Orvil had asked to be present at the first uncovering of the entrance to the cavern. Two of Frederick's private staff of gardeners, from another project upstate, were brought in to crack open the new mortar floor of the storeroom, and to dig down to four wooden planks directly below. When this was accomplished, and before the planks were dislodged, the two men were sent away.

Late on a cold Saturday at the end of November, the Carriage House was empty and locked. The door to the storage room, whose brick walls made it virtually soundproof, had been bolted from the inside. Frederick and Orvil stood over the freshly opened hole as if over an empty grave. A lighted gas jet jutted from the wall, and Frederick carried a lantern.

Frederick lowered himself down onto the exposed wooden planks. With some difficulty he dislodged one of them and slid it aside. A moist, cold breath of air wafted up from the black, reverberant pit. He took a rock the size of a baseball and dropped it through the slot. Falling, falling, it hit the distant bottom with a chocking, stony sound that echoed back up to them. Orvil selected another rock and handed it down. Wordlessly Frederick dropped it into the black void. Again the stony echo.

"How deep it is," Orvil remarked, "and how chill and dark."

Frederick lowered the lantern like a man on a cliff, and Orvil peered over his shoulder. Replacing the plank, and with the other's help, he hauled himself out of the hole.

"In the morning," he said, "we will build a covering to disguise the entrance."

"Disguised as what?" Orvil asked.

"It will be fitted with a bin, or movable shelving of some weight, so as not to be dislodged or discovered by accident. It will take a knowledge of the mechanism to move it aside."

"Very well . . . and the vents?"

"They will be seen to in the coming week, one by one. I have placed one of them to connect with a heating pipe. Another will pass by the forge. It will be possible, theoretically, to force heat down through these two vents into the cavern. Otherwise I fear your workmen will suffer no small amount from the cold and damp. They might wait until the weather turns, but by then the Stable and Carriage House will both be in full use."

"My men are well paid," Starkweather declared, "and are used to the hardships of working with stone. Unless I hear to the contrary, I will tell them to begin in a week's time."

Stage Two, Orvil's decoration of the Temple, was a meticulously planned, almost military operation carried out in relative silence —for the building of the Temple, according to Masonic lore, must be silent, with no sounds of construction on the site—and almost exclusively at night. Throughout the construction of the Stable complex, stonemasons and craftsmen had worked together in a warehouse owned by Orvil in Brooklyn, assembling the Temple exactly as it would stand underground, cutting and fitting marble veneers for the walls, mosaics for the floors, ranks of columns, marble stairs, plinths, pediments and other classical odds and ends. In addition, over the past two years Orvil had privately commissioned the following articles:

  · A pair of massive (thirty-five-foot) columns of brass, one light, one dark, hollow and cast in sections for transportation and ease of passage through the secret entrance in the storeroom. Cast in Wilmington, Delaware.

  · An altar of hardwood covered with brass, eight feet across, ornamented with huge wooden horns overlaid with brass, one for each of the four corners. Across the top of the concave surface a grating of iron hung in the hollow; for burnt offerings. Cast and constructed in Virginia.

  · A smaller additional altar for incense, also made of hardwood, covered with beaten gold, three feet across, with four rings, two on each side, through which staves of wood overlaid with gold were passed for carrying. Pennsylvania.

  · A laver of hammered bronze, being a large bowl, five feet across, to hold fresh water, standing in a font like a cup in a saucer;

the saucer, to catch the overflow, made of stone, seven feet across. New York State.

· A large gong of brass within a gilded ebony frame. Vermont.

· A golden candelabrum with six branches, each holding a lamp large enough for sufficient oil and cotton to burn all night; of beaten and chased gold ornamented with knobs, flowers and bowls. Height eight feet, width five feet. Made in Brooklyn.

· A table of hardwood rimmed with gold, four feet by two by three, with four rings and two staves sheathed in gold for carrying; set with a service of dishes, bowls and covers, all of gold. The table from Connecticut; the gold service, Tiffany and Co., New York.

· A model of the Ark of the Covenant, five feet by three by three, overlaid with gold, unembellished, with rings and staves for carrying. Brooklyn.

· A cube of agate, two feet on a side, encrusted with a triangular plate of gold on which, in precious stones, was inscribed the Tetragrammaton, a delta: the sacred and ineffable name of God. Quarried in Vermont; set by Tiffany's.

The cost of these articles, together with certain others, was nearly two hundred thousand dollars, plus another eight or ten for shipping, all of it paid privately by Orvil Starkweather.

As planned, at the end of the following week, with the air vents connected to the chimneys and the storeroom entrance convincingly disguised, Olmsted declared the cavern ready for Starkweather's craftsmen and designers. Orvil had divided his men into two crews. The temple in the warehouse in Brooklyn was dismantled, its parts numbered and loaded into wagons to be carried by night to Manhattan. One crew prepared the shipments in Brooklyn, the other received them in the Carriage House and lowered them into the cavern for reassembly and embellishment. Only Orvil's Tiler and Deputy knew the eventual location of the finished Temple. The workers and artists were brought in blind-folded. These men, reduced to the minimum number, and themselves sworn to the Craft, were afterwards comfortably paid off and returned to their homes, all out of state. The advance work in Brooklyn, the dismantling and transfer to Manhattan and reassembly on the site, cost Orvil another three hundred thousand dollars in material, labor and bribes, bringing the total spent on Temple Park to something like a half million. An equivalent sum today might be closer to five million, both for what the Temple might cost to duplicate and for the emotions attendant on the accomplishment. Orvil paid for it all quite cheerfully.

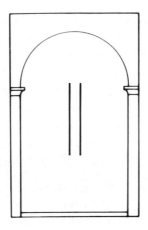

The Dedication of the Temple took place on a night in late May 1863, a formal affair. In April Orvil sent the following invitation to the thirty-two members of the Cabal, the general Brotherhood not being included or even informed of the occasion.

Orvil Starkweather
Grand Master of the Antient and Accepted
Order of Freemasons
Commands
Your Presence and Attendance
At Dinner
24th May, 1863, Eight O'clock
At the Broadway Lodge

Dedication of the Temple

White Tie, Orders and Regalia   (+)

A solar cross in parentheses at the bottom of the invitation indicated a state occasion involving only the Cabal, and therefore of the highest secrecy. It meant also that no excuse for absence was acceptable. Even the Civil War at its height, in which some of the Cabal were involved at government levels, would not signify. The generous advance notice contributed to a sense of command, as did the engraved formality and instructions for dress. And as if to underscore further the importance of the occasion, Orvil also sent personal notes to the officers of the Cabal. To the Grand Secretary, Giles Springer, he wrote:

> As my most admired intimate in the Craft I wish you to know the night of the 24th May marks a historic moment in American Freemasonry, and to understand that within the confines of the secret which burns in my heart, you shall know of it somewhat sooner. Please come to the Lodge at seven on the appointed night.
>
> O. S. GM

The Grand Secretary had kept his office as long as Orvil—longer, insofar as he had also held it earlier under MacNaughton. He had his intimates as well, and after comparing notes, speculation ran high. The wording of the invitation—Dedication of the Temple—was understood to be metaphorical. The only certainty among them was that everyone would attend.

On the great night, Secretary Springer arrived at the Broadway Lodge slightly before seven as urged, carrying a small suitcase of regalia, there being too much of it in his station to wear in the streets anywhere outside Baghdad. In the cloakroom he donned his sash of office and Masonic apron, which depicted a red pomegranate on a white field. He entered the hall to find long tables set for a banquet, with draped white cloths and flowers and red candles, and waiters standing about already bored. In the adjoining lounge Orvil sat in a comfortable chair. A maroon and gold ambassadorial sash, matching and obscuring two of his ruby studs, crossed the linen expanse of his chest in a glossy proclamation of power. *Grand Master,* it read; or rather, *and Mast,* for only that much of it was visible. Orvil's fringed apron depicted a green palm tree on a yellow dune.

"Giles," Starkweather declared, not rising. "Thank you for coming early. Champagne?" He indicated a tray, ice bucket and twelve empty glasses nearby.

"Here come the others," he murmured, disappointing Springer, who had thought the interview would be private; and the Senior Warden, the Marshal, the Treasurer and the Tiler entered the lounge, each also in a different colored apron with gold fringe, like shirt fronts pulled out of their pants. "Gentlemen," Orvil said, rising. "Good evening. This is delightful. Yes, yes, have a drink and be comfortable whilst I tell you why we are here . . . Well, you had no great difficulty in the traffic. . . ."

They all allowed not, and took a glass from Giles Springer, who poured.

"Well, well," Orvil began, lifting his glass in a toast. The others looked at him expectantly.

"To a historic evening," Orvil said. "The night of the new Temple." He drank his champagne and threw the empty glass into the fireplace, where it smashed with a gratifying sound. With visible surprise the others did the same. For purity of drama, they thought, none could match Orvil; and as a reassuring detail of intelligent planning they all now noticed the remaining six glasses, thus explained. Springer poured out the rest of the bottle and turned it upside down in the bucket. "New Temple?" he inquired politely.

"I will save my explanation for the banquet," Orvil replied, "but I wanted you all to know first that I have caused a new Temple to be built, and that tonight we will be performing the ceremony of its Dedication. Charles here," meaning the Tiler, "for logistical reasons, has known of the project for some time, and all advance preparations for tonight's formalities have been seen to by him and his Deputy . . ." Orvil paused, for his guests were looking at him and the Tiler blankly, or apprehensively.

Springer said again, "A new Temple? You've built a new Temple? Where?"

"In the Central Park," Orvil replied simply.

"But how?" the Marshal asked. "I have heard of or seen nothing like that in the park, and we drive there frequently."

"It can't be seen from the park," Orvil replied. "It can't be seen from anywhere. It is hidden." Orvil had never been happier. They were stupefied.

"Hidden!" the Grand Secretary exclaimed. "You've hidden a temple in Central Park?" and the Treasurer said, "Who paid for it?"

"That is not your concern," Orvil snapped. "It's all paid for. To be frank, I paid for it myself—as my gift to the Brotherhood."

"Is it to replace this Lodge?" Giles Springer asked.

"No, no," Orvil replied. "That problem still faces us. The Temple is for special occasions—Initiations and Investitures, for instance. Only our little group will ever know it exists, or where."

Some of the regular Brothers of the Cabal were arriving, somewhat early, and Orvil put his fingers to his lips. "You will of course not spoil my surprise. All will be explained before long. I ask only that you keep this to yourselves until *after* dinner."

"When can we see it?" the Marshal asked.

"Oh, tonight, tonight," Orvil replied with a smile. "We are all going up there after dinner. Now, not a word."

Commensurate with his office and responsibility for the evening, Orvil had reserved for himself a thronelike central position among the tables, which were laid out in the form of a solar cross. Seen from above the effect was striking, for a second, floral cross—in red roses and candles—had been arranged on the crossed white tables. Orvil began the banquet with a short speech to explain the evening's theme, but succeeded only in tantalizing his guests further.

He said, "Tonight is a night you will always remember. And were it not that we are bound to keep it ever the direst secret of our lives, it is a night history itself would record. For tonight we become something beyond Freemasons. Tonight we return to the mystical center of our heritage, forswearing none of our ideals or oaths, but assuming others lost in the shadows of time. Tonight is the beginning of a new era of Masonry in America. I invite you, my Brothers, to join me in the resurrection of the Order of the Knights Templar!" And to a sudden silence which then was gradually filled with a murmur of approbation and conjecture, he sat down and signaled to the captain to begin.

The meal had come down from Delmonico's, and went on for over an hour. In the middle of it one of the Brothers stood up and rapped his glass with a knife for attention. His name was George Goelet and his family owned, among other things, much of the East Fifties; but although a respected member of the Cabal, he had no particular influence in the group. What he stood up to say was thus all the more significant, for it represented a sort of common consent. "I give you," he said, holding up his glass, "the Knights Templar!" and everyone stood and drank. It was doubtful that Goelet or anyone else there had the least notion of what it meant or entailed to take up suddenly a toast to the history or identity of the Knights Templar. It was only a likely and interesting idea to be pursued, another game, of the sort one came in for often in the Masons.

In that most civilized lull, cigars among men with full stomachs, and after the waiters had been sent from the room, Orvil at last got up to explain.

He stood for a moment at the head of the white cross of tables, solemnly beginning with the sort of simple theatrics that are basic to a good speech. They would all have patiently waited for another minute, but Orvil kept them a mere thirty seconds before speaking.

"My Brothers and friends," he began, "in a moment we are going to get into hired coaches for a drive uptown. You will find a number written on the back of your placecard—one, two or three. You will board the corresponding coach as we leave here and arrange with your own drivers, if you have them waiting outside, to collect you at the corner of Fifth Avenue and Fifty-ninth Street at one A.M. Otherwise a hansom will take you home."

Orvil paused again and rolled the tip of his cigar in an ashtray in front of him. "I have had to decide exactly how much to tell you of tonight's great dedication—whether simply to let you come upon the glories and surprises in store for you, or to pique your interest in the goings-on with a hint beforehand of what we are about to see and do. On the whole, I think it better to tell you our destination and purpose so that you know something of the significance of the occasion.

"We are Masons—as others before us have been for hundreds of years, with a rich heritage that stretches back, we have been told, through the Middle Ages to the dawn of civilization, to the building of the Great Temple of Solomon. This we have been told and taught, and this we have on faith believed. But it has fallen to me now, as Grand Master, to correct that misconception. It is not true." He paused again and looked slowly around the room.

"We did not build Solomon's Temple, nor were we there to witness its building. This is myth, a wishful legend.

"But I will tell you what we are. We are the descendants of the Knights Templar, a holy order of soldier-monks who fought in the Crusades, and who got their name from the fact that they lived and stabled their horses on the *site* of Solomon's Temple.

"In the East the Templars discovered the solution to the mysteries of existence, the secrets of life, the great questions posed by all men and women to their gods: Where do we come from? Where are we going? What happens to us after death?

"This knowledge was power—over ignorance, fear and superstition. Little wonder that the French king, the pope and his bishops took them for heretics; for this the Templars were—and heretics of the most dangerous sort.

"Brothers of the Craft! I invite you tonight to a rededication of the Temple of Light, the Temple of Enlightenment and Triumph over Ignorance, the Temple of the Power of Imagination! Join me! Come with me to a magic place." Orvil held up his hand. "I adjure you now, under the Masonic oath and pain of death, that the place to which you are about to be taken will remain ever secret from all people outside this room, and for all time. Swear! Swear!"

Rising, and as one voice, and holding up their hands, they declared, "I swear! I swear!"

Orvil waited in the ensuing silence. "We are going now to the Temple. It has been hidden underground in the new park. Its architect, bound by the same sacred oath as ourselves, has built it in such a way as to be unknown even to its artisans. Those who know where it is are themselves Initiates sworn to silence."

A man stood up. His name was Robert van Rensselaer, and his family had helped in a way to invent New York City. "Are we actually going to see a temple tonight, or were you speaking metaphorically?"

"Both, sir," Orvil replied.

They filed into waiting coaches, the officers riding, without Orvil, in Orvil's carriage. Coming up Broadway, they passed through Union Square to Fifth Avenue and drove straight uptown. At Eighty-fifth Street the line of coaches turned into the park, at which point, sitting up with the lead coachman, Orvil lighted an amber lantern. As they rounded the curve of the transverse and approached the Carriage House, a sentinel in its first skylight caused a set of double doors to swing open, and all three coaches and Orvil's carriage disappeared inside.

The thirty-three men stepped down simultaneously, looking about and openly wondering why they had stopped there. Some suggested that for secrecy's sake they would now proceed on foot or make a change of carriages. Others guessed the Temple must be below.

With a great clatter the empty coaches departed through the westernmost doors, which were then closed and bolted. The Tiler said, "This way, gentlemen," and led them toward the storeroom at the far end of the building.

Its doorway stood open, guarded by the Tiler's Deputy, who marked off the name of each Brother as he entered. Inside, the little room had been altered, its walls draped with black cotton from ceiling to floor. All that was visible in the torchlit space was the top of a spiral stair disappearing into a light-filled hole in the ground.

"You are to remain silent from this point on," the Deputy murmured as each man passed into the storeroom and down the spiral steps.

At the bottom, on a landing some twenty feet across, they were made to wait, conscious of the flickering torchlight in the gloom, the cool drafts, the rough-hewn stone walls that echoed back their footfalls and nervous coughs. As instructed, no one spoke. An alcove to one side showed the top of another spiral, leading downwards. Before them, beneath a stone arch, a monumental marble staircase descended into a large vaulted room hung with tapestries and lighted with torches.

The Tiler spoke again. He indicated the other spiral stair. "You will go down to a room at the bottom, where you will strip and be given robes and weapons. The Deputy will assist you." Silently and carefully they circled their way down another flight. Orvil had disappeared.

Minutes later, back on the landing, each of them wore the white, monklike pallium of the Templars, a knee-length flap front and back cinched with a leather belt and embroidered with a red solar cross. Each also wore sandals and carried an unsheathed sword. With officers in front, minus Orvil, the Brothers were arranged into three ranks of nine, facing the descent of marble steps. The Tiler again addressed them.

"Brothers, you are about to assume knighthood in the Secret Order of the Knights Templar. Any who reveals the mysteries learned in this place will die at the hands and swords of the others here present. So swear! Swear!"

"I swear! I swear!" The sound echoed like a growl through the vaults. Then the Tiler, followed by each rank of nine, descended the staircase into a vaulted room forty feet long, its marble walls studded evenly with torches. Tapestries depicting maps of the Holy Land and scenes from the Levant were hung at intervals, while from the vaults were suspended flags, pennants and gonfalons of the Knights Templar, commemorating a hundred ancient battles. In the center of the long wall opposite the stairs a pair of massive doors of gilded bronze were flanked by the two hollow brass pillars Orvil had commissioned, one dark, one light, representing the porch columns of Solomon's Temple, called Boaz and Jachin. Slowly, from the inside, the huge doors swung open, revealing Orvil dressed in the glittering robes of Jacques de Molay, last Grand Master of the Templars.

For the execution of this costume Orvil had chosen to emphasize its priestly as opposed to its warlike allusions, and it evoked the hierophantic dress of a great state occasion: the pope, in fact, an impression enhanced by the tall white mitre whose double tail of purple silk strips hung halfway down his back. Beneath a long cape emblazoned with a red cross, a white surplice of cotton fell to his gold slippers. Framed by the great doorway and the thirty-five-foot brass pillars, Boaz and Jachin, the response he evoked in the gaping Brothers was one of papal, imperial awe, as theatric as Grand Opera. Now, with grace surprising in one so short and corpulent, and extending his arms in a sort of open embrace, he beckoned them to enter the huge room.

Within, the Holy of Holies was a domed circle sixty feet across and fifty feet high, the outer ten feet separated from the inner circle by a ring of twenty-four columns. The columns of white marble were forty feet tall with sockets of silver cast in a filigree of lilies. In the ceiling a blue glass dome was studded with gold stars that caught the light. In the center an oculus, like a smooth gold dish, reflected downward. Between each of the columns on the outer wall, high-fired gas jets were mounted with mirrors that angled their brightest points of light up toward the dish in the dome. The combined light of these twenty-four focused beams collected in the dish and shot downward in a single shaft to the central Altar, with a cumulatively greater brightness. The High Altar itself, with its massive gold horns and a white fire in the grate, shot heat back up to the dish, which then fanned warmth in swirling circles throughout the huge room. Beneath the grate, which had an open hole at its center, in a space created by the Altar's four legs, stood a model of the Ark of the Covenant, all of gold. Placed directly below the currents of heat and light, a glowing ball—white, like burning magnesium—filled the empty Ark. The impression, in the big room, was of daylight, even of sunlight, and of a mild, comforting warmth.

The Brothers stood in an inner ring in front of the columns so that each had a full view of the Temple, sword points down like chess pawns. The floor, depicting the duality of existence, was a checkerboard of black and white marble squares, or diamonds, depending on how the eye was turned. The Tiler stood at the doors, which now, with the help of five men, were pushed shut and bolted.

Orvil walked around the Altar greeting each of the Brothers and smiling in benediction. Ritually, he spoke to them in French. *"Bon soir, mon fils,"* to which some of them replied and some of them did not, *"Bon soir, mon père."*

They had been chilled in the damp chamber below, but now the altar's light and warmth, permeating the room, induced in them a near-hypnotic state of lassitude and comfort. George Goelet, who had got up at the banquet to toast the Templars in a show of spirit and credulity, and Robert Van Rensselaer, who had wondered if the Temple was metaphorical, stood beside each other in the wide circle. Orvil stopped in front of them.

"You will light one of the lamps, mon fils," he said to Goelet. "And you will assist him, Robert." Orvil gestured toward the towering gold candelabrum standing in their quadrant of the circle. "Take a flame from the Altar and light one Lamp of the six, from the left." And he added, *"Au plus beau,"* meaning, Smartly, the Templar motto.

Goelet handed van Rensselaer his sword and approached the Altar. The Marshal gave him a long wax taper. Extending his arm at full length, he lighted the wick, shielding his face from the intense radiating heat of the fire. As Goelet lit the first of the oil lamps, Orvil said, "Light from the light of lights to dispel darkness."

The two men returned to their places and Orvil passed into the next quadrant of the circle, containing the Censer. He himself put incense from a small gold pot into the Censer bowl and lighted it. "By this holy scent shall you know the sanctified." And the smell of attar of roses began to fill the room.

In the third quadrant stood the Gong, a large dish of brass suspended from a gilded frame. Orvil took up a mallet and struck it once, twice, three times. "Sound, from the sound of time, to hear the world," he said as the hollow note drifted gradually off.

The next quadrant contained the Laver, filled with water. Pointing to another of the Brothers, he said, "You will bathe in this pool. Remove your garment."

David Wellman, the youngest man in the Cabal, hesitated a moment, embarrassed by the request. Then he removed his belt, pallium and sandals. He was twenty-eight and well formed, with a gold-white-rose glow to his skin. The water in the Laver was ice-cold; he stepped into the tub and stood shivering, the water up to his thighs. Orvil directed him to kneel, and taking up a gold dipper, poured water over the young man's head.

"Water of life," Orvil intoned, "to bathe the spirit."

Shivering, his genitals shriveled from the cold, Wellman stepped out of the Laver, replaced his robe and sandals and returned to the circle. Orvil signaled the next man, and thereafter each of the Brothers was baptized.

When all of them had been bathed, the Tiler brought in a young black goat, which was thrown unceremoniously, bleating and screaming, onto the flaming Altar. To the scent of roses was added the odor of burnt hair and seared meat.

"So, in a moment," Orvil declared, "did the Grand Master and his Templar martyrs perish in the flames."

The goat was consumed by the fire. When it had been cooked through, its charred carcass was removed from the grate and pulled apart, the pieces placed in gold dishes and bowls on the table, also in the fourth quadrant; and Orvil said, "Food from the flesh of life is an offering to the Lord."

In the four corners of the square encompassing the circular outer wall of the Holy of Holies were four triangular rooms, each with a door behind the ring of columns, obscure but not concealed. In two of these rooms were kept fuel for the fire and water for the Laver. Another contained a staircase to the lower level by which the Master came and went unseen. A fourth room also contained a staircase, this one leading down to a Treasure room.

The lower level consisted of five chambers and a passageway. Together with the Treasure room were a changing room with lockers, a lavatory, a storage room like a large closet for regalia and robes, and a room for the Grand Master. The Treasure room, however, could be entered only from above, using a small spiral staircase. In it, together with the gold implements of Temple use, Orvil had stored a fortune in gold bullion, now to be the treasury of the Cabal, and reproducing the treasure of the Templars.

Orvil had converted roughly half of his holdings to gold. With each bar worth sixty-three thousand dollars, the Treasure room held three hundred and twenty-two bars, worth twenty million dollars. To have thus converted more of his wealth would have risked insolvency, for stored gold was relatively useless. Given the earning power of such an enormous sum, it cost him something like fifty thousand dollars a day to keep it out of commission. On the other hand, gold was gold, and its value in the vicissitudes of a great Civil War could never decrease. Here, in fact, in bulk, it more or less kept pace with its steadily rising cost on the market.

According to Templar lore, Orvil ought rightly to have stored the gold inside the hollow pillars, Boaz and Jachin, on the Temple porch. But this would have precluded the possibility of viewing it, which now, in a long, slow line going down and up the staircase to the Treasure room, he allowed the Brothers to do. Of all the sights they had seen this was the most impressive, not only for the worth of the gold but for the commitment it represented on Orvil's part. They could see that he had held back nothing in the recreation of the Temple, having surrendered even his worldly value to the obsession.

They returned to the Holy of Holies and stood again in a wide circle around the altar. Orvil addressed them.

"Knights Templar, you have seen all the wonders here but one, and that one I cannot show you. The Sacred Stone. Its value is greater than gold. It is the secret glory of the Knights Templar recreated here. It is the embodiment of mystery. It is itself the secret—the will, the word, the name of God.

"The great treasure in the room below will be the resources of our Order. We will soon double it, and more."

They all stared, as thoroughly subdued by the effect, by the endless preparation now made evident, by the theatrics and glamour, as by the stupefying treasure stacked below; the Temple unfinished—not of heavenly wisdom or earthen stone, but of gold; a temple of the power gold could buy.

"This one thing is left unseen," Orvil said mysteriously. "But I can tell you its story.

"Enoch, son of Cain, built a temple underground on Moriah, a mountain sacred to the Lord. Enoch dug nine vaults, situated perpendicularly one under the other, deep into the ground, and communicating by apertures left at the top of each vault.

"In the ninth vault Enoch placed a triangular plate of gold, each side two cubits long, enriched with precious stones—the gold plate encrusted upon a larger stone of agate. On the plate was inscribed the Tetragrammaton, a delta: the sacred, ineffable name of God.

"And the son of Enoch, Methuselah, who lived for centuries, and his son Lemech also worshipped the stone in the ninth vault, unto the time of Noah.

"After the Great Flood, Noah's Ark came to rest on Mount Ararat, also sacred to the Lord. But King David, digging the foundation of the Temple on Mount Moriah, found a certain stone in the depths of the excavation. This stone, a perfect cube, he removed and placed in the Holy of Holies."

Spreading his arms in benign benediction, Orvil signaled that the ceremony was ended.

THREE

·

THE
BLUE STAR

Chase was still handsome. He seemed to have just hit thirty when we were both in fact thirty-eight. His eyes were bright, his hair intact, his face smooth and taut. But his skin had thinned and a certain high color had gone, and the lovely integration of features —the way they fell together—had simplified into something approximate. He was less rare. I thought he had begun to look like the faces on Mount Rushmore, particularly Jefferson's: the deep chisel marks, the flattening, squaring planes of his forehead and cheeks had obliterated all boyishness to give him a monumental aspect. It had always been a head that would do for stone; now it was character and interest—in the calm, handsome façade— that would lure the sculptor. Looks-wise, he said, it had all been a moot point after twenty-four. He knew the league he'd been in; standards there were too high to maintain. Now he was in another, parallel league, no less exalted, but based on other values than beauty and youth. Peering this way and that in the mirror, he declared, "I think we'll manage another few seasons . . . possibly three." He saw now how he would look as a charming ruin.

Something else had taken over—something he allowed to happen instead of the automatic sexual reflex that so often had got in the way of so much. He would never have indulged himself with one of the Botanical guards, several of whom were available; however, he would frequently miss days of work because the command for sex had come at three in the morning. Now he said to himself oh please, and stayed home. This change in habits and personality I observed in myself as well. This was the color that had gone.

It seemed that in the preceding years we had become equalized. I had remained as I was, reasonably, humanly attractive, while Chase had come down from the gods. I had seen the display and effects of ideal beauty with Lorenzo. Chase, if he had ever possessed such power, had relinquished it.

Happily for Olympia and the plan, Chase was not at the moment engaged, other than by his work at the Botanical and, on weekends, by his own garden upstate. In five years the Farm had acquired the illusion of maturity, even of age. It was, as Chase's father often termed it, a showplace. Using some of the old trees as backdrops and with judicious but expensive plantings, Chase had given it the look of a third-generation garden. During the week the Botanical was perfect in that he needed to be institutionalized, needed somewhere to focus his knowledge—on rare specimens, objects, theories, history, horticultural and floral controversy. Some people, Chase among them, held that the next age would have botany at its center. From the plant world, as in Darwin's time, we would yet learn the secrets, the meaning of life. This philosophy and excitement unified his life, whereas when he was younger he had accomplished it momentarily only with sex.

At the Farm he was constantly rushing out to the blue and white garden—four wide borders facing each other across a small square of lawn—hovering, bringing his face as close to the floral event as he could. He would say excitedly, "So much going on, every minute is different." It was a frustration to miss any of it. One night the evening news—the only television he would watch —ran a three-minute, stop-time condensation of a day in the life of a spring garden. Plants jostled each other, thrusting their little faces at the sun. Stalks danced about like singles at a discotheque. Bleachers of color opened and closed. Clearly you could make out selfishness, pushiness, pride, passion, triumph and fatigue. "There, you see!" Chase exclaimed, pointing at the screen. "That's what I see all the time." He loved the naive predictability of plants. " 'Plant a radish, get a radish,' " he would sing gaily over his spadework. Plants did not disappoint, or if they did, one need not take it personally, as with people. A garden gave back fidelity, like a pet, and in place of love it was lovely: to Chase the same thing, if not an improvement.

I don't think a real connection ever took place for Chase in any of his four long and semi-long love affairs. Perhaps his love required of its object the passivity of plants; yet to deal with him and to love him back took strength. This paradox was difficult to sustain beyond, it seemed, a few years, after which a certain sexual vision paled. With two of the four he had fallen deeply in love; the other two were milder events, taken on the rebound. Physically they were all different, though he was sure to favor ethnic types: dark-haired, green-eyed if possible, short, very New York. None had been as gifted as he, and in each case the match, to his friends, seemed lopsided and doomed. Two of them, however, the two he loved, had remarkable intelligence, cunning attentive sensibilities and great humor. Chase forgot all anxieties if he could laugh or be amused. Boredom made him neurotic and difficult.

I had met each of the four immediately, having had them presented to me in turn formally, as if to Chase's mother for approval, although my approval always was expected and could not, in the event, have been withheld. Purely a formality. Chase would say, "My oldest and dearest friend," I would invite them to sit down and I would pour, having learned by now to pour a handsome cup of tea, and would divine in their initial responses to the situation the chances of their making it through the winter. During all of these affairs Chase was at first happy, fulfilled, homey and devoted. His parents had been excellent models in this regard, and it pleased Chase to be as openly affectionate and demonstrative as William with Juliet. If one side of him was less than original and fresh, it was this soft, sentimental, affectionate part of him—at other times perfectly hidden, but with his lovers exposed, even flaunted, like the odd courting extravagances of a male bird on display. Soon however, usually within six months or a year, I would hear of trouble in paradise. As Chase's intimate I would be sought out by the lover for advice, first casually and then assiduously, as a sympathetic neutral who might understand and commiserate, if not help. I learned a great deal about him from these conversations.

The one he loved best—a male nurse—stayed with him the longest, nearly four years. The nurse was a specialist in terminal cases and was not accustomed to giving up on anyone, no matter how terrible the symptoms. His specialty was the final hours and he considered himself expert at "seeing them out." Though Chase was never ill he certainly at times behaved like a terminal case; and then Carter, the nurse, unlike his bewildered predecessors, was in his element. This was the secret of his longevity with Chase: Carter responded to every neurotic device with professional calm, and under his regime, perhaps because of the gift of love exchanged between them but also because of this medical know-how and unflappability, Chase seemed far less changeable and neurotic, far more organized and ambitious and successful. He was crushed when Carter suddenly left, practically without warning, he said, although Carter had been talking to me about it for weeks, if not longer. It was, ironically, the nurse business that ruined the affair. What, in this special case, was the reward for maintaining Chase as a happy, functioning human being, free of all medication? Was it money? Was it loyalty and fidelity? Was it a sensational sex life? Carter said on the phone that he had glimpsed the end and that this time he could not wait for it. He left a note and went to California. A forlorn and total weakness seized Chase for months. He never heard from Carter again except through friends—news that brought the old weakness back like a relapse. He wondered what on earth he had done to prompt this sudden cessation of feeling. Or had Carter never loved him? Had anyone really?

He was content to amuse himself. He would have preferred selected company—a good friend or, ideally, a lover—but being much alone he made the most of it and was good at it. This was clear at the Farm, where he rose early and quietly. Quiet was the charm of being up alone in the garden early. Dawn and just afterwards held special magic: standing in the damp grass with a cup of coffee in his hand and the first of forty cigarettes, he inspected the subtleties, the ongoing narrative of miracles and treachery, life and death, beauty and delicacy—all the random surprises and disappointments of his kingdom. Soon something requiring immediate attention would seize him, or he would begin the endless round of chores he kept in his head. He was, for instance, that season growing potatoes in the compost heap; these must be plucked like jewels from the muck. Sooner or later something must be done to everything, endlessly, in an order that came to him naturally, or seemed to. I was able to converse on the level of the decorator, "Decorator of the Interior," he called me, as opposed to the botanist or gardening maven; that is, in terms of shapes and colors and positioning, of vistas and concepts. This we would do by the hour.

At Chase's suggestion, and to earn a little money, I sublet my apartment in the city until fall and spent the next three months living at the Farm. He came out, usually with one or two guests, for weekends; during the week I was there alone, writing, thinking of Lorenzo, while Chase went to his job at the Botanical. I wrote and received long letters from Lorenzo. These I rather liked sharing with Chase on Saturday, sitting on the porch in the afternoon.

> I have just come back from calling you so I have nothing to say except I miss you and all the things it embarrasses me to say on a phone in the post office. I think only of this yacht and being on it with you. In Egypt even. This is not easy to believe, plus the difficulty of telling my wife that it is an antiques convention in Genoa, and organizing a show to cover the excuse. The show is nine days long, with two days to set up and take down. She will at the last minute want to go, but I will say what about your children? and that will be that. But I must actually send the furniture away and then back again—all for the joy of the trip. The dates as I said are September 5 to the 14th, not two weeks and will seem like nine minutes as you said, but to have any time is miraculous. I will have to stay out of the sun. It is so dangerous. I do this only for you because you know why. Do *not* have Olympia call me. This is a terrible idea, like the ones you have sometimes that scare me.

"What an enterprising boy," Chase remarked. "It will of course all backfire in the most charmingly Italian way." I agreed. "Too complicated," Chase said, drawing deeply on a cigarette. "Too many things to go wrong. He can, however, in the middle of the show, call home and say it is such a success that it's been extended another week."

He rocked and smoked. "I must say, *you* didn't make it easy for him to refuse. He sounds like he'd crawl through the swamp in a white suit to get on Miss Olympia's yacht . . . but then, number four. . . ." Which of us wouldn't? "Not very affectionate today," he went on, referring to the letter. Chase loved to moue over the love bits sometimes added at the end. These he found exciting because so direct. He had asked me to read this part of an earlier letter several times: "The other night—I was thinking of you—we broke the bed. She said it's because the bed's an antique but she was very pleased."

"I must say la moglie gets her share," Chase had commented, then rocked and sighed and added, "Oh dear, no one will ever break the bed with his wife on my account."

Three times during the summer Renzo called, at prearranged hours. I had been so used to empty stretches of time—years on end—with nothing but a glimpse of his photograph, that the immediacy of speaking with him long distance verged on the miraculous, as if we were speaking from one dimension to another, or one planet to another—something to account for the rarity of it, and the excitement. I longed to be casual and calm, but instead within moments would lapse into wretched clichés of love and loneliness. On the other end he would simply say, "I know, Piero. Anch'io."

In August Olympia sent me a ticket to Rome and enclosed an open ticket round trip from Pisa to Cairo for Lorenzo. In addition she sent a check, made out to me, for three thousand dollars—for additional expenses, she said. I was astonished, but Chase explained. This was to cover his costs too, while sparing everyone the indelicacy of Olympia directly offering money to her husband, who could, it was to be understood, manage quite well without her help.

"This shows great tact," he announced approvingly. "I suggest we buy clothes with some of it. And my ticket. The rest you may spend on trinkets for the child," as he sometimes now called Lorenzo. "A cigarette lighter I believe is customary."

"What do you mean?" I asked, not liking an inference that had seemed to be an undertone in many of his remarks recently —that Lorenzo was in this for the money and glamour: meaning that he was not really in love with me.

"Simply jealous." He saw the look in my eye and, as usual, cut to the finish. "None of this would be happening, after all, if it weren't for Miss Olympia and me, and I much prefer your part of the deal."

I made a similar leap. "Does it mean anything," I asked, "that if you were ever to touch Lorenzo I would cut your throat?"

"In gardening," he replied after a moment, "we would say you are overpowdering your roses."

I thought, how almighty is love, that Chase would consider this move, then not take the trouble to deny it; and that I would immediately comprehend the temptation—all because each of us understood the power of the need and defense of love—from everything and everyone, even from one's friends. Thinking back over his life, over four unsatisfactory love affairs and countless lesser if more glamorous encounters, Chase would rather have traded it all up for my romance with Lorenzo—as if this could be accomplished quickly, with cunning, mere cold treachery and his still great physical charms—perhaps on the yacht. Not that he could see himself through, actually, to doing the awful thing; the contemplation of it, the implied idea itself gave satisfaction.

Whereas I had done so much less with my love life than Chase, having devoted fifteen years to an idea; and now, just a few months to its realization, I thought how mean, how rude, how unfriendly, really. For me the idea had practically the force of the event. And if he took satisfaction in wicked contemplation, I felt suddenly that beneath all the years and laughs and good times, really, you might not find a strong connection between Chase Walker and me. At the bottom was an age-old agreement to be friends.

Not jeopardizing my chance of seeing Lorenzo again meant letting disillusionment subside. Chase had not done anything, or even said he would; he had only thought of it, out of selfishness and unhappiness. Was this not perfectly understandable and pardonable? It was. We let it drop. In the following weeks, although I received several more letters, I read none of them aloud on the porch, nor did we again discuss Lorenzo except in passing, at which times Chase adopted a manner of studied respect.

I had always thought the secret of our friendship was the lack of demands—emotional, temporal, financial—we made on each other. We did not expect or require anything except mutual affection, respect, tact, amusement, loyalty—the basics really—within the framework of the idea that we knew and fundamentally liked each other. Still, we took a great deal from one another, although I'm not exactly sure what Chase got from me—something perhaps as simple as the idea that you hold onto and finish things once they're begun, or that principles matter. Certainly I learned more from him, for he introduced me to the specifics of a whole spectrum of life I had heard of but had never seen or understood. I suppose you would call it refinement, since it must be called something, but the word is lame with unpleasant connotations.

I have not said anything of myself as I was before arriving in Florence the first time in '63, because in that year I changed from one sort of person into another and my earlier self is beside the point. I was a callow, under-educated, middle-class boy raised to be a productive heterosexualist professional—perhaps a doctor, perhaps an architect, at least a businessman—who instead had discovered himself to be a gay artist manqué, in the eyes of the world and his family a stunningly useless combination of human characteristics, the worst imaginable, leaving out crooks and deadbeats. But I was intelligent and might come out right in the end, and anyway no one knew anything of the homosexuality, not even myself until Florence. I was a sensitive dreamer, an emotionalist. As a baby I held my breath when angry until my face turned blue. But even stubbornness can be interpreted positively in a world where everything and everyone shifts with the wind. Perhaps in their own pride everyone thought I would eventually hit on something useful.

The trip to Florence had been undertaken in the nature of an expedition into myself, financed by my father. If I had said no to medicine, no to architecture, no even to journalism and business, then it was up to me to find something within myself to which I might say yes.

The attitude of refinement to which Chase introduced me was not based on the having or the spending of money, but on the tenor of your perceptions, priorities, tastes, the pace of your existence and pursuits. These had all, until Chase arrived in my life, washed like a vast crystal wave over my head. It was a question of not noticing things—the most glaring error of the young —of not appreciating anything of which you are not the absolute center; of expansion and growth in directions other than those pointed out at home, in school or by childhood friends. No one I had met, before Chase, was equipped to help me over the old barriers of habit, superstition, class, geography and custom. Perhaps sexuality was the real key, but Chase showed me that its strangeness and difference from the usual did not make it wrong.

From the beginning he was conscious of my admiration; most of us are either students or teachers, and fit together accordingly. But being himself also young and not fully aware of his originality, he did not overplay the role, while it was understood between us that he had seen more than I, and that I might in some way like to catch up in certain areas, among them art, music, clothes, manners. This was pointed out as a matter of course, amusingly, lightly, as we went along. And this, from the start, was our basis of friendship. After Florence, with Chase back at Harvard and me in graduate school, it went on as before, by letter, with hardly any of the essentials lost except the visual. This was more than offset by the style and freshness of the letters themselves, from which, I see, I learned as much about writing as I ever did in school.

Dear thing, I don't know what came over me in Food Town but I've come home with enough kidneys to feed nine, and there are only six of us tonight (Big Bear, Little Bear, Mousekin and the dolls—and the dolls scarcely eat anything at all). Standing at the sink, slitting kidneys, I thought now's a good time, whilst the milk leeches the urine out of the kidneys, to write to Peter.

B has been staying with me on vac and last night we went through the whole thing of raiding my Hyde closet to find him something suitable to wear downtown, then had a couple of tokes. B then balked at the excursion saying I was capitalizing on his apprehension of the place (The Big Dollar), feeding it, rather than smoothing it away, and he pulled off my Army boots and said he wouldn't relive my initiation for me. This threw light like a magnesium flare on some elements that have remained cryptic in our relations, Peter, yours and mine, I hope you have never resented the multitude of times I have beguiled you into performing the role of initiate for me. I think of all those excursions at eleven o'clock from the Bardolini, those ritual investitures in my room, calculating an effect that was a shade farther out than you were willing to go, exposing you to comment on the platform; my air of easy familiarity in the low places, while I obscurely hoped that at least your heart, since no longer mine, was in your mouth; even the gifts of various shreds of Leather paraphernalia, for which you could have no serious use. I think of your infinite grace in every outrageous situation, your good will and bland courage and confidence that the hints I passed would not lead you into desperate straits, the stance you took up in the theatre of action: aloof, intelligent, amused, mysterious—and always the hint of danger I let drop at every turn, as if to keep you prudent, but I know covertly to keep it all thrilling to me. The cues you took from me in all this are part of what has bound us together.

195

Rereading this I find it sounds like egoistical assurance that I have taken the lead in everything. Not it at all. I was just trying to point out the extent that I've been using you in that arena.

And this after a trip to Florence when Lino was small:

I was afraid there might have occurred an impassioned scene with O in the last hours, when she helped me pack. If it weren't so necessary to treat each woman like a lady, much more might be possible. Conversely, if I were prepared for female sexuality, I wouldn't be appalled when a lady acted like a woman. More later, lest we descend into burlesque.

C

None of this seems diminished twenty years later. At the time I found these letters utterly, entrancingly convincing, like the artifacts of a world counter and superior to the regular world, the one existing in the interstices of the other, a place where everyone felt as we did; where, if provoked, all babies held their breath until blue, to show in this simple and dangerous way a commitment to their own feelings.

When we met later, after school and the publication of my novel, after he had begun working at the Brooklyn Botanical after the failure of his first serious love affair, our altered selves still fitted together, but differently, as equals, which was of course more comfortable. He still retained a sense of glamour and specialness, but I felt I had learned what I could from him; while he himself felt, I think, that some of it had proved false, or, like his fat ties, had gone out of style. I cannot say what the change in him was; disappointment, disillusionment, perhaps, or the feeling that a peak had been left behind, receding imperceptibly day by day; or that his assessment of life would not serve; or that he might not, would not, ever be properly loved; or that to be homosexual was a social curse; or that his mind, like his body years before, had been raped. Some extra faculty that had worked so well was barely functioning. Whereas he had ridden smoothly on the crest of a wave, now he fell slightly behind and felt the current tugging at him, if not yet pulling him under.

A most peculiar thing happened when he announced at work an intention to postpone his vacation, from August until September, in order to go on the cruise. He was told that his vacation was a matter of indifference, since his services at the Botanical were no longer required. Cutbacks in the endowment necessitated a reordering of the etcetera.

His firing was part of a massacre with, practically, blood on the walls, but Chase didn't, couldn't, see it that way. At its most personal perhaps he had stepped onto the wrong piece of a disintegrating iceberg, having befriended the losing faction in a political situation—and it was of no comfort to him that twelve other people lost their jobs with him. For the first time fate had proceeded in a manner prejudicial to his cause. He no longer felt favored.

He was stunned. He arrived at the Farm, announced the news—I suppose like a husband out of work, or as close in his life, or mine, as we might ever come to that situation—and took immediately to his bed. Later he got up and went into the garden. He began potting around, then lost himself in chores until dark. I went out and found him sitting in a chair in the now, at dusk, exclusively white sunken garden.

"They've ruined mother's day," he said softly.

Although I was sorry for him, I selfishly wondered if this would prevent our trip and my chance to see Lorenzo again. Also, for me as for Chase, it was still a new concept that things could go against him, as they did against everyone else, and perhaps I did not yet quite believe it could happen. I refrained from asking the obvious or necessary questions, and we sat on in the gathering dark. Suddenly night came, and everything went flat and matte like silhouettes on a darkened stage. High up behind us the hilltop and sky reversed. The vast, still-luminous bowl tilted down on either side; one by one little points of light glimmered on. The garden had quite disappeared. Crickets made a din. Chase's flowers, now invisible, sent out their sweet, delicious, exaggerated scent.

The cruise aboard Miss Olympia's yacht however was to be in no way affected. Also it appeared that Chase had been for some time unhappy at the Botanical. Now he felt that in his dissatisfaction with the job and its few responsibilities he had allowed himself to make several crucial if insubstantial errors, not worth discussing. "We engineer these things ourselves," he declared.

"The man's a pig," he said at another moment, referring to the head of the department. "He defecates into a plastic bag worn at the waist which, ironically, makes him behave imperiously. *En plus,* he is made nervous by the sight of leather pants in daylight. The situation was hopeless."

"But it's all very convenient," I suggested. "We might simply stay on the yacht all winter."

"We might," he agreed. "Certainly it begins to look as if this cruise comes at the perfect moment for all of us—me, when my career in weeds needs rethinking; you, when you would like to see Il Magnifico; Olympia, when she has decided to reconstitute her *mariage blanc.* Niccolo on the other hand is old, and Lino young —always the best reasons to do anything. It's all very *Bridge of San Luis Rey.*"

I thought this very unlucky, and said so.

"Peter," he replied, "things never happen the way they do in novels. That's what makes them novels."

"That's nonsense," I said.

"Well, perhaps," he agreed with a smile.

As in the old days we had suits made for the occasion. And now that Chase no longer reported for work each day we rather freely roamed back and forth between the Farm and Manhattan, assembling what would be for me an extensive, and for Chase an enormous, array of baggage. "We must be prepared for every contingency," he said. "I can only assume we'll all be in danger of sinking under the weight of Miss Olympia's wardrobe. And Niccolo, if he chose, could make Coco Chanel seem like a nudist. We must keep up our end."

We spent all of Olympia's check—on Chase's ticket, our clothes and a few gifts, including shirts and sweaters, for Renzo. Several days before we were to leave we assembled everything and packed it into six large cases and several smaller pieces. It would have done for a trip around the world, in three if not four seasons —I had drawn the line at anything suitable for the dead of winter. The bags were sent ahead. Chase said he refused to pass through three airports "like Elizabeth Taylor." We would claim it all in Pisa, where Olympia would send a car to take us the rest of the way.

The night before we left, Lorenzo called from Florence, as arranged, to say la moglie had not been aware he meant to stay in Genoa the *entire* duration of the Antiques Fair, and was now, as expected, threatening to visit him in the middle of it, in order to make a holiday for herself and the children. Lorenzo was desperate and didn't know what to say to keep her at home. How had he got himself into this terrible mess? What should he do? The cruise seemed to hang on some viable suggestion from me. Otherwise he would actually have to attend the Genoa show, instead of pretending to, and we would miss each other.

"Tell her—" I said, "tell her you need a complete change —to be away from everything for awhile."

"But I've already said that," he called into the phone. "She cannot imagine that a rest from everything would include her."

"What about the boys?" I said. "Don't they have school in September?"

"She's thinking of the weekend," he replied. "The second weekend."

"Oh my God—"

"What am I to do?"

"I'm sorry, Lorenzo," I said finally. "You'll have to figure this out on your own. We will wait two days in Capri. After that . . ." I paused.

"Yes, yes, I know," he cried.

I gave him the directions Olympia had given me for finding the yacht in Cairo, should this be necessary. Being two hundred feet long, it would not be difficult to spot. The name was *La Stella Azzurra, The Blue Star.*

Leghorn has come into the language as the American navy's name for Livorno, a key port in World War II and after, and also as a hat, a woman's hat—wide-brimmed, of smooth plaited straw, and usually black. Chase and I were not there long enough to find out why. A car and driver, sent by Olympia, had collected us in Pisa and twenty minutes later we pulled up beside the largest and quite the most beautiful yacht imaginable. In all the port of Leghorn nothing that was not military could touch her.

The description of ships, like the description of people, depends on your own view of them; what you require, or admire, may be what you first notice or remember. *The Blue Star* was huge and elegantly shaped, but beyond that you saw first the stunning whiteness—a fresh, unmarked purity of white that dazzled in the Italian sun, as if the whole thing were lighted and pulsing from within. She was of that generation of yachts, built previous to the fifties, that gloried in detail, reflecting complete indifference to cost and maintenance. Tall, with three full decks —main, shade and promenade—and probably three or four more below, the impression overall was of long, graceful horizontals; a white, spearlike shape to cut smoothly through wind and waves, with a round, attenuated, breasted stern—like the flattened arc of a champagne glass—canting out a full thirty feet from the rudder. The clipper bow, a long pointed shaft supported by a gilded beam of carved scrollwork, gave the ship an oriental elegance, like a smart woman wearing a fan. "So," all this said, "she has been East."

While the driver unloaded the bags, Chase and I stood regarding the ship in happy surprise. I had expected something big but not so grand. For once, temporarily, Chase was unable to fish up a smart remark. We stood looking this way and that, fore and aft, as if at a slow tennis match. "My God," he murmured finally, to say something. "Number five."

Niccolo's servant appeared and came down the covered gangway, followed by a number of stewards in white coats. *"Buon giorno, Signori Dottori, e ben venuti."* In a world of titles and respect, *Dottori* was the best Igor could do for us. Our bags were hoisted by the stewards, and with a gratifying sense of arrival we boarded *The Blue Star.*

The stewards and luggage went off in one direction down a long corridor and Igor asked us to follow him in another, and presently we were shown into a saloon that looked like the sitting room of a large country house, with white paneled walls and pilasters, a shallow-domed ceiling and big, comfortable, over-stuffed furniture.

Niccolo and Olympia were seated. Standing over by a lavishly curtained porthole, Lino, taller, blonder, had seen us arrive and was watching the door. He and his father looked directly into each other's identical eyes before Olympia and Niccolo knew we were there. Then, with a start, Olympia kicked her legs uncrossed and stood up, and a set of easy if slightly self-conscious greetings ensued. Lino and Chase shook hands, then Chase pulled him closer and kissed his cheek. Olympia giggled once involuntarily. Niccolo, though stately, had tears in his eyes.

We were given drinks, and Chase and Olympia smoked. Lino returned to the porthole, apparently feigning indifference but watching every move. Olympia had darkened her hair and was conventionally and exquisitely made up; she asked after Chase's parents, whom they had not seen in fifteen years. Niccolo said what a splendid idea this all was. Lino said, *"Si parte,"* and the dock moved slowly away through the window. After a moment a faint tremor from the engines could be discerned, which then was equalized. Ovoid circles of sunlight drifted forward across the carpet and up the walls as we set out through the harbor.

"Oh, let's go out and look," Olympia exclaimed, taking Lino's hand. We went on deck and aft to the stern. Livorno dropped to port and the Ligurian sea lay flat and gray green into the haze. We assumed a lordly pace, the pace of a horse-drawn sleigh, an impression enhanced by the soundlessness of the engines and the swish and tumble of the water. After a few minutes of this Olympia said no doubt we would like to freshen up and rest before lunch; or perhaps skip lunch altogether. Igor would show us to our cabins.

Mine was aft, and we came to it first. Chase's, I saw later, was *en suite* with Olympia's and connected to it by a sliding wall arrangement that Chase found startling. All the cabins were generous and smartly done; most of them, like mine and the owner's suite, large and opulent. Niccolo's even had its own sitting room. The corridors were wide, fitted with brass railings and carpeted in deep burgundy. At intervals crystal lights and beveled mirrors at once illuminated and confused the issue. The look below was Italian-English—streamlined but overstuffed and comfortable, rich, modern and timeless, studded with antiques—all of it beautifully kept and arranged. At a glance you realized that nothing need be shifted. Everything was perfectly placed and then bolted down to keep it that way.

We sorted out our luggage; I showered and changed into the first of fifty possible outfits and went up again on deck. Lunch was served in the stern with everyone in dark glasses, with little place settings reflected in each lens. The food was astonishing, especially after the airplane. Olympia had hired someone from Sabatini's, who had cost, Niccolo declared, practically as much as the yacht. Talk of money embarrassed Olympia, but later, because Niccolo loved anything resembling gossip and had been raised on it, he informed us privately that the yacht had been chartered at a cost of seven thousand dollars a day, plus daily expenses of approximately another thousand, plus fuel. It cost eighty-seven thousand just to fill the gas tanks, but once would do. The charter money however could be put toward the yacht's purchase, if so desired. The asking price was two million, all found. Niccolo said that if Chase liked the idea, Olympia would gladly buy it, simply to show him the extent of his influence.

We retired until dinner. When I awakened I picked up the phone and asked for Chase's cabin. "Where are we?" he murmured.

"Blue heaven," I said. "Are we dressing for dinner?"

Recollecting himself and in a stronger voice he said, "Miss Olympia was here. I think she wanted to see if I had aged. Oh, God!" he exclaimed and hung up.

I called him back. "White jackets on deck in a half hour," he said tersely and hung up again.

Leaning on the rail he hissed, "The phones are bugged. It's just like La Favola, only electronic . . . Whisper!"

"You're joking," I whispered.

"Well, wouldn't it be?" he said.

I pointed out that Miss Helena was dead.

"But it all goes on anyway, with or without Helena."

"What does?"

"Family intrigue. They can't stop themselves. It goes on by itself, like a machine."

"What does?" I insisted.

"*It!*" He looked at me. "You must make an effort to keep up."

We gazed across the empty sea to starboard, with the coastline behind us. The sun had gone; now the last light colored a line of soldiers at the edge. Their undersides reddened while the tops turned yellow. Soldier clouds meant fair weather to a point.

"They've had plenty of time to have the whole yacht rigged," he said softly.

Niccolo came along the deck supported by Lino, both in white dinner jackets glowing in the dusk. From a distance we must look like balls of light on deck.

"Buona sera," Niccolo said ritually, pleasant as usual. Lino smiled beatifically. Niccolo walking seemed twenty years older than Niccolo at rest; he moved like shaky sticks. We sat down and Chase asked Igor to bring us champagne. The moment, with its darkening orange light, was perfect for Olympia's arrival, and well she knew, wafting toward us along the deck in a long white caftan and enormous gold pendant earrings. We rose, except Niccolo, who gestured with his hand to indicate both desire and regret. Olympia's perfume had been brewed to subdue—had each of us not been either too old, too young, or immune; however Chase was gallant. "You look lovely," he said, then turned to Lino and said, "Doesn't your mother look lovely?"

Lino, the little prince, was at fifteen a subtle mix of child and adult. This had long been true, but lately the weight of his personality had gone over to the adult side with childlike exceptions. One of these was the capacity to keep silent for hours. He was not merely taciturn—an adult idea; he was secretive, withdrawn, observant and intense at intervals. He had heard someone say that a wise man spoke every other thought; Lino held that every other *other* thought would be added improvement. He did not seem ever to have a vacant look, as children and adolescents often do. When in range of Olympia he lost his insouciance and stared at her, both the child in him and the adult fascinated by his mother.

Moreover, he wore his dinner clothes as a miniature adult, and looked natural and elegant in them. The jacket was a trifle big, no doubt because Olympia wanted it to fit beyond the next few months. He seemed to be virtually growing in front of you, like certain vines that snake perceptibly along the ground. His sense of reserve and concentration could have come from the violence of change he observed daily within himself—so much to catalogue and conceal. To Olympia, in word and gesture, he was miraculous compensation for all worldly deceit and disappointments. Her love was obvious, a respectful adoration. A code of expressions existed between them—short looks, abbreviations, raised eyebrows, wry smiles, single syllables. The subject, or possibly the verb, would do for the whole remark; as now she said, "Lino, the sky." And he looked at the sky and formed his own conclusions, keeping them to himself. When, every so often, he bestowed a reaction on her, she rewarded him with a short flashing smile. This he took in like a small electrical charge; and so on. These three—Olympia, Lino and Niccolo—formed the event, which observed itself and went on, in endless permutation.

The ship at dusk had whitened to a blur—the same white as our jackets, in blurred scintillation. The yacht pulled your attention. It made you think in these terms. Just consider, it said; I will take you anywhere, in pure, silent floating splendor, in stately procession, etc. This induced a reflection of something suitable to the decor, a way of being that complemented the luxury of the yacht—this need hardly have been pointed out to Niccolo and Olympia, to whom it was all rather natural, or even to Chase. It did seem like Villa La Favola, its opulence and glamour making you rise to it and behave differently.

At dinner it was mentioned that the following day we would be stopping, in Capri, at the Marina Grande, of which we would occupy half. I could not wait to see Lorenzo. I excused myself to call him at the Bardolini.

Signora Zá-zá answered the phone. Lorenzo had just gone out; she would give him the message—Capri, the ship's number —in the morning. I had just hung up when Olympia knocked on my cabin door. Her face was moderately flushed. She said, "I thought you were my friend. You said you would help."

I asked what had happened. She entered and surveyed the stateroom.

"What's turned him against me?" she asked.

I said I had done nothing except try to help them both.

"That's what I mean," she went on. "Your loyalties are with him."

"My loyalties to him do not conflict—"

"Why is he so distant?" she asked. "He hardly says a word to Lino."

"Lino?"

"Lino is just a child." She looked again, idly, at the room. She sighed. "I had such hopes."

"Olympia," I began, "I'm not sure you can make a husband out of Chase. . . . A companion, perhaps—a friend."

"A friend? Does he make a good friend?"

"An amusing one. He's not always around, but you're used to that."

She thought about this and gave me a look that said I could have no idea what she was used to. "You know," she said, "he's very remote."

"It's only the first day."

"Yes, you're right. I must be calm. . . . Are you comfortable here? Do you need anything?"

"No. . . . Mineral water, perhaps."

She opened a cabinet in the night table containing a small

refrigerator filled with drinks. She peered inside. "Gas or non-gas?" she asked, switching over to the side of her personality she inhabited as a self-possessed expert, capable of a direct and intelligent approach to whatever came up in life, moment to moment. This included conversation, protocol, contingencies, one's comfort and moods. She removed a bottle, opened it and put it into a silver canister on the desk. Standing there, she mentally passed a hand over the objects on the desk's surface—a matched leather set from Pineider—and I saw how familiar the room was to her. She had in fact already bought the yacht and had it redecorated, a labor consuming the three months since our last meeting. By what for us was only the first day of the cruise, she had already seen and felt much. Having lived aboard to make sure it was done properly, she was by now completely at home, and while the rest of us wandered hesitantly through the three-dimensional maze of decks and hatches, she and Lino, who had spent the summer with her, knew and used the companionways and shifting spaces to appear and disappear suddenly, moving quickly and silently from place to place in moments. From the ship's interior, in size and looks, you would have taken it for an ocean liner, or a royal yacht, I suppose. It would be difficult to find anything more sumptuous that was not also in bad taste. I saw that Olympia was proud and very fond of it all.

She turned to leave. "So you're not against me," she said.

"To tell you the truth, I was thinking mainly of seeing Lorenzo again."

"Of course. . . ."

"I was thinking of flying to Florence. Would you mind? We'll meet you in Capri."

"Oh, Peter, you're not going to leave us alone?"

"There's Niccolo and Lino, and the servants and crew. You're hardly alone."

"But he seems to behave himself better around you." I looked at her. "Oh, all right," she said. "How can I blame you?"

Olympia in English was fluent, direct and idiomatic to whatever extent the Italian metaphor matched the English in translation, with nothing at all American about her. This perhaps was the problem, too simply put, between her and Chase: he had enough of the European in him to attract and confuse her, and not enough to help her understand.

"Aren't men difficult?"

"Yes," I agreed.

"Most situations in the world favor them," she said philosophically. "Except having babies and dying."

Chase had once said it was easy to have a baby, difficult only to beget one, meaning the act was distasteful. "Sometimes," I said, "they die well."

"Keats was the last man to die well," she announced. "Although, since then, there may have been others. Helena died well —after a long life, as to her bed for a nap."

I asked why she thought dying was easier for women.

"Well, not easier; more familiar," she replied. "Women are changed by life in ways men never are."

"You mean physically?"

"Men are afraid of change, afraid that *they* will be changed. We accept it."

"Death is more than a change," I said. Olympia, while apparently intelligent, studiously hid her light. I agreed with her about women, but was inclined to remind her that all men were not men, or women women. I said this.

Lifting her hand over her head, fingers splayed dramatically, she said, "Why must you two drag that subject into everything?"

"We—I—don't drag it in, except as a fact of life."

"Yes . . . I'm sorry. You have every right. Most men are obsessed by sex at some time in their lives. It may all be the same."

"Clear the air with Chase," I said. "You can't hope to spend any time together if you don't understand—"

"Probably." She leaned forward and kissed me lightly on the

cheek. "Peter," she said, "I'm so glad you're here with us. Please hurry back."

The next morning in Capri I left the ship, took a hydrofoil to Naples and flew to Pisa. I wanted to show Lorenzo, by arriving suddenly and unannounced, that such things could be easy and magical. Suddenly we could be together, instead of suddenly apart. I went to the shop and peeked through the window. He was talking to a woman customer. Out of the corner of his eye, perhaps by instinct, he saw me, so I went in. I should have waved and walked on. The woman was la moglie. He introduced us and she smiled quite cordially, as did I. She was not at all plain. She wore a smart beige suit. Her hair was long and lustrous. She did not seem to think I was anything but a client of her husband's from America. After a few moments she shook my hand and left.

"Lorenzo, I'm sorry," I said immediately. "I thought she was a customer."

"*Fa niente,*" he said unconvincingly. "What are you doing here? Is there something wrong?" He went to the door of the shop and looked down the street to watch her go. "Oh my God," he said, coming back in. "Another moment and she would have been gone."

"Does it matter? She doesn't suspect anything, does she?"

"No, of course not."

All I could think of were compliments. We gazed and smiled. I asked what had happened with the Genoa plan.

"*She's* going instead," he said with a sudden dazzling smile. "She's going to do the show herself. She's taking the boys, plus someone to set up and mind the booth."

"And what about you?"

"She thinks I should go away, by myself." He clapped his hands together once. "It's all set."

"But how did you do it? What did you say?"

"I said I was fed up. I said my life was a bore, that I hated selling furniture to ugly Americans with fat bellies and not so fat wallets."

We laughed and I said I had come to take him back, to Capri.

"But she thinks I'm going to Ischia, and not until tomorrow."

"Tell her you've decided to go with me now, to Greece. If she thinks you're in Ischia and available, she'll try to call."

He thought about this. "Tell her I'm going with you? Tonight? What about Egypt? Aren't we going to Egypt?"

"Yes, but tell her it's Greece, which in a way it is."

"Greece," he said.

He closed the shop and in the back room we made love. Afterward, stirring ourselves like drunks having coffee, we separated and he went to pack and explain to la moglie. Two hours later we met at the train station and took a taxi to the airport, rather like the getaway I had had in mind months before. Four or five hours more, and we were on the last hydrofoil to Capri; and just after midnight we stepped quietly onto the gangway of the yacht. Igor said everyone had retired, and we went immediately to my cabin—as if beds, rooms, cities, regions had not been changed in the intervening hours, being back again in his arms.

In the morning I felt the jitters of a great undertaking. So might I have led a movie star from my bed to breakfast in the stern— which I knew they took together at a certain hour—and I thought, Better all at once and ceremoniously. Italians of this type could perform such simple social rituals in their sleep. And I could count on Chase to give it lightness and, if necessary, charm.

The four of them, however, were surprised by Lorenzo's appearance—that is, by his presence and his looks, to the degree that they saw no reason to hide it. Niccolo audibly gasped, Olympia jangled her jewelry, Lino stared and blushed, Chase excused himself and left, but returned a few minutes later wearing something else. Having declared his interest and absorption, Niccolo had his chair moved closer to this object, at which Lorenzo smiled becomingly. Lino tilted his head like a bird or puppy. Olympia offered coffee. The scene went on in fragments for twenty minutes, with none of it holding together into a conversation, or even a meal, constantly breaking up into pauses and brief remarks.

And there we were, together at last, Capri falling astern, sailing away on Olympia's yacht. It should end here, but these things never end when they should. Lorenzo and I excused ourselves so I could show him over *The Blue Star*. I saw it now as he did, as I had not until then—as one of the great private yachts of the world—in fifty whites and fifty blues; teak, brass, chrome, enamel, canvas, rope, leather, silk, crystal; impeccably arranged between the sea and the sky, gliding forward between two planes of color, one vivid, one soft; falling forward down a blue chute. I showed Lorenzo deck after deck, cabin after cabin, down the long corridors, the small pool under the dance floor, the library, the military bridge, the romantic, theatrical stern that ledged over a constant waterfall. Who could not be happy, amid all of this, could not be happy.

This was Olympia's accomplishment. She had transformed *The Blue Star*—rather a bagatelle, from a financial point of view, the money she had put into it as nothing compared to the hopes and dreams invested in every treasure selected for the cabins and passageways. She had had the loot of two palaces to choose from. Some of the larger spaces had the look of terra firma, like palace anterooms, with only the light shifting up and down the walls to show you were at sea. Some of the cabins were like ledges or balconies on the water, their whiteness merging with available light and changing color with the hour. Olympia had done this. It came to Lorenzo, however, through me—at last a suitable offering.

Having at first held compliments in reserve and then spent them anyway, more was demanded with nothing left. Lorenzo uttered small cries of helpless delight, or said nothing at all. He seemed most impressed by the quality of the furniture and antiques. For instance, the Empress Catherine suite from Helena's rooms at La Favola had been installed in Olympia's rose-colored cabin.

"You have no idea of the quality," he said in amazement. I had, because Chase had already vetted all of it to the penny. He had said if this were dumped all at once on the art market it would depress antiques for fifty years and fetch something like fifty million.

"Lire?"

"Dollars. It's fabulous," Chase had said, "and perfectly terrible for the furniture. Wait till we get to Egypt and everything begins to pop like pistol shots."

The ship however was temperature- and humidity-controlled, having passed all insurance requirements. Policy premiums amounted nearly to the former daily charter. Niccolo called it the Floating Exhibition of Treasures, including, in his own sitting room, the Caravaggio from Florence. Even this I was able to show Lorenzo, who did not notice the resemblance.

Resting beneath the painting, Niccolo invited us to come in and sit a moment. With Lino's help he stood to touch Lorenzo's shoulder and the cap of his hair.

"If I were twenty years younger, my boy, or if you had twenty more yourself, we would meet somewhere for an hour in the middle, of which I might now live forever merely on the memory —you are that perfect."

From Dante, I imagined. Lorenzo turned red and dark, which showed like a huge engine powering up, and Niccolo watched fascinated.

Later at tea, Niccolo himself looked younger, and was dressed and made up with great care. He raised a toast with his teacup. "You may cart me off after this one," he said and smiled sweetly. "But do let's do it for more than a few days."

Perhaps any pretty new face would have been welcome. To

them Lorenzo was the ship itself springing to human form, the one eerily matching the other in degree. Everyone seemed fascinated by him, except perhaps Lino, who never showed his feelings—Lino did not behave according to his feelings, so you could not tell what they were. But Olympia loved the finer examples of anything, and Niccolo was frankly in the god's thrall, with no hope of return. He was like Rashid, whom he had been like in the first place. And I expected Chase at any moment to hurl himself theatrically across the stage like the Firebird.

It all held through dinner, the ingredients of which, had they been analysed, would have made layouts for six different magazines, and over which Lorenzo presided—a visiting dignitary and honored guest who conveniently spoke a form of their language. He was inscrutable, unreachable, inviolate, though puffed with potency and warmth.

Lino asked a question, a rare occurrence. "Are you," he asked quietly in an awkward lull, "able to fly?"

Misunderstanding the question, Lorenzo answered, "Yes, we flew here last night." When I looked again Lino was gone.

Regarding the empty chair, Olympia put her elbows on the table and said, "All his life I have told him of the existence of angels. I hope you don't mind."

"The child is quite right," Niccolo declared. "Look at these men." He indicated the three of us—Lorenzo, Chase, even myself. "They are the angels of God, come to find one righteous man."

"I believe it was ten," Chase corrected. "Only ten righteous men, that the cities of the plain might be spared. Nowadays it would be ten decent pairs of shoes."

Like the Czar's family we went on deck for coffee. The night was velvety dark, like a tunnel. The ship's bell rang out four or five crystal notes that floated over the Straits of Messina, where we had anchored. Now and then small boats surfaced into our circle of light. They contained fishermen who had rowed out from a coastal village to get a closer look. You could see the white points of the ship's reflection in their dark eyes, two points of light at the top of each dark silhouette. The crew shooed them away.

Gradually it had become understood that conversation was not required, that in fact the whole event went more smoothly without it—Lino's way: every other *other* thought. This was after all the pace they would have hit on for a country weekend. Coffee was brief and we split up. Niccolo officially retired. Chase and Olympia took a turn on deck. Lino had disappeared. Lorenzo and I went to our cabin.

Lying in bed I said to him, "Chase believes the cabins and phones are bugged." I whispered this in his ear.

He sat up and asked why anyone would go to such trouble; I told him about the secret passages and intrigue at La Favola.

"But why?" he asked. "What do they have to gain by it?"

"Well," I replied, "I suppose they could watch us make love."

"They could?" He looked around the room, searching for a hidden lens. "Would they really?"

"Niccolo would, if he could arrange it. He'd do anything to see you."

We lay quietly for a while and he said, "It wouldn't matter really, if they're watching. Whoever has gone to such trouble"—he indicated the luxury around us—"deserves anything they want." He got up. "Let's go look at the water."

On deck we encountered first Chase and then Olympia stalking the ship looking for Lino. Chase was calm, she nearly hysterical. The crew had been set to turn the ship upside down and they were everywhere—young Italian faces none of us had seen before. "He's gone," Olympia kept saying. "He's gone." She would suddenly think of a corner where he might be hiding

—he did this all the time wherever they were—and would rush off.

Searching Niccolo's room, they disturbed the old man; he sat up in bed. They explained the intrusion.

"My angel?" he said uncertainly, and went back to sleep. The space under the bed, all the closets were empty.

It was not known what to do next. Had we been under way the captain might have ordered the ship turned around. Local police would be less than useless. There was no one to complain to and no one who could help. Olympia stared out into the night, smoking and fretting, walking from one end of the ship to the other, never sitting down. The three of us wondered what to do and did nothing.

Then about two o'clock something butted against the hull and we looked over to see Lino standing in a small boat, shaking hands with its sailors. He came up the steps and into his mother's arms. Olympia carried on.

She held him at arm's length and asked if he was crazy. Hadn't he realized she would think he had drowned? She touched his clothes. They were wet. "Lino!" she cried and held him again. "What did you do!"

Lorenzo leaned over the side and asked them in the boat to say what had happened. The man at the tiller replied in a thick dialect, incomprehensibly. Olympia caught some of it and gasped. Chase and I waited for Lorenzo to translate.

They had come out to see the great ship and happened to see someone fall or jump overboard. Fished out of the water, the boy claimed to be swimming.

Where had they taken him? Lorenzo asked.

Ashore. The boy had said he was in danger and must flee. He was adamant and forceful. They had gone in to ask what to do and it had been decided to bring him back. Here they were. They thought he might be a little odd, no disrespect. Olympia said, "Pay them," and called a mother's blessing on their heads, from which they pulled their caps and bowed. Chase handed down a roll of bills and they drifted off into the dark.

Lino was put to bed. Some minutes later Olympia came rushing back to say that his body was covered with bruises and marks. She was wild with anger at the fishermen. What had they done to him? *Why* had she not brought a doctor? What did it mean?

"He says they are pinch marks," she cried. "He says they teased him but were very kind."

"Teased him?" Chase said.

"Pinched him, tickled him."

We looked at each other. "Tickled him?" Chase said.

"Oh my God!" Olympia exclaimed. "It's not possible."

Chase went off to look and returned to say Olympia had greatly exaggerated the bruises. The boy had a few red marks on his ribs and back, a bruise on his thigh; he was sound asleep. We all went to bed.

The next morning on the open sea, as if released from night, sleep, dreams, nothing seemed more than a few minutes old. *The Blue Star* cut through the water in heavy gliding state, white water tumbling below the bow, rolling in the wake. No one mentioned Lino's escapade. The child himself sat in the stern reading books about our destinations, his gold hair riffling in the breeze. We were to reach Piraeus sometime in the afternoon.

"What happened, Lino?" I asked him quietly.

He looked up at me over the book, the white from the pages reflected under his chin. He regarded me for a long moment before speaking.

"I tried to fly," he said. "I was going to circle the boat a few times and come back."

"Why did you think you could fly?"

"I often fly."

"You mean, you dream you're flying."

"Yes, I guess I mean that. It's the same thing."

"It's not the same thing," I said. "One is real, the other is not real but a dream."

"It seems real," he said, and closed the book.

"How did you get those marks on your body?"

"The men played with me. They threw me about."

"The fishermen? Why?"

"To make me laugh. For luck."

I asked what luck had to do with it.

"They said the whole thing was good luck—the ship coming last night, the way I jumped—"

"Good luck?" I said.

"Apparently."

"Did they . . . interfere with you in any way?"

"One of them bit me." He turned and touched his buttock. "Here."

"He bit you?"

"As they were throwing me about, one of them pulled down my pants and laughed and bit me. Not seriously."

"I suppose you were lucky they brought you back. They could have kept you."

"Why?"

"They eat young boys along that coast. That was Sicily."

"I have heard that," he said solemnly, with Chase's eyes.

"Your mother was upset."

"I can't help that."

"People cannot fly."

"Lorenzo can," he said.

"Lorenzo was talking about coming here in an airplane, from Pisa. He didn't mean with his own wings. You were thinking he's an angel . . ."

"He *doesn't* look human."

"Of course he does. He's simply good-looking."

"Is he . . . your friend?"

I nodded.

"I know all about men . . . and men."

I thought he would have had to by now, but I said nothing.

Later in the morning when Niccolo came out on deck I brought up this conversation. Had Niccolo told him about men?

"Why, yes," the old man said. "If only to counter the gibberish Olympia was preaching. Wicked of me, wasn't it?"

"The boy was kidnapped last night," I said, "and for some reason brought back."

"Is that what happened? What a lot of versions! Jumped, tried to fly, was kidnapped by gypsies. Only I would sleep through such a thing."

"What did happen?"

"I was asleep," Niccolo replied. "But Lino is fanciful. With exquisite taste . . . Your Lorenzo is just as much an assault to his nervous system as to mine." He said this while looking and smiling at Lorenzo, who stood beside me. "What must it be like," he asked him, "to go through life having people react to you in this way? Do you not come to feel that everyone else is small and ordinary?"

To his credit, Lorenzo neither smiled or made reply.

"Is Lino so unhappy he would want to fly away?" I asked, picturing Lino perched for an instant, his arms raised over the railing of the stern, followed by a soundless instant of flight and a small splash.

". . . Or so exhilarated," Niccolo said proudly. "Only the prince would find *The Blue Star* confining."

Chase approached. He stood over us, and by way of explanation I said, "You know, you of all people, that he may have been forcibly had by those fishermen and can't speak of it."

"If anyone was had, darling, it was the fishermen," he replied flatly.

"Children are not like that," Niccolo said. "They do not profit by the situation, as we would."

"He knows what he's doing," Chase said. "He does not seem the worse for wear."

It was dropped. In the afternoon we went ashore in Piraeus. Olympia had flowers sent to the ship in enormous armloads, having bought out a corner vendor. She and her maid Elvira arranged and placed them all over the yacht. Chase bought a quantity of cocaine in the street and we lay up on the sun deck ripped in the heat. Lorenzo and I never appeared for dinner. The next day we started through the islands. We spent the night in the harbor at Hydra, though we were too large to approach the dock, and came and went by launch. Someone aboard another yacht tried to make Olympia's acquaintance, purely on the coincidence of two such leviathans being there together. Olympia read the invitation, ascertained that none of us knew the name, and ripped it up. "What cheek," she said, throwing the pieces overboard.

On Hydra we walked to the top of a hill to a moonscape view of islands to the south and the Peloponnesus. Lorenzo and I made love on pine needles over a cove after swimming, then went to a café in the harbor, with *The Blue Star* riding at anchor halfway out. It was immensely satisfying to sit on shore tethered in the mind to this huge, lovely ship whose presence struck everyone. "Will you look at that," a woman at the next table said to her husband. "What a life . . . What can it be like, I wonder."

"There are those who wonder what it's like to go traipsing through the Greek Islands in the first place," her husband replied sarcastically. Betrayed, she glared at him, then looked back to *The Blue Star.*

The next night we anchored in a beautiful lake-like cove that turned into an amber cave at sunset, which then dimmed and darkened while the sea went completely flat and birds and bats came out to feed on insects.

"What's today?" Olympia asked of no one in particular.

"The Saturday, September ninth," Lorenzo answered, the only one conscious of such details.

"Could it be the moment for Egypt?" she wondered.

"On the whole," Niccolo mused.

She picked up the phone and invited the captain to dinner. At table she said it might be pleasanter to forego Mykonos and Rhodes and head straight for Alexandria. She said we were ready now. During the night we set sail.

After the incident with Lino and the fishermen I lost touch with everything and everyone but Lorenzo. Nothing but him interested me. The two of us kept to ourselves and were so dichotomous by now that a kind of autism had set in, plunging us into each other—within the bright blue-white bubble of the yacht, under vacant skies, on and on, anywhere you pleased. I knew much must be happening but could not bring myself to ask Chase about it, though curious about him and Olympia and whether it would work out and be that kind of life. When she encountered Lorenzo and me, Olympia would smile. Niccolo, I realized, was drugged. This came out over the cocaine, which Chase had not simply connected for by chance; he had been sent looking. Why else stop in Piraeus?

"To the tits," Chase said.

"Constantly?"

"He's in another world. Has been for years."

I could not really be surprised. Niccolo was not always serene, and I had often thought the same of Olympia.

In the seventies Chase had done a crash course on LSD with Carter, the nurse. Since then he had never been interested in drugs, beyond the odd reefer, and was just short of contemptuous of those who were. Now Niccolo was excused because of his age.

This was an old story Helena had told Chase, as part of the character job on her son—to show Chase what he was saving them from. The homosexual disaster. Meanwhile Niccolo believed that beyond a certain age cocaine was an elixir of life; this from South American natives.

"Witchcraft at its most expensive," Chase observed.

"But—" I said.

"Yes, I know," he said. "Number four."

Like Niccolo, he did not mind talking in front of Lorenzo and I asked how it was going with Olympia.

"Olympia already has the strangest kind of marriage—to Niccolo. I'm not sure at this point where I'm supposed to fit in. They share a weird set of dynamics—husband/wife, father/daughter, mother/daughter—as efficient as anything you would find in a large family."

"But Olympia loves you," I said, under the circumstances valuing love above all. And Chase, whose tongue had been loosened by the unaccustomed drug, replied, "Peter, I thought you had realized that nothing with these people is ever what it seems." His idol's eyes looked inward. "You think life is a big white yacht with your lover, sailing to Byzantium."

I said that was precisely what it was at the moment.

"There are those," he said, "for whom life is a big white yacht without your lover."

I said he could be swimming alongside, or still at home like everyone else.

"Love has made you cruel."

"Perhaps," I said. "Perhaps the point is to enjoy yourself."

"Well, I do," he replied. "I enjoy *The Blue Star*. It makes you think the world is a romantic place, when we all know it's a sewer filled with turds and reptiles."

It took two days to reach the Nile delta. In the surf after the water had turned ineffably brown, a pilot was engaged to guide us to

Alexandria. He scrambled half naked from a felucca to the glistening pinnacle of the bridge, as if clambering over the altar of God. His life now would be different. His wife and children would obey him and show respect. In Alexandria he was paid and sent away. It was not thought wise to trust a pilot's knowledge past any major event in the river. Each section had its experts, who thus were never far from home. Each claimed superior knowledge of the river. As a result, ships were safe from all impediments.

Lorenzo and I stayed up in the wheelhouse most of the time, watching the river or one now gradually approaching, now receding bank or the other. A pilot would leave in the same felucca as his arriving replacement. Their delicacy of tact with the captain and navigator varied. Water or beer was acceptable, tea preferred, but on the job. The most impressive individual was old and blinded by cataracts, like the river itself. He traveled with a boy who spotted debris and indicated landmarks. The old man wished to know how many hundred passengers were under his care. Six people, he was told, not counting crew and servants, of whom one was a foreign princess.

"Six people!" he exclaimed, and sipped his tea.

Olympia herself appeared and the captain had a raised chair brought, into which she climbed and lighted a cigarette. "Where are we?" she asked. Below us, in the bow, Lino put his face into the smoothing wind. Niccolo and Chase were somewhere aft, deep in conversation and the consumption of cocaine. Our position was noted for Olympia.

"We are here, madam," the blind pilot said, putting a third finger to his forehead.

The captain said, "There . . . Cairo," indicating a line of low buildings with towers and palm trees in the undulating distance.

14

The Livery Stable complex opened in the spring of 1863 with, ironically, a public ceremony featuring the Masons. Under Orvil's leadership an era of the most profound—you might say criminal —secrecy proceeded beneath a veneer of increased public visibility. No self-respecting realtor in New York would christen a new building without the grand ceremonial participation of at least one marching band and the Masons in full regalia. Also in 1863, Frederick Olmsted again resigned from the Central Park, this time moving to California to run a gold mine called the Mariposa Company, owned by John Charles Frémont. Vaux resigned with him, and in their absence Andrew Haskell Green—by now also a powerful figure in city politics—continued the development of the park according to a precise interpretation of Greensward. During this short period of innocence it was not fashionable to miss the weekend promenades along the Park Drive. Many of the vehicles and horses displayed were hired by the hour and day from the Stable at Eighty-sixth Street, reservations being absolutely necessary, and most of the better carriages and animals being on standing call by such notable families as the van Rensselaers, the Wellmans and the Goelets.

Then in 1867, in the tenth year of the park, even Andrew Green lost his footing in the advent of the Tweed Ring. The Park Commission, like the City Commission and indeed the entire city and state government, was overrun, and from 1868 to November of '71 the most malicious damage imaginable was committed in the park. Greensward was abandoned in favor of a ribald array of private schemes and interests, with harrowing episodes of corruption and graft, of artistic and horticultural carnage. Among the saddest of these was the destruction of a project by the English painter and sculptor Benjamin Hawkins, who had planned to build twelve life-size models of prehistoric reptiles and dinosaurs and install them in a paleozoological museum in the park. Earlier in London, in 1854, a conclave of Victorian scientists had dined *inside* Hawkins's first life-sized restoration of a dinosaur, as part of the Crystal Palace Exposition. Now he devoted himself to this even grander scheme. Hawkins had built an immense *Laelaps* and seven plaster casts when, under the order of Ring Commissioner Henry Hilton and with the blessing of "Brains" Sweeny, vandals smashed the models, carted off the pieces and buried them in the park. Hawkins, no less shattered than his models, never attempted anything in this vein again. Ironically, only a few weeks afterward, Tweed himself was broken by another Englishman. The British editor Louis Jennings, hired by the *New York Times*, exposed frauds perpetrated by the Ring, which resulted in a loss of political power and the prosecution of its leaders. Meanwhile the Commission reverted to the capable hands of Andrew Haskell Green.

There followed, at the end of 1871, the worst winter in New York history, killing eighty thousand trees in the park. In '72 Olmsted and Vaux were enjoined by Green and the Commission to return, not as partners but as Superintendent (Olmsted) and consultant (Vaux), to undo the havoc wreaked by the Tweed Ring and the bitter cold. Disappointed with the Mariposa venture, and for the sake of the park itself, Olmsted, and then Vaux, agreed. Restoration took four years, and by 1876, nearly twenty years after it was begun, Central Park was considered complete.

Orvil Starkweather was carried off in the same winter that killed the trees and, in ironic fulfillment of his name, rather in the same way: by the bitter cold. He fell asleep, alone, in the Master's room beneath the Temple, which itself, for reasons of comfort, was not used in winter months; his body went undiscovered for weeks. Finally the former Grand Secretary, Giles Springer, as baffled as the police by the great man's disappearance, thought to check this haunt and found him sitting up at his desk like a waxwork, frozen through. Officially the body was never recovered.

The other surprise for the Templars—as the Cabal now called themselves—was the disappearance of all the gold from the Treasure room. According to a carefully kept diary left in his library safe on Eleventh Street, Orvil used the gold for some great purpose, not specified. In light of his final arrangements, including a note to the Templars enjoining them not to destroy the Temple in a mad search for the gold but suggesting that they drop his body into one of the ensuing excavations, it appeared his death was a meticulously planned suicide.

Isn't there always a diary? This one—in the same neat little block letters in which Orvil had listed the holdings of the Cabal on the Lodge blackboard—recorded every detail of the plan, execution and disposition of the Temple, its decoration, rites and Treasure, in terms that seemed like inspired fantasy, rather like a novel, but that Chase, who inherited the diary from Grandmère, believed to be completely true and real. Orvil had striven for years to manifest his obsessive secret, had gone to wild lengths and enormous expense to fashion the apparatus surrounding and supporting it, and had no intention of allowing that secret to die with him, or of entrusting it to the Templars. Even the Temple, he saw, was not enough; or the gold. Beside mystery and legend there must be a tale, to be told after he was gone.

The diary was mentioned in his will in the following terms: "This book," which Orvil had caused to be bound in black leather with the title *Secrets of the Temple* on its cover, "I bequeath to my son Franklyn Starkweather, together with that part of my worldly goods herein stipulated, and of which this is the greatest jewel, with the command that his eldest issue receive it likewise after his death, and so on down through generations to come."

That the family had quickly run to the distaff side—no less a river, but underground—had perhaps lessened the force of the bequest; what in any case was a person to do with such a book? But the Chases and the Walkers had been no less studious in observing Orvil's wish than if the spear side had prevailed. Grand-mère Chase, however, chose to bypass her son William. At her death in 1959 the diary, to which Chase had already been alerted, went to him; it was with him in Florence, where he read much of it to me. He thought that for style and commitment it ranked with some of the best work of Melville, and he quickly convinced me, as he himself from the beginning had been convinced, that the Temple was real.

•

Frederick Olmsted had returned to New York in the late spring of 1872, five months after Orvil's disappearance. Contrary to Starkweather's promise, Frederick had not been invited to revitalize and cap his Masonic career with an advanced degree; nor would he have wished to, and the two men had not seen or communicated with each other in the intervening decade.

Like Chase a hundred years later, every time Olmsted passed the Carriage House on his rounds he thought of the Temple beneath it. He had quit New York just before the formal Dedication in late May of 1863, and had last visited the site before any of Orvil's embellishments were brought in from the warehouse in Brooklyn. For ten years he had been curious to see it finished. Throughout that time, on rare visits to New York, he had thought it dangerous to reassociate himself in any way with Starkweather, or to be seen skulking around the Carriage House. It had seemed prudent to leave it all alone.

But now, with Orvil missing and presumed dead, he thought the time bomb of his involvement with the Temple might at last be defused, especially since he had resumed a position of responsibility in the park. What he and Starkweather had done together was still grossly illegal, but with the passage of time and the intervening atrocities of the Tweed Ring, perhaps the authorities and the public would be less amazed at such private indulgence. Perhaps, with so many other revelations, the whole thing could be laid at the feet of the Tweed Ring itself. The question in Olmsted's mind was whether to risk exposing his own connection to the Temple by accusing the Ring of building it, or to forget it forever. He had been assured the Masons would never know of his involvement as builder, although it would not take a genius to implicate him automatically; now with Orvil gone, no one could prove his part in the affair. Had he known of the existence of the diary he would not have been so complacent.

But beyond a vague fear of exposure, Frederick was practically overcome with curiosity to know how the Temple had been finished and what had become of it. He had never heard of the Cabal, and wondered how an organization as large as the Masons could keep such a thing a secret for so long. Almost immediately upon his return to New York he quietly undertook a plan to discover if it was still in use.

His method was simple: he hired a private detective to work undercover within the park's mounted police, based in the Stable complex. After a short time this man was able to make a preliminary report: everyone in the Carriage House was a Mason, including the manager. Without exception they had worked there for years, most of them from the beginning. Only lately had parts of the building been appropriated for other uses—concrete drinking fountains were cast from a mold that resided in a room on the second floor, for instance, and occasionally when the main dormitory over the Stable was filled, men of the mounted police slept in a smaller dormitory over the Forge, at the western end of the Carriage House. Olmsted had imported the detective from Buffalo, hoping to minimize both the risk of exposure and a presumed self-interest. The detective was instructed to pay close attention to the arrivals of carriages and coaches after dark; to facilitate this he was himself to spend the night whenever possible in the Carriage House dormitory.

According to Orvil's diary, during the nine years after the dedication of the Temple the Templars met there on the average two or three times during the spring and summer. Both the Temple and New York being uncomfortably cold the rest of the year, Orvil in this period of his life took to wintering in Europe. Moreover, he believed that overuse of the Temple would rob it of its glamour and mystery; it was used sparingly and only for Templar investitures, which were rare, and grand ceremonial funerals. Sometimes these two ceremonies overlapped in the same event.

Some weeks after he was hired, the detective reported that the night before, toward eleven o'clock, a number of large coaches had suddenly clattered into the Carriage House. The racket of wheels and hooves had awakened him in the dormitory above and he had crept halfway down the staircase unobserved. Wordlessly many men disembarked and went into the Forge room, or so it seemed, for the detective dared not follow them further. Then the doors were closed behind them. After several hours, during which a perfect and eerie silence reigned, they reemerged, got into other coaches and departed. The detective counted about thirty of them. He could not be certain of the number; all were well-dressed, most of them middle-aged, some young but some quite old. Olmsted paid the detective and sent him back to Buffalo.

Knowledge that the Temple was still in use led Frederick to forget the idea of exposing its existence, for this meant that every man using it would become his enemy. But now more than ever he yearned to see what it looked like. Without Orvil's protection the risk was great, but late one night, using his own key, he stole into the western storeroom and bolted it from the inside.

He shifted the bin covering the entrance just enough to squeeze through with his lantern and started down the spiral steps.

Below, it was cold, damp, smelling of smoke and, faintly, of incense. As he came upon them he lighted several torches jutting from holders in the wall, and gradually the space defined itself— a large, castle-like room with stone walls, black alcoves and receding staircases. On the landing he stood still and listened. Somewhere in the silence he heard the drip of water and, after a moment of fear, what he took to be the scurrying of rats. Before him, down a wide flight of marble steps, was the huge, dark void of the porch. He put aside the lantern, lighted a torch and removed it from its holder. Pale figures in the tapestries lining the walls leapt into relief: knights on luminous horses, white-robed Arabs fleeing for their lives, crosses, spears, flags, palms—all stood out in the yellow torchlight. And before him, rising to the vaults, the two enormous brass pillars shimmered hugely on either side of massive, gilded doors. Frederick could only gape at it all. He lighted more torches and examined the tapestries, the mosaic floor, the huge pillars. He pushed on the doors with all his strength but was unable to move them.

He had brought with him the old architectural drawing, and saw that by taking the other staircase on the landing to the lower level, he could reach the main room from below. He went back to the landing and down the other stairs. At the bottom it was five or ten degrees cooler. Torchlight flattened the narrow spaces into trapezoids that loomed and shifted oppressively, as if the stone walls themselves might close in on him. The L-shaped corridor led past several chambers—a changing room, a lavatory, a large closet filled with robes, helmets and long swords in stands like umbrellas—to a room with a desk and chairs, table and leather couch: the Master's room. Through another doorway at the back he found the staircase he was looking for, and cautiously he climbed back up to the main level.

He came into a tall triangular room, filled with gilded ball-room chairs stacked in a mass of upended legs, and resembling a staging area. In the convex wall was a small door, unlocked. Opening it, he saw first the bases of several white columns. Eerily, others faded in an arc to either side—the ghostly, receding wings of an arcade encircling darkness. The torchlight caught something huge and golden in its midst.

Frederick passed between the columns. Even by the flickering light these glories were evident, overwhelming: the golden Altar and dome, the sparkling blue glass and stars overhead. The silver sockets atop the tall columns, the clean dazzle of white marble, the tall, perfect intervals of light and dark in the surrounding circle, like matched moments. Frederick tried to guess at the look of the room when properly lit, and of course knew nothing of the splendid laserlike effect of lighted gas jets focused into the gold dish above the Altar. Here, in Olmsted, if Orvil had only lived to see and orchestrate it properly, was the response he had looked for in his Templars; for Frederick saw, even in these shadows, the surpassing beauty of the place. He felt a momentary pang of loneliness, of depression, as one would before the forgotten work of an artist, or within a lovely, abandoned house. He wished for company, for someone to see it with him—if not Orvil, then his wife Mary; even his partner Calvert would have keenly appreciated it. He felt the same immediate conviction as when Orvil had first shown him the drawing of Temple Park—that this great effort of beauty and effect was wasted, hidden under the ground. It should not have been kept secret. Who now but this pack of Odd Fellows would ever see and appreciate it?

He examined everything. Consulting the drawing, he made his way through another of the triangular corner rooms off the Temple and down to the Treasury. It was empty. Its floor of cobbles had been dug up and replaced. Orvil, like a great Bishop, lay buried here beneath his cathedral, where the gold had been —not that Frederick knew anything about the gold, or for that matter anything really about Orvil Starkweather.

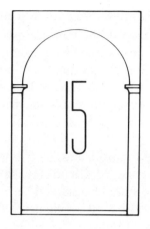

We spent the following week on the cloudless Nile. In Luxor
Lorenzo and I said goodbye on the deck of *The Blue Star*. His
time was up. He sailed back to Cairo and flew to Italy, as the rest
of us would do a week later.

In the Valley of Kings Niccolo suddenly fainted, apparently
from the heat, and was taken first to a nearby infirmary and then
to the yacht. We started our return up river and at a place called
Minieh he died in his sleep. From Cairo the yacht, empty but for
the captain and crew, sailed back to Livorno.

To my surprise Olympia was devastated. It had not been
clear how much she loved Niccolo, as Chase had said—like a wife,
mother, daughter; but now she wept and was inconsolable. It had
seemed to her as to everybody that Niccolo like Helena before
him would go on for some time. When he fainted between tombs
in the merciless sun, she knew he would die. Standing over him
she thought him already dead and saw herself alone. She had lost

all resistance to her love for Chase, and in a brief flash of feeling transferred her needs to him. Niccolo went into the ship's cold room, meticulously wrapped by Igor against freezer burn. Elvira outdid herself in the production of mourning clothes in the middle of nowhere. Chase made decisions. Despite the sad alteration of the circumstances, we still travelled in abject luxury, these many miles from home, unaffected by anything so grossly immediate as Egypt.

Drifting up the Nile toward Cairo, with Lorenzo gone, Niccolo dead and everything changed, Chase and I sat by the hour watching the river, under empty blue skies. The pilots came and went in reverse. Sometimes Lino sat beside us, close enough for Chase to reach an arm around him for five minutes. Lino insisted that Niccolo was still on the ship, asking questions, suggesting what we have for dinner, telling anecdotes. Chase expected that the boy would not cry before Niccolo disappeared.

I felt the same about Lorenzo. I still smelled him, still tasted him. Incessantly, he spoke my name behind me. His face appeared periodically, as reflex to a feeling of emptiness, as the reason why.

Chase lay back and relaxed in the riverine breeze. He was depressed by Niccolo's sudden death but frankly pleased that Lorenzo had gone. He now had back, he said, my exclusive company.

"How many times have we said to ourselves, 'Number five?' Where will it all lead us? . . . Now we know—Death on the Nile."

He and Niccolo had finished the cocaine. This had taken them days, sitting in Niccolo's cabin talking. All of it was on tape; Chase said that one day he would play it for me. It was all on tape and all on film. The yacht, as he had surmised, was extensively bugged.

"By whom?"

"By Niccolo. Olympia never noticed the extra workmen,

there being so many. . . . You remember Niccolo's album. His album grew. It became multi-media."

"You mean, Lorenzo and I—?" I began in horror.

"He practically dropped dead watching that."

"Did you see it?" I asked.

"No, of course not. I averted my eyes."

I was stunned that there should be a record of all of that, and witnesses—among them Chase. "You mean it killed him, I hope."

"Probably. It certainly got his heart going for one last blissful week. This was really quite beautiful. Niccolo was aware he was going to die."

Later Chase said, "Coke makes you totally susceptible and truthful. He told me everything. His version . . . We're only here because of Niccolo. *He* suggested the yacht idea to Olympia. He certainly knew his game. And do you think Miss Olympia believed two New York homosexuals wouldn't drop everything to go up the Nile on a yacht?"

In the cool of the shade deck all afternoon and then the following day, before reaching Cairo, he told me what he had learned from Niccolo, who, perhaps because of the drug, had thought it time to unburden himself. His version went further back than Olympia's, to accommodate his own part in it.

"It turns out we were distantly related," Chase said.

"But Olympia said you thought that was nonsense."

"I did. I never heard of anyone in my family marrying an Italian. But according to Niccolo his great-grandfather was Orvil Starkweather."

"Your Orvil?"

"There's nothing about any of this in the diary—how secretive can you be?—but after his wife died Orvil went to Italy, married again and had another family, all of which he kept from the American Starkweathers."

I said, "Chase, I can't grasp this. Surely people like Rudolfo and Helena would know their recent ancestors—in a family like that."

"Of course they knew. *I'm* the only one who didn't. That's how Helena knew Grandmère. Niccolo said if I thought I had been arbitrarily chosen I would be more likely to accept, rather than if I knew it had all been arranged and *depended* on me accepting. It's also where much of their money came from," he added.

"Money?"

"The Temple gold. I think the Temple gold ended up with Orvil's Italian family. . . ."

In 1865, late in life—after the death of Dorothea and the completion of the Temple—Orvil traveled in Europe, rather like a touring head of state, to make the acquaintance of Masonic leaders in England, France and Italy. In Florence he met the Malatesta, a Renaissance family, the *capo* of which was Grand Master of the Italian Masons. The Malatesta, like many Florentine families, had done duty against the Medici, and like them had been expelled for their efforts. By Orvil's time the Medici had died out, but despite the absence of a great fortune, the Malatesta were brilliantly connected. Maria Malatesta at eighteen was exquisite, and Orvil's reaction went beyond enchantment. A whole side of his personality, freed perhaps by the success of the Temple or the passing of his wife, sprang to life. True love inspired him to pursue Maria Malatesta. In his ensuing last years, from 1866 to the winter of '72, when he died, he led a more secret life than was indicated even in his diary. Half of each year he spent with Maria. Had it not been for the Temple, the Cabal and his oblivious American family, he would certainly have expatriated himself altogether.

At first, because of his age, corpulence and nationality, and despite his wealth and Masonic eminence, the Malatesta would not seriously consider Orvil's proposal. But with the gold, tons

of it, arriving in a long, ever-increasing amazement of bribes—
million after million, according to Niccolo—Orvil wore them
down. And finally, gagging with greed and delight, the family
relented. In 1866, at age sixty-three, Orvil and the twenty-year-
old Maria were married. The following year a child was born, a
daughter. When he died, having disappeared so mysteriously,
the difficult name of Starkweather was Italianized, and as Anna
Beltempo, Orvil's daughter was raised among the Malatesta,
quite the richest little girl in Florence. The addition of great
wealth to pedigree attracted the dynastic attention of European
aristocracy. In 1884 Prince André Odischalchi married Anna
Beltempo, who in the next few years gave birth to the principal
branch of the family in Italy, among them the father of Rudolfo
and Helena, who then, together, gave the Starkweather saga its
circular shape in the end.

"So," I said wonderingly. "It was arranged by Rudolfo."
"Rudolfo, Helena and Grandmère."
"Grandmère!"
"Grandmère," he repeated. "You don't remember, but—"
"I remember."
". . . Grandmère gave me Niccolo's name. I knew all about
him. She said if ever I was in Florence it would help to know
someone smart, to show me around. And you know, I have this
vague recollection that she brought me to them as a child.
. . . You know, that's the way children live their lives. Someone
makes a clever suggestion. Grandmère could have recommended
the moon, and I'd have become an astronaut to get there. If you
look at anything long enough you see a pattern."

The funeral was large, with Niccolo buried in the family church
near La Favola. Everyone from the old days appeared, including
Donna Carlotta and Donna Rita, whose presence as representatives of the last Queen, Maria José—still in Spanish exile—was

official. So much for the Virgilianos, everyone said. A fascinating story. As a family they had made genealogical history because nothing invents like life and necessity.

Margi and Marco attended, and Lorenzo brought la moglie, serene in her invisibility at his side. While she was talking with someone I leaned over and asked Lorenzo why she had come.

He said, "The yacht . . . in the papers. Your name . . . she saw it all. Instead of being suspicious, she was impressed. I had to bring her. From her point of view it was natural she come." His skin was tanned and his eyes perfectly gray. He smiled lightly —as much as one would dare at a funeral—to show he knew, as ever, my feelings for him. The smile flickered over his lips and up to his eyes, and was gone. He saw his mistake, and blushed. He backed away and la moglie took his arm. They withdrew.

Chase's requested presence at the reading of the will did not seem unusual under the circumstances—that he had been with Niccolo at the end of his life—and Niccolo's last wishes came as a surprise only to Olympia and me. Chase was given joint guardianship of Lino with his mother, together with Niccolo's money; both palaces went to Olympia—all in separate lifetime trusts for Lino. Thus Niccolo bound them together as best he could. He was familiar with the idea of a last grand gesture from the grave— something to give direction to the proceedings for some time afterward. Upon long consideration and as part of the complicated plan, this was the best way to do it—to think of the child. It did not compete with Helena's posthumous accomplishments; it augmented and completed them.

Chase and I flew back to New York—he on his way to the Farm to prepare for Olympia's and Lino's arrival, and I to the city to pick up the threads. I had sublet my apartment until October, thinking the cruise would last until then, and in the meantime stayed with Chase in the West Eighties. Olympia and Lino were due at the end of October, a month away, and Chase wanted them to be comfortable. He bought new sheets for all the beds, and odds and ends no one would notice. He tried to see the Farm and his apartment as Olympia would, as Lino would. He assumed that having lived all their lives in palaces they were oblivious to their surroundings, on the theory that only the poor are truly appreciative. He lamented the lateness of the season. At the Farm his garden was dropping off for winter and would be dormant and gray by November.

I went up for a weekend and we sat out in the by now blowsy blue and white garden over coffee. "I have a job," he said simply.

"You do?"

"I've been hired by the Parks Department, part time." He had often mentioned this eventuality—always in connection with Orvil and the Temple. It seemed to him now that his life, almost fatalistically, had been bound up in the incidents and results of Orvil's existence. The idea of a real temple under the Eighty-sixth Street transverse obsessed him.

"I went by," he said.

"Went by where?"

"The Carriage House."

"I don't understand. You mean you have a job in the Carriage House? You mean, cleaning up?"

"What did you expect—Superintendent?" He got up, went into the next room and returned carrying a uniform—green khakis and a shirt with Parks Department shoulder patches. "When they gave me these the guy said, 'Should I wrap them, or will you eat them here?' "

"But you'll be a common gardener," I said.

"I *am* a common gardener."

"You're doing this to look for the Temple. It has nothing to do with gardening."

"You're quite wrong," he said, "as usual."

"Do you intend to look for it; I mean, actually?"

He nodded his head. "You know, if only they would let me

clean up the whole thing at once. If I could just run around making the park as pretty as it really is—"

"You're mad," I said. "You don't even know what you want."

"I want to do what I'm doing," he replied excitedly. "I have a wife, a child, a job, a house, an apartment, two palaces and a two-hundred-foot yacht."

"Somehow the job doesn't seem to fit," I observed.

"Why? Olympia won't care. While she's out shopping I'll be working in the park. And Lino will be in school and I'll come home and wash up and have supper and we'll all go to the movies."

After a moment I said, "Supposing it's not there—"

"Yes, I know," he said. "It doesn't have to be. Orvil could have made it all up."

"And if it is there," I said. "What would you do then?"

"Do?"

"What would you do about it? Would you tell anyone?"

"I'd tell you."

"Yes, I know. And then what?"

He looked around at the garden. "I'd tell Lino. I'm not sure what else I'd do. But just knowing, one way or the other. . . ."

We had been back a few weeks when I received a letter from Lorenzo.

> Piero, I can't understand why I haven't heard from you or how you could leave again without saying goodbye. If you write I have the same post office box. You must tell me what happened. It's not right to disappear after all. I miss you.

I sent this familiar reply:

> Realized finally how impossible it was. I can't hide. Can't sacrifice myself to the sensibilities of your wife, or spend my life wondering when I'm going to see you again. Our lives

don't fit beyond the few hours it takes to show we can love each other. This is not enough, and was supposed to be the beginning, not the result. We are too different and far apart. You are one thing and I another. I could never resist the temptation to love you if you were near me—if our lives crossed in some natural way—but they don't. I still love you, but within myself, the way it used to be.

to which Lorenzo wrote the following:

Piero, I will never release you, whether you come back or not, whether I see you again or not. I love you. You love me. You are wrong to give up. Please don't.

Olympia and Lino arrived. They were driven to the Farm at a high moment in the fall display, transfixed by a show of color they had seen only in sunsets over the Arno.

"It's the same in a way," Olympia observed, meaning the end of summer and the end of the day. She thought the Farm adorable, something of a doll's house nestled in the hills. For the first few days she behaved utterly like a guest, which she had seldom ever been, doing nothing except make up the bed— less meticulously each day. It would occur to her suddenly, in the kitchen, that they were alone, and that she had left her underwear strewn about for Elvira. Climbing the narrow stairs, which seemed to her like the attic stairs of a huge old house, she would snatch her things into the cobra basket Chase used as a hamper.

He was teaching her to cook so that in the spring he might be free for the garden. He asked if this would suit her and she replied, "Could I possibly do a little of each? Or neither, if the mood struck?"

She wondered about Elvira and Igor. Perhaps they could construct a little servants' hut in the field.

I warned him that the whole thing would begin again, the

same intrigue. He said, "It's not intrigue. It's our lives. You of all people." We might now say "you of all people" frequently.

Taking his silence and self-containment with him everywhere, Lino fitted in seamlessly, disappearing into the hilly woods and high meadows, turning up only for dinner. Chase took him into the barn next door and introduced him to a horse leased from the neighbor. Lino stared up into the animal's enormous eyes and spoke to it soothingly in Italian. The horse nuzzled his neck. Lino embraced his father, mounted and rode off through the fields, their fears of boredom dispelled. At meals he mapped the countryside for miles in every direction, learning the names of everything from Chase.

"A triumph!" he declared on the phone.

"He's a special child," I said.

". . . Now that he's got Niccolo in him."

"Is that how it works?" I asked.

"Apparently. The dead pile up inside you and you become a kind of committee."

"You've added something," I said.

"Yes—as his father. But it's sweet of you to say."

Olympia and Chase were sleeping in the same bed, sleeping together. This had begun on the yacht—the cuddling and holding occasionally translated into action by Olympia's receptive desire.

The three of them went walking, following Lino on one of his circuits, up to a clearing on the hill where all the trees were stripped to a height of eight feet and the ground was stamped bare and flat, streaked with white, like salt. Inside were the cool and dark of an empty chapel, and in the air, like the feeling of slight damp, was the notion that many people or creatures had just left. Olympia said, "Chase, what an odd spot."

"It's where the deer come to rut," Lino volunteered.

"Lino, stay away from the fucking deer," his father advised.

"Is it *really?*" Olympia asked, looking around in wonder.

"I don't think so," Chase said quietly. "Though it does look as if something happens." Outside the ring of trees the hill dropped away and the green valley lay off below.

Olympia looked out and remarked, "But wouldn't the house sit better up here?"

"Sit better?" he asked.

"The view," she replied. Below, amid fluffy hills, a gold light played over the fields, the neighbor's pond, the burning-ball tree-tops. It dropped down from the clearing like the view through a well-placed window, as if she had already built the house she had in mind. The old one would then do for Elvira and Igor.

A week or so later, all seasonal chores completed, they returned to Chase's apartment. This was found inadequate for the three of them. Lino was enrolled in a local private school for diplomatic children. Chase began menial duties in the park, gardening on rather a larger scale. Olympia looked for somewhere suitable for them to live. Instinct led her immediately to the East Seventies.

Chase's job was a clever, direct way to gain access to the western storeroom of the Carriage House. It lay casually un-locked. Inside was a common tool shed, now electrified, its shelves stacked with materials and implements used in connection with the big forge in the main room; six or eight feet by about ten feet, with brick walls behind the high shelving and a cement floor. A square wooden bin filled with coal sat in the middle. The bin, he thought.

The bin was less than half-filled and appeared to be deeper than the floor by a foot or more. Its outsides were sealed at the bottom within a second layer of mortar over the original floor. Nothing about it was movable.

The actuality of the building, the small physical certainties, the reality of the little room did not seem to bear the weight of hidden stairs, a temple, an altar to something sacred and secret. Here instead lay an unexpected and too-deep bin of coal and the evidence of alterations made sometime in the past hundred years. Yet, he thought, it was possible—given that the Masons must at some point abandon the Temple—they would logically seal its entrance in some permanent way. Or, conceivably, Frederick Olmsted—in service to the simplicity of preserving the secret, as the only way of preventing its discovery—might himself have sealed the entrance with an extra layer of mortar. Chase would have no way of knowing, short of absolute authority or the wrecker's ball, if any of it was true.

•

The present has overtaken us. Signora Zá-zá runs the Pensione Bardolini exactly as before. Lorenzo has three children and will inherit the place. If ever I return to Florence we will make love in one of the rooms.

Chase and Olympia divide the year into some kind of schedule between New York and Italy. Chase has worked his way up within the Parks Department from Carriage House menial to assistant to the Superintendent. It is his intention one day to be Commissioner.

Lino is nineteen. His principal titles, none of which he uses, are as follows:

Don Niccolino di Virgiliano-Odischalchi, His Serene Highness, Prince of Tuscany and Liguria, Fourteenth Count of Arezzo; plus, if he chose, Hereditary Keeper of the Sacred Stone, Bishop of the Order of Jacques de Molay, Grand Master of the Knights Templar, Worshipful Master of all faithful Brothers sworn solemnly to the Craft.